BETWEEN WALLS

The City Between: Book Six

W.R. GINGELL

Copyright © 2020 by W.R. Gingell

Cover by Seedlings Design Studio

All rights reserved.

No part of this book may be reproduced in any form or by any electronic or mechanical means, including information storage and retrieval systems, without written permission from the author, except for the use of brief quotations in a book review.

To keep up with all the latest news and learn whenever there's a new book coming out (plus free chapters of ongoing work) sign up to The WR(ite) Newsletter!

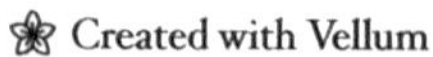 Created with Vellum

For The Kid and Kid Number Two.
This book has no tractors, but will hopefully still enthrall.

CHAPTER ONE

Change is a funny thing. Sometimes it creeps up on you like *someone's* flamin' pong of a cologne, overtaking the room in minuscule, unseen increments until it's in your lungs and hair and clothes, tinging the air in the room with a faint blue cast.

Sometimes it's obvious, like the murderous look that the vampire tosses at the huge, white fae at the head of the table over breakfast. Or the cold, emotionless look with which the fae meets that fiery glance, and the blunt words, "Don't show your teeth at me unless you want them ripped out of your head, Jin Yeong."

Sometimes it's soft and subtle, like the fae steward with the brown waistcoat murmuring, "Perhaps we could refrain from unpleasantness at the breakfast table, my lord? The pet has barely settled in again."

And then sometimes it's something as big as your former owners coming to rescue you and a leprechaun who got caught up in someone's anti-Family machinations instead of leaving you to die with the dropbears, even though they're no longer contractually obliged to do it.

"I want to meet your human friend," said Zero at the breakfast table that morning, roughly a week after the Great Dropbear

Incident. Maybe it was in deference to Athelas' plea, but he had turned his chilling blue eyes away from Jin Yeong's liquidly murderous ones.

"No," I said. "Givus the jam, Jin Yeong."

Across the table, the vampire turned his eyes from Zero and let them rest on me. He considered me for far longer than it should have taken to decide whether or not he was going to comply, then picked up the jam in a desultory fashion and put it down precisely in front of me.

To Zero, he said, "I have met the friend. You do not need to."

There was that idea of change again: Jin Yeong being weird. Well, weirder than usual.

"Pet," said Athelas, on something of a sigh. "Is it really necessary to argue upon *every* point?"

"Yeah," I said, because sometimes...sometimes the change is so faint that if feels like nothing has changed at all.

It wasn't so much that *everything* needed to be argued, it was just that I was still trying to figure out the things I should be objecting to. It made me more martial than usual, but so far I hadn't found a good way to differentiate between the things I should object to, and those that were fine. Mostly, over the last week, I'd fallen into the habit of doing what I was told when it came to Zero's orders on Behindkind stuff, and pushed back on everything that had to do with humans. My three psychos weren't the best judges of what was best for humans, but it hadn't stopped them deciding stuff anyway. Usually their decisions left humans out in the cold when it came to trouble with Behindkind: that was exactly what I was here to stop.

Or at least, that was what I'd come to believe.

"Anyway," I said to Athelas, feeling as though I needed to defend myself. "Unpleasantness at the breakfast table isn't my fault: Jin Yeong's being snippy again."

He was being more than snippy, actually; he was being downright stroppy.

"I'll give you credit for not *starting* the fight," conceded Athelas, and I was left with the impression that, in some way or other, he still blamed me for the unpleasantness.

That was flamin' rude, because I hadn't even been downstairs yet when stuff started flying around the house; including Jin Yeong, who went flying through a wall. I'd been sleeping in because I'd about had it with pretty much all the inhabitants of my house and didn't really feel like getting them breakfast. I didn't know exactly what had started the fight, but I did know that Jin Yeong was looking pretty worse for the wear when I got downstairs, and that Zero was looking slightly less ice-like than usual, which meant he'd been getting exercise.

"I will wait to meet your friend," said Zero, and if before I'd got the idea that Athelas hadn't changed *his* mind earlier, I had that feeling much more strongly now. Zero hadn't decided that he didn't need to meet Morgana; he had just decided that he didn't need to do it *right now*.

Well, that was something, anyway.

Pushing it a bit, I asked, "Who was that at the door this morning?"

"Detectives," Zero said briefly, surprising me.

I was gunna have to get used to the new state of him actually telling me things. Maybe when I got used to it, I'd be able to start working on learning when he was telling me part of the truth, and all of it, 'cos I hadn't been clever enough to work that into our interim agreement.

I felt Athelas' gaze on me and flicked my eyes over to meet it. As usual, he was looking serene and a bit amused; I wouldn't have bet very highly against him knowing exactly what it was I was regretful about.

"Perhaps you'll remember that we had another death in the area recently, Pet," he said.

He wasn't just talking about a death; he was talking about a Death—the latest in a series of similar murders that had begun in my area with a dead body outside the window. Which series was, itself, part of a series of similar murders all over the world; and, apparently, all through the trifle of layers that was Behind (the fae world), Between (the weird, squishy bit between *us* and *them*), and the human world. The victims had been a mix of Behindkind and humans, which was why my three psychos were involved in the first place even though they didn't care about the fate of humankind in general or humans in particular. In fact, the killer was one of the very few Behindkind I knew—and I was assuming he was Behindkind, because what else could he be?—who didn't seem to discriminate between human and Behindkind.

Yanno. For what *that*'s worth.

"I remember," I said. That last body had been just over a month ago, before I left home and adventured by myself and came back home. A lot had happened between then and now, but I wasn't likely to forget it: like the first body I'd seen, it was pretty memorable—a human hanging in front of a house, its insides on the outside thanks to a long, deep slash from neck to lower stomach, dripping gore on the grass. Throat cut almost right through the neck.

It had also looked just like one of my old friends, but that had only been a glamour, thank goodness.

"Thought you blokes had already looked into it," I said. "What were you doing while I was out of the house, anyway?"

"It was a singularly enlivening time," said Athelas. "I believe that none of us were bored, if that was what you were suggesting."

"I was *suggesting*—"

"We have been looking into it," Zero said, before I could continue. "But we are in need of a significant amount of evidence that has...gone missing."

"What, Upper Management stole it before you could? Flamin' rude, that!"

"My lord was of the same opinion," said Athelas, holding out his teacup when I proffered the teapot. "We fancied we'd have to do something about it."

"Yeah, can't have other Behindkind pinching stuff before you pinch it," I said, and I wasn't completely tongue-in-cheek. If it came right down to it, at least my Behindkind were trying to do something about the deaths. Upper Management seemed determined to hide what was happening—hide it, or profit from it; I wasn't sure which one, yet. Either way, they were good at making sure there were no witnesses or records left behind of stuff they didn't want left behind, and they were pretty deeply entrenched in the police force in Tasmania, too.

"What'd you do about it, anyway?" I asked. "You go knocking on their door or something? I don't recommend that; it's flamin' dangerous."

"We're aware of that," Zero said, with a cold, blue look in my direction. "That situation wasn't of our making, and I would have chosen another way to bring about that outcome. Walking into the bowels of Upper Management by yourself wasn't the best choice."

Jin Yeong gave an impatient mutter, and when Zero turned an icy gaze on him, said aloud, "We did not *need* your outcome; we did it by ourselves."

"Perhaps this would be a good time to mention," said Athelas lightly, "that as exotic as the scent of harpy undoubtedly is, it is making even the banshees restless."

"Thought Zero got rid of those?"

"I did," Zero said, his eyes narrowing. "They came back."

"Hang on," I said, catching up with the implication. I turned an accusing look on Athelas. "You saying I stink?"

"As painful as it is to me to admit, Pet—"

"You," said Jin Yeong, pointing his knife at me, "certainly stink. More than before."

"That's flamin' rich!"

"First you smelled of dead person—"

"Daniel bought me those clothes."

"—now you smell of harpy again."

"Well, you always stink, so—" I stopped. This morning I *had* put on the clothes I'd worn to confront Richard the harpy; maybe they needed to be washed again. "Yeah, whatever. I'll wash my clothes and take a shower."

"Bath," Athelas suggested. "And perhaps soak."

"For three hours," Jin Yeong said, his eyes narrowed at me.

If I didn't know better, I'd think the pretty little git was trying to pick a fight with me. I'd been mostly ignoring him for the last few days; I was still pretty cranky at him for pretending to be my friend when he was just following Zero's orders. Maybe he didn't like being ignored.

"Yeah, fine; I'll soak," I said. "What did the detectives bring you, Zero?"

"Information," he said. "Enough to start us on the trail of the murderer again, anyway. More evidence will arrive later: the physical evidence will be sent to us—"

"And the body?" asked Jin Yeong, brightening.

"You were just complaining about me smelling like a dead person!" I protested.

"Yes, but you are alive. I object to you smelling dead."

"Double flamin' standards, that is. Anyway, you can't keep a dead body here: I just filled the freezer with that half-a-cow you ordered from the butcher and there's no way you're putting a body in our fridge."

"I want the body," Jin Yeong said, glaring at me. "How can I investigate if I do not have the body?"

"You can't have the body," Zero said. "That was one of the pieces of evidence I haven't yet tracked down. It was processed for a very simple autopsy and then transferred to a secondary location for a more thorough examination."

"Lemme guess; it went walkabout?"

"It went what?"

"Walked off."

"I fancy you're confusing this body with a zombie," said Athelas. I was pretty sure he didn't fancy anything of the sort, because his grey eyes were dancing.

"Okay," I said suspiciously, "'Cos I was pretty sure there was no such thing as zombies."

I was still pretty sure, if it came to that: Athelas teased me a lot more often than Zero did.

"Really? Your belief system is remarkably fluid; I should have thought it easy enough to believe after all that you've seen over the last six months."

I mean, he wasn't wrong: I'd seen a heck of a lot over the last six months. Still, it had been something of a comfort to me that I'd never seen any of the bodies I came across stand up again and start walking.

"You mean some of those suckers get up and walk again after you kill 'em?"

"There's no need to sound so appalled, Pet," he said equably. "A very specific set of circumstances is needed to bring about a zombie—much like bringing about a vampire."

"Zombies are much harder to make," Zero said shortly. "You don't need to worry about them. They need a power source as well as—don't pull faces at me, Pet."

"Sorry," I said. "It's just gross, that's all."

Athelas laughed gently into his tea.

"How'd you lot lose a body, anyway?" I asked. I didn't mean it to, but my voice sounded accusatory. "Woulda thought you were keeping an eye on it so that stuff like this didn't happen, and I know it wasn't the last body that we found, 'cos Detective Tuatu texted me about that one this morning."

"We were...distracted at the time."

I narrowed my eyes at him. "You blaming me for this?"

"No," said Zero briefly. "If we were distracted, it was our fault."

"Hang on," I said, realising something. "That one disappeared when we were running around trying to find Athelas, didn't it?"

Athelas looked down at his tea with a faint smile, and I had the impression that he was trying very hard not to laugh. "Ah, I wondered if that would occur to you," he murmured. "Yes, Pet; it was my fault. I have already spoken to my lord on the subject."

"It was also your fault," Jin Yeong said. "After Athelas, we were running around after *you*."

"Didn't *ask* you to!" I said at once. "You're the one who wriggled your perfumy little way into the house I was—"

"Good heavens," said Athelas, faintly startled. "I see you're still quite annoyed, Pet."

"Anyway," I said. "We're about a month and a half late, right? And you've got no idea where the body is?"

"There will be another soon enough," Jin Yeong said, with a dark certainty that suggested he would be the one providing said body if it didn't turn up under its own impetus. "We will have evidence enough when that happens."

"I prefer not to wait until then," said Zero, with finality. "For now, we'll go through the evidence we can find. At least in the human world we tend to find evidence more easily than Between and Behind."

"Is that because it's easier to make humans talk?" I asked. This time I was very careful not to sound accusatory: I was genuinely curious, not trying to shame them.

"Only partially," said Zero, surprising me again. "The laws of the physical world are different here—well, perhaps not different, but we tend to examine things Behind in the light of different parts of that physical reality."

"Magic instead of forensics," I said, nodding. "Why not both?"

"That would require a greater deal of cooperation between the two worlds," Athelas said. "And a sharing of technology. One doubts that it's possible."

So what you're saying is that the human forensics provide more evidence than you usually get Behind through magic, was what I wanted to say. I didn't, because Zero was playing nice and I should be, too. Besides, he might stop playing nice if I was too snide.

Instead, I said, "I reckon that's the sort of thing that Upper Management are trying to do."

"Yes," said Zero, frowning.

"Very worrisome of them," Athelas added, speaking what Zero hadn't.

"Yeah," I said, with a heart-felt sincerity that made Athelas look at me in surprise. I explained, "Got nothing against Behind-kind and humans working together—"

"Yes, one feels it would be rather hypocritical of you to feel otherwise," he murmured.

"But I reckon it should be working *together*, not Behindkind enslaving humans or making weird bargains that only benefit Behindkind. I don't see why we can't all have cool stuff if everyone can work together."

"I see you're rather more sanguine about the idea than am I," said Athelas, delicately cutting into his toast with a knife and fork. "May I ask why the worried look, Pet?"

"Dunno," I said, "but if there's anything that would make me sure you're a psycho like the other two it's you cutting up jam toast with your cutlery. You know you're meant to get your hands dirty when you eat toast, right?"

"My *cuffs*, Pet!" he expostulated. "I absolutely refuse to sully them with butter fat!"

Jin Yeong said offendedly, "*Nan aniya!*"

"You're the psychoest of the lot," I told him. "At least the other two don't drink blood."

He stiffened very slightly, eyes darkening. It was weird. If he was a human, I'd think I'd really hurt his feelings. Lucky for me, Jin Yeong is a psycho, not a human, and his feelings are about what you'd expect from a psycho who spends a good portion of his time ripping out throats and drinking blood. It was important not to trust him when he was pretending to be nice.

"You," he said. "You, human. Make me *kimchi* again. There is none left."

"My name isn't *human*," I said. "It's not *you*, either."

"To do Jin Yeong justice, you've not given us another name by which we may call you," pointed out Athelas, very gently.

"You never asked for one," I told him. "You just came in and decided you were gunna call me Pet or whatever you wanted to call me."

"It is better if we go on calling you Pet," Zero said levelly. He directed a decidedly warning look in Jin Yeong's direction. "All of us."

Jin Yeong showed his teeth very slightly. "*Shilleoh.*"
Don't want to.

"You called me Pet before!" I protested. I didn't know why I was even arguing. It wasn't as if I *liked* being called Pet, but I still found it hard to think about telling any of them my real name.

"I shall not call you *Petteu*," he said, putting his nose up. "Because you are a *bad petteu*."

I must have accidentally rolled my eyes, because he bared his teeth at me, too.

"All right, don't get your knickers in a knot!" I told him. "I'll make you kimchi! You'll have to wait for it to age, though. I can make you some fresh radish stuff to hold you off until then. Seriously, dunno what's wrong with you. Any self-respecting vampire shouldn't like garlic as much as you do."

"I," said Jin Yeong coldly, "am *special*."

"You're telling me."

"Do not say it like an insult! *Hyeong*, make her stop saying normal things like insults!"

"Good heavens," sighed Athelas. "It really seems as though we're not likely to get any peace at the breakfast table. Bring me another pot of tea when you're finished with Jin Yeong and the breakfast dishes, won't you, Pet. I feel as though I'm going to need the solace."

I DIDN'T REALLY NEED TO GO SHOPPING THAT MORNING, BUT I went anyway. The house felt too comfortable, too normal: too much like it always had. That was better than the house trying to follow me into another house like it had recently, but when things were supposed to be changing around here, it felt a little bit stifling for everything to be as usual. I didn't want the usual; I wanted something new.

So of course I went out to buy onions and a tray of snags to go with our half-a-cow on the barbecue. Someone followed me as I went down the road, but that was nothing unusual, either. Still, I'd have to check and make sure I knew who it was following me before I went too far; didn't want to encourage the wrong sort of stalkers.

As I walked on, gazing discreetly into the reflective glass of the windows of passing houses for a sight at the follower I was certain was there, I felt my phone buzz in my pocket. That would be another message from Morgana. I'd been living with her up until a little while ago, and although she hadn't said anything out of place when I left, I was pretty sure she was hurt that I'd just gone off without so much as a good explanation. I mean, what explanation *could* I give?

I'm sorry to leave you with the werewolves, but the two fae and the stroppy vampire I live with need me back and they've promised to behave this time, so I gotta go?

I'd just told her I was moving back home; I hadn't expected to hear much from her after that.

Well, that's not quite true. It was more that I'd decided I couldn't see more of her; she was already infiltrated with were-wolves, and even if they were nice ones, they were still reason-ably stinky and carried a pretty good chance of leaving fleas on the couches. Fleas were about the best thing that could happen when you invited Behindkind into the house, too: everything else was downhill from there. It was safer for everyone if I stayed away.

I took out my phone and briefly swiped up to look at the message, but turned the screen off as soon as I saw the name that flashed up. Yep. It was Morgana. I preferred not to see what she wrote: I would have blocked her if I thought it would do any good.

Or maybe there was still a little bit of hope in me that one day I would be able to meet up again with my only real human friend who wasn't law enforcement, without putting her in danger.

I sighed faintly and put my phone in my back pocket again.

"Oi," said a rough voice from over my left shoulder. "You ignoring your texts, or what?"

"Don't you growl at me," I told him.

It was Daniel, of course: I saw him leaning against the wall of one of those little gardens that are all through North Hobart as soon as I turned around.

Even though his voice was rough, he was smiling. "Long time no see," he said.

"It's been less than two weeks," I said.

"How many messages is it that you've ignored now?"

I checked my phone. "Yeah, 'bout that many."

"I tried to tell her not to bother you."

"It's not...it's not bothering me."

"Yeah, I know. I told her you wouldn't talk to her: I told her you probably wouldn't even talk to me."

"I don't mind talking to you," I said to him, shoving the phone back in my pocket. I started walking again, and he came with me. "I just can't be talking to her. Zero's done something to the house to make it safer, and it's better if I don't go showing up there again."

"I'm not the safest person to be around the house, either,"

Daniel pointed out. "It's not like I'm not on the Behind Wanted list."

"Yeah, but you're more likely to keep her safe than you are to get her killed," I said. "Why are you here if you're not trying to get me to speak with her?"

"Dunno where you got that idea," he said. "That's exactly what I'm here for."

"But you said—"

"I said that I told her you wouldn't come; not that I wasn't going to try."

I looked at him accusingly. "Are you *sure* you're the alpha in that house?"

"Nope," he said, grinning. "But I am when it comes to the wolves, and that's all that matters."

"So you say," I said suspiciously. For someone as small and physically weak as she was, Morgana had a habit of extending a very great field of influence. Over Daniel, at the very least. "I'm not going back to the house."

"You haven't heard what I have to say yet."

"It's not gunna *change* anyth—"

"Morgana needs help."

I stopped walking. "What's wrong?"

He grinned at me.

"What?"

"You're really predictable, you know that?"

"What's wrong, and why can't you do something about it?"

"I can't do something about it because I don't have friends in law enforcement, and because I'm wanted, myself."

I raised a brow at him. "It's something that needs the cops?"

"Well, not necessarily the cops," he hedged. "Maybe. Not yet. It's mostly a missing person situation, but there are a couple of things that need to be checked before we can involve the cops."

"Story of your life."

"Shut up, Pet."

I grinned at him. "No promises. If I can get Zero to take it on, we'll come to the house. He wants to meet Morgana, anyway."

Immediately suspicious, Daniel said, "Why?"

"Dunno; probably wants to see what the pet dragged home. Are you sure this is something you can't just tell me about and have me go and check?"

"Yeah." He was serious immediately.

"Who's the missing person?"

"She says I can't tell you. You've gotta come to the house."

I narrowed my eyes at him. "If this is just a plot to get me to the house so she can make me practise putting on eyeliner again—"

"It's not, Pet."

"'Cos if I do this, I'm bringing Zero in on it. I told him I wouldn't go off and investigate my own cases, and he said he'd help out when I asked for it."

Well, he had said he would help out on human cases I brought him if they had a Behindkind element to them, but I wasn't going to mention that little qualifier to Daniel right now; not before I'd even brought the case up with Zero.

"Even if you've gotta bring Lord Sero into it," he said. He was still very serious, and that worried me. Daniel usually fluctuates between annoyed, slightly stressed, and mother hen. "She's really serious about this."

"Okay," I said. "Leave it with me; I'll come around tomorrow morning. And stop following me, all right? I've already got another follower and it's getting embarrassing, how popular I am."

I left him there protesting that he wanted to know who else was following me when he had been sure he was the only one, and kept going on my way to the supermarket. That got rid of one of my followers and left me with the same amount I'd thought I had in the beginning: one old mad bloke.

I checked a couple of windows again as I walked, and sure enough, it was him. He'd gotten himself another new t-shirt since

I'd last seen him; reckon he thinks of it as a form of camouflage. At any rate, every time he's supposed to die, he gets a new one.

That probably needs a bit of explanation, but it's kinda convoluted, so I'll keep it simple: the old bloke was supposed to have died about a month ago—a body looking like him was the last one we'd picked up from the murderer Zero was chasing. It wasn't the only time, though; we'd thought he was dead at least three times, and he'd come back alive every time yet with a new t-shirt.

At any rate, if he feels like he wants to follow me, who am I to tell him otherwise? It's not like I'm gunna put him in more danger than he's already come through, at least, and sometimes it's nice to have a weird, raggedy shadow that wriggles his toes in the sunlight through the holes in his shoes as he waits for you to cross the road.

And that reminded me: I'd have to get him another pair of shoes as soon as I could.

One problem at a time, though. I took out my phone again as I walked, and swiped up to look at the message again, this time more carefully. It said, *Please, Pet. I just need ten minutes.*

I didn't answer the text then, and I didn't later on when I found myself pulling my phone out while I waited in line at the cash register, either. I left some food and a bottle of water in a bag next to a bush as I crossed the road, and I didn't answer the text while I was using the camera of my phone to make sure the old mad bloke picked up the bag, either.

Daniel would tell Morgana I was coming. There was no need for me to answer the message, no matter how much I wanted to know if she was okay. It was better if I still kept contact as little as possible until everything was done. Then I could walk away, knowing that Morgana was safe, and happy, and didn't need me in her life.

All I had to do was bring it up with the psychos this evening at dinner. Even if the three Behindkind weren't open to helping humans for the sake of helping them, they seemed open to doing it if it meant keeping me nearby and out of trouble. Well, and keeping the secrets held in a certain USB close to them until they could get their mitts on them, anyway.

And lately I'd thought that for Zero at least, it wasn't entirely that he didn't want to help humans: it was more as if the wanting to help had been beaten out of him so badly that he'd never wanted to try again because he already knew it wasn't going to work and he didn't want the aftermath.

Maybe that was just me hoping, but I don't seem to be able to help it. That's something I've learned about myself, I s'pose. I can't help hoping, but if I can't help hoping, at least I can make sure I keep my expectations under control. As much as Zero might secretly want to help, that wish is buried *deep*, and I know exactly how much it takes to pull it out of its grave. I also know that if it comes to a choice between me and Zero, Athelas will follow Zero every time. Jin Yeong's the same, the little rat.

Still, things are still just that little bit different these days. And I know that I can say no, now: I've got that much strength. I already know the worst that can happen, and I'm not afraid of it anymore.

Or maybe I'm just not afraid of them anymore. I'm not sure which one it is, but it gives me more freedom than I would have guessed.

So I just asked Zero instead of beating around the bush. And I mean, yeah, I made him a flaming good meal and made sure he was already eating before I asked, but that's more like bribery than appeasement, after all.

When everyone was digging into steak and sausages, I slid a sunny side up egg onto my plate and said, "You lot got a bit of spare time this week?"

I already knew they were fairly busy: I'd seen the boxes of physical evidence as I came back into the house with the groceries, and more of them had been steadily arriving as I cleaned the house all afternoon. The last boxes didn't arrive until I started making dinner, either.

Zero looked at me briefly over the pile of sausages. "We'll make time," he said.

I didn't mean to smile at him. I must have smiled pretty brightly, though, because he looked back down at his steak-and-egg sandwich and said, "We have an agreement until you finish your demands and bring them to me. I said I would do as much."

Flamin' fae. Can't be seen to be showing emotions. *Oh* no. You gotta be emotionless and untouchable.

"Don't roll your eyes at me, Pet," he said, with a full mouth. "I suppose you've found a case for us."

I grinned. "Not exactly. But there's something dodgy going on."

"Where?" he asked.

"Morgana's place. Well, she says she'll explain when we get there, anyway," I said, shrugging like it was no big deal. "I said we'd look into it."

But even though I shrugged, I felt like I could have hugged him.

Because sometimes change is just your fae, former owner asking simply, "Where?" when you tell him that there's something dodgy that needs looking into.

CHAPTER TWO

WHEN I WOKE UP THE NEXT MORNING, THERE WAS A BOTTLE-cap on my windowsill. Under normal circumstances it might have been possible for a bird to have dropped it there, except around here it's never normal circumstances. And except for the fact that my windows are hidden from the outside by fake shutters and no one on the outside knows there's a bedroom there.

Oh yeah, and the fact that the bottle-cap was on the *inside* windowsill.

Maybe I should have been more worried, but it wasn't like Zero didn't have a hundred and one protections on the house, and it wasn't like the house itself didn't have a particular bent against letting anyone in if it didn't want them in.

It was just a bottle-cap. Definitely not where it should be, but just a bottle-cap. It didn't even have anything of Behind to it—that particular sheen of *otherness* that meant it could be something else if you wanted it to be, depending on how you saw it. For all I knew, it could even have been the banshees that left it.

I put it in my pocket, where it spiked my leg with the little bits of plastic that had once joined it with the seal, and promptly forgot it. It was time to make breakfast for my psychos in some sort of payment for taking on the case for me.

Technically, it wasn't a case that had to do with fae. They didn't need to agree to look into it for me even if I asked, because the interim agreement we'd come to only included looking into things that had to do with Behindkind hurting humans, not random cases for random humans that had nothing to do with Behindkind.

I shouldn't have been so hopeful about what Zero taking the case meant—what it meant that all of them were coming along, actually—but I couldn't help myself. It sprang up regardless of my reservations: the hope that my psychos weren't quite as much psychos as they had been when I first met them.

I just had to make sure I was *cautiously* hopeful: I couldn't forget that Zero had let a human die when he could have saved the man, or that he was still happy to refer to a human as a pet. That he still thought of humans as lesser than his own kind.

There wasn't anyone else advocating for humans around here, and if I didn't do a proper job of it, that was it. No one else cared —no one else *knew*. I couldn't afford to be blinded by my closeness to this particular set of Behindkind; not when there were always lives at stake.

All three of them were sifting through evidence downstairs in their own ways when I got down there. They don't need as much sleep as I do, so they'd probably been doing it all night.

Jin Yeong, surrounded by physical samples in bottles, plastic baggies, and boxes, was methodically going through each and either sniffing, licking, or touching each one, which was gross but also pretty much par for the course. Athelas, his teacup balanced on the leather arm of his favourite chair, was paging through crime scene photos with a professional kind of interest that's probably not the profession you're thinking.

Sitting on the floor with his broad shoulders leaning against the wall beside the bookcase, Zero had his eyes closed and his arms crossed over his chest. There were files all around him, but there were also books, which probably meant he'd been doing magic type stuff to try and follow leads, or was thinking about what sort of magic type stuff would be the most useful in this situation.

I trotted into the kitchen to make them some breakfast, and by the time it was half ready, they were all at the table, waiting, their boxes of evidence abandoned.

"Heck," I said, when I turned around. "Anyone'd think you lot hadn't been fed in a month or two!"

"I believe I have already mentioned that I do not list cooking among my accomplishments," Athelas said. He said it carelessly, but his eyes followed me around the kitchen just as much as Jin Yeong's—even, possibly, as hungrily. "I've not yet recovered from the time you were away."

Zero's eyes went just a shade lighter: he was laughing. "Neither of you starved," he said.

Athelas, slightly pained—whether at Zero's assertion or at the smell of the eggs scrambling—said, "Well, my lord, Jin Yeong *could* be said to have run away from home."

"I ate *very* well," said Jin Yeong, with a far-too-smug look in Zero's direction.

I left the eggs to their own devices while I madly buttered the toast that was popping up from the toaster and starting to smell ready from the grill as well. "Well, you've been eating well again for a little while now," I said. "Just don't forget that I can go on strike."

"Believe me," said Athelas, with a smile lingering on his lips. "None of us will forget that."

I brought the whole skillet over to the table and went back for the tower of toast. Over my shoulder, with a touch of anxiety, I asked Zero, "You didn't forget we're off to Morgana's today?"

It wasn't that I expected him to have forgotten exactly: it was more that I was afraid Zero might have changed his mind. From the looks of the living room, which seemed to have exploded overnight with case paraphernalia, they were neck deep in what they were already doing, and they were already a month behind on it. It might mostly have been because we were out looking for Athelas, but at least a bit of it was my fault, too.

"We'll be ready to go after breakfast," Zero told me, helping himself to the mountain of scrambled eggs before Jin Yeong could get to them.

Athelas went for the toast first, declining to get into a scuffle for the scrambled eggs, and piled that toast high with eggs once the other two had decimated them. Since he had behaved better than the other two, I gave him his tea before the others got their coffee, even though it meant I had to wait for my coffee, too.

Zero didn't say anything, but I saw him looking at me, and stuck out my tongue at him. His eyes went a bit bluer still, and his lips curled just slightly at the edges, making me grin in triumph. Heck yes! Got a real smile outta the ol' iceblock!

"I wish to have coffee," said Jin Yeong, rather thickly, through a mouthful of eggs.

"Isn't ready yet," I told him. It was true, but only because I'd deliberately made sure I did Athelas' pot first.

Maybe he was still sulking about that when everyone finished breakfast, because when Zero rose and made for the door without giving me time to clear the dishes away, Jin Yeong said coldly, "I have not showered yet."

"Wanna know the funny thing about that?" I asked him. He didn't answer, but I told him anyway. "You'll pong worse afterward than you do now."

"Do not say that word at me," he ordered. "I do not like it."

"Well, *I* don't like your per—"

"You have as long as it takes the pet to clear the dishes and wash up," Zero told him, and added briefly, "We won't wait for you."

Like me, he must have suspected shenanigans—or at least sulking.

"I will catch up," said Jin Yeong, and disappeared into the bathroom.

To my gleefully ill-natured delight, Zero really did leave without him once I'd finished with the dishes. Athelas and I followed, and perhaps there was another little change around the place, because Zero neither told me to hold onto him or to use the door properly. He didn't object when I followed him through Between and the door alike, either.

Between: a squishy place that isn't quite the human world and isn't quite the world Behind, but holds elements of both those places. Human constructs aren't quite real when you're Between, and can quite often be walked through. And when you're Between, Behind items that look like other things in the human word show their true forms.

We didn't come right out of Between, either. Zero and the others tend to slip Between to get through inconveniences like doors, but they don't usually stay there for too long. This time, however, we stayed Between the entire way to Morgana's house, which shortened the travel time by a good ten minutes. We came out just at the gate, sending leaves scurrying with the suddenness of our arrival. Zero must have known just where to slide back into the human world, because as we kicked through the leaves, we passed from behind the last of the hedge in front of Morgana's place, and I saw a flash of her watching us through a shard of mirror as we emerged.

I shot a look up at Zero, and thought he looked *very* faintly smug. He also avoided my eyes, so I'm pretty sure he thought he wasn't even allowed to have smug feelings—pity knows he doesn't let himself have any others, so I mean, at least he's being fair about it.

Athelas, his head turned to gaze over the front garden as we took the path to the front door, displayed very little interest. I would have liked to know what he saw in the garden, but if I'd asked him he probably would have charged me for the information. I kept my eye on him to see if I could figure it out for myself, but he returned his attention to the house when we were under the small awning at the front, and that was that.

Someone, no doubt Zero or JinYeong, had rearranged the mirror there to prevent Morgana from seeing us as well as she normally could. That would annoy Daniel—Morgana would send him down to move it again, which would annoy the kids, who apparently liked to be the only ones who did things for Morgana and also didn't like Daniel.

The door was already open a crack, so I didn't bother to knock; I let myself and the others in. There was a scattering of movement from the living room, and a few growls, but those stopped as soon as the first human-form werewolf poked his head around the corner and saw me.

"It's just Pet," he said. "You going to cook for us, Pet?"

"Nah, I'm here on business," I told him.

At my heels, Zero and Athelas stepped into the hallway, which didn't try to move around them like it might have done if it was connected to Between in the same way that my house was.

Zero looked around at both the werewolves and the house, frowning. He could have been looking for a way to get to Morgana, but I had the feeling that he was almost looking *through* the walls instead of around at the place. As if trying to understand how and why it had so little of Between to it when he was used to houses—well, places in general—being well connected.

"Upstairs," I said helpfully, as if he really were looking for Morgana. The mirrors could be confusing if you didn't know the path they took to reflect a version of the outside world to Morgana. Besides, I didn't want to encourage him to stay around the werewolves if he was inclined to disapprove of them being where they were.

"Yes," he said, still frowning. "Who else lives here?"

"A pack of werewolves is enough to be going on with," Athelas said, looking around rather fastidiously. "They're rather...a strong presence. And some lingering effects from our Pet's visit, I should think, to confuse the whole."

"It's just a few humans and a werewolf pack," I agreed, grinning at the few werewolves who had given up watching telly to come and stare at us. "Oh—make sure you're not too loud in the hallway. Morgana's parents live on the floor above and she might not want them to know you're here."

Athelas smiled slightly and sat down as Zero started up the stairs.

"What, you're not coming up?" I asked him.

"Oh, I think not!" said Athelas, crossing one leg over the other. He grimaced a little at the dog hair that already clung to his trousers, but appeared to leave it there as a hopeless case with the house so full of lycanthropes. "It will be far more entertaining down here, I rather suspect."

That was probably because Jin Yeong had just walked in and the lycanthropes still didn't much like him. Growls rumbled low and threatening around the living room, and I glared at him, too, for good measure. The annoying mosquito hadn't worn his suit out of the house as usual. I mean, it wasn't as if I *liked* his perfectly pressed, perfectly cut suits—especially not when I was pretty sure he'd never paid for them—but the annoying thing was that he was wearing jeans and a yellow knitted jumper.

I knew those particular clothes very well: I'd bought them for him when I thought he was my friend. When I thought he had bled and very nearly died because he was trying to protect me.

Jin Yeong met my glare with one raised brow and a very small smirk. "You cannot tell me what to wear," he said in Betweenlaced Korean, so that I could still understand him. Then, to my utter astonishment, he said in very careful English, "You. Don't. Own. Me."

"I can still put holy water in your shampoo!" I yelled up the stairs after his retreating back, when I'd recovered from the shock.

I followed him, taking the steps two at a time, and came through the door just in time to jostle with Daniel by the foot of Morgana's bed. The room wasn't a small one, but it was already looking pretty full with Zero hulking over by the window, not to mention Jin Yeong's cologne.

Morgana, looking slightly alarmed beneath her already pale makeup, asked from the bed, "Pet? Who is this?"

Since she already knew Jin Yeong, I said, "That's Zero. Don't worry, he's house-trained."

Zero's eyelids flickered shut for a very brief moment before he shot a cold look at me.

"Wait, is this the one that kicked you out?" demanded Morgana, scowling at Zero.

"Yeah," I said. "But he asked me to come back, so—"

"That doesn't count for much," she said. "It just means he's clever enough to know what he's missing."

She didn't stop scowling at Zero, and I saw one of his eyebrows tilt up slightly. Jin Yeong openly smirked.

"He's come to help you, though," I said.

I could understand being annoyed with Zero: I often was, myself. But it was a pretty big step for him to be here at all, and I thought that was something that ought to be encouraged.

To my relief, that made Morgana stop scowling at Zero, even if her voice was slightly stiff when she said, "You'd better sit down, then."

"Pet tells me that you need some help," he said, without acknowledging either the previous scowl or the cessation of it. He sat down by the window, facing her, and asked, "Is it about the house?"

"What? No," she said. "It's a friend of mine: we play *City Fae* online together."

Grinning, I asked, "You play what?"

"Don't judge me!" she said. "It's actually a really good game; the graphics are great, and so is the world. It's a kind of urban fantasy cross between an FPS and RPG, but actually it's an MMO. You can't just interact with everyone, though; it depends on your level."

"Pet," said Zero. "Translate."

Morgana giggled. "He's not a gamer?"

"Nope," I said. To Zero, I said, "Reckon she means your viewpoint in the game is first person—like, you can see your hands but not your body—and it's an open world, so you can explore everything, but you have to play it online. And you create your character to start with."

"Right," said Morgana. "You need an internet connection. So I met this boy online last year; he calls himself Blackpoint, but his real name is Joel Santino, and he's nineteen. I'd just started *City Fae* then, so I wasn't very high level, but I managed to unlock a perk that shot me a few levels higher in the game, and that's where I met Blackpoint."

Zero shifted a little. "When was that?"

"Last year about this time. We've been playing together for just a bit longer than a year."

"Did he tell you his real name?"

Morgana made a tiny, chirruping throat-clearing. "No. I um, found it out when I was looking for him. I couldn't get in contact with him and I got worried, so I started looking for him."

"When did he disappear?"

"About two weeks ago."

"Could he have gone away somewhere without telling you? Travel, or—"

"No," said Morgana firmly. "You don't understand; he's like me."

Zero frowned. "Like you?"

"Sick, I mean. He can't leave his house: he has cerebral palsy."

"Did he tell you *that*?"

Morgana gazed at him curiously. "Yeah, he told me that. Why? Is it important?"

"Yes," said Zero briefly, but didn't explain any further. "Then could he have gone to the hospital?"

Morgana shook her head. "It wasn't just that. You don't understand: he was in the game *all the time*. That's all he ever did. He didn't leave. Not to eat, not to bathe; not at all. It was always running, and if he was going to be away for more than a few moments, he left a message up so his friends could see. The game's still running on his computer, but there's no away message and he's not answering over there."

"Pet said that you want us to go and check on him. You have his address?"

"Yes," she said. "I've got it. I just want someone to go over there and make sure that he's all right."

"You don't think he's all right?"

"No."

"And you think there's something strange about his disappearance? More than usual."

She looked up at him solemnly. "Why do you think that?"

"You could have gone to the real police." Zero gazed at her for a few moments longer, and added unexpectedly, "Or did you come to Pet for a different reason?"

"It's weird," she said. "Daniel already went to check the house, but he couldn't get inside. He says no one's there, but it didn't look like there'd been a struggle or anything."

Knowing Daniel, he'd probably found that it didn't smell like there'd been a struggle—blood, for instance—but that wasn't something I was going to say in front of Morgana. Unlike me and my psychos, Daniel wasn't capable of passing through Between easily, so he probably wouldn't have been able to get inside.

"We'll check," Zero said. "But first, tell me about the game."

Morgana frowned. "Why is the game important? I just want you to go and check his house."

"We'll do that," said Zero, unexpectedly patient. He wasn't that patient with me. "But first, there are other things I want to know. They may not seem pertinent to you, but they will be to me. You said you were only able to meet Blackpoint because your rank improved unexpectedly by a few levels. He was already high level and that meant you couldn't interact with him until you got higher?"

"He's been playing for two years—since the game came out—so he's technically higher than I am, but when you get to higher levels you can also pick who you interact with."

"So if you're a beginner, you can't interact with anyone who doesn't want to interact with you, or anyone the game doesn't want you to interact with?"

"Right," said Morgana. "It's completely hierarchical. It also blocks you from advantages, because they make it so that you can't see them; perks, cheat codes, all that sort of thing. If someone doesn't want you to see them, you don't."

"What is the point of this game?" asked Zero. He had leaned forward with his elbows on his knees, taking up far too much space.

From him, that was practically begging for information.

I shot him a curious look, wondering what it was that had engaged his attention. I hadn't really gone into this thinking that it had something to do with Behindkind or fae, but given Zero's reaction, I was beginning to wonder.

"There isn't one specific goal," Morgana said, her eyes sparkling. "There are *heaps*! It's what makes this game so addictive. It's hierarchy based, so of course you're trying to advance, but there are a lot of different ways to do it: you can marry your way to the top of an influential family, or try to partner with the right kind of person; you can work your way up from the bottom with your own guild, or wriggle your way into someone else's and work your backside off or kill the right people to keep moving up. You can even be an assassin if you want, but I don't recommend it."

I shouldn't have been shocked, but after the last couple of months, maybe it just hit a bit close to home: art imitating life to this extent, that is.

"You can murder your way into power?"

She nodded enthusiastically. "You've gotta make sure you don't get caught, but if you can make the world work for you, you can do it. If you get caught, that's it."

"What, you lose the game or something?"

"Yep. It just stops, and the next thing you know, you're at the start of the game again. You have to start all over again with a new character; you don't even keep your previous level. Doesn't matter if you save your progress or if you don't—you're back where you began. Do you know what the funny thing is, though?"

"Surprise me," I told her, though I had a feeling I wasn't going to be surprised.

"You don't lose the game because you got *caught* exactly. You lose it because once you're caught, you're visible, and no one will ever work with you again. Even if you don't face justice, you're toast."

"What other things kick you out of the game?" asked Zero. "Loss of face? Marriage into the wrong family? An injudicious alliance?"

Morgana looked at him in awe. "I thought you said you hadn't played?"

"I've run across something similar," Zero said, with something of ice in his voice.

"Oh," said Morgana. She looked as though she wasn't sure if the ice was directed at her or something else. "You can lose the game if you lose face bad enough. Basically you drop dozens of levels and you can never rise again, so you might as well start over; it's also really easy to lose if you make a bad alliance, especially if the alliance is marriage—if your partner is more powerful than you and they die, you die too. If you join someone's uprising and it fails, you're kaput, as well."

"I see," said Zero, even more grimly than before. "Has anything unusual ever happened while you were playing the game?"

Morgana gazed at him with black-ringed eyes for a few moments, then asked, "D'you mean did I meet any creeps, or actual weird stuff?"

"Both," said Zero, after the barest pause.

"Well, there are always creeps, but they were all the normal kind—oh, except that one bloke, but I blocked him straight away. I had a few weird power surges the first time I played, then a couple when I got to the higher levels. There was an attack on my firewalls a few days ago while I was playing the game, too, but—"

"Pet," Zero said. "Translate."

"It's like a security spell," I said, without thinking. "Stops someone getting into your place and tells you they're trying. But for a computer."

Morgana gazed up at him in wonder. "It's like you're *really old* or something," she said.

"I am really old," Zero said expressionlessly.

"You don't look really old."

"You should know that appearance isn't everything," he told her.

It sounded vaguely remonstrating: as if he was telling her something that she, of all people, ought to know. Morgana looked roughly as confused as I felt.

"Yeah, I suppose," she said, and I saw her look across the room at the mirror on the far side of the room. Reflected there was her face: pale and perfect with makeup, her eyes black-rimmed and dramatic, matching the black lace of her choker.

It was a lot of makeup, but it wasn't like she'd look significantly different without it, so I didn't think that's what he was talking about.

Zero asked, "Tell me about the—the unusual creep."

"Well, he's a creep: you know, the sort you find on the internet when you're a girl who games."

Zero gave her a brief, perplexed look. "I don't know what that means."

"You're really sheltered, aren't you?" Morgana said wonderingly.

"I beg your pardon?"

"Don't you spend a lot of time on the internet?"

"None," he said.

"Oh," said Morgana, taken aback. "That's—are you joking me?"

"No."

"Oh. Well, he does stuff like sending messages and pictures and trying to get me to talk to him when he's in-world. I blocked him everywhere and usually that's good enough because I'm quite good with stuff like that. This little pervert managed to get through my firewalls and into my message-box even after I blocked him, though. That's pretty unusual: I still don't know how he did it."

"I offered to go visit him," said Daniel, with a very toothy smile. "She didn't want me to do that."

Zero turned a very cold look on him. "You're here on sufferance. I'd advise you not to make trouble."

"I didn't tell him where the guy lives," said Morgana, frowning a little. She might have misunderstood by whose sufferance Daniel was actually in the house, but she certainly didn't seem to like Zero threatening him. "So you don't have to be annoyed at him."

Daniel opened his mouth to say something, his expression stormy, but I elbowed him in the ribs.

"You don't know when a little creep like that is going to have a knife," Morgana explained, at the same time. "And even if they don't, it's not worth going to jail for trying to teach them a lesson."

"Do you know where this little pervert lives?"

Morgana, warily, said, "Depends. If you're the cops, I've got no idea."

"We're not the cops," said Zero. "We're connected, but we don't do things on the same level that the police do them. We have a little more...leeway."

"Oh," she said. "Well, I've got a bit more leeway, too."

"You *take* a bit more leeway," said Daniel, grinning.

"And it's not exactly legal, the way I do things," she added.

"I don't care about that," Zero said. "Do you know where this person lives?"

"Yes. But what good is that going to do you? It's my friend I can't find, and I've already written down his address for you."

"Give me both of them," ordered Zero.

"Do you think this creepy bloke had something to do with Blackpoint's disappearance? Why?"

"Because people in power don't like it when high-level denizens interact with low-level denizens," Zero said.

"I don't know what that means."

"Don't worry, he's just being mysterious for the hang of it," I said. "You'll get used to that."

"Does that mean you're going to help me?"

Zero, as always the soul of brevity, said simply, "Yes," and got up. He took the written addresses from Morgana and passed through the door in one movement, leaving me and JinYeong looking at each other. JinYeong shrugged slightly, but his feet shifted toward the door just as Zero's head popped back through the frame.

"You said there are hierarchies in the game. What are the ranks?"

"There are actually two sets of hierarchy," Morgana said, gazing up at him. "Character, and Class. You start out as one kind of a character, and everything else is tied to that; you can only change it under certain circumstances. Mostly you have to level up through the classes as the same character: each new level gives you new advantages and disadvantages, but they're specific to your type of Character. My latest character made a bad alliance just after I got to about the mid-level, so I had to start again. I'm back at servant class right now."

"How does a servant interact with the world?" asked Zero.

"Servant is pretty good," Morgana said. "People don't notice you a lot, so you can get away with a lot if you're clever about it. Class is a big thing in-game, so you can use that to your advantage. But the bad thing is that you can't lie if you belong to one of the servant classes, no matter what kind of Character you pick."

"Hang on, what are the characters?" I asked. I was starting to get a really bad feeling about this game—and about what may or may not have happened to Morgana's friend. "Bottom to top."

"It's kinda rude," Morgana said. "Human is right at the bottom, then there's goblin, assorted hobgoblins, werewolf, merperson, fae. I think there's some hidden classes that have extra perks, but those ones need a cheat code to get. The ranks are servant classes—chattel, indentured, paid, steward—lower noble, middle class noble, upper noble, royalty. It's hard to get to the higher classes if you pick Human, though. That's why I play as werewolf."

Great, I thought, as Daniel coughed a bit beside me. Flamin' fantastic. The whole game was a fae plant. For what purpose, I didn't know—I didn't even know it was possible for them to use computers, if it came to that—but I was betting it was a really bad purpose.

"Very well," said Zero, and vanished again.

"So what, he's going right now?" Morgana hazarded, confusion written across her face.

"Looks like it," I said, shifting toward the door.

"I thought—I thought you could—" She stopped, and sighed faintly. "Will you come back and tell me how it goes?"

I should really call her instead of visiting, but it wasn't like we weren't all going to be around for a while, after all. "Yeah," I said. "I'll come 'round when we know a bit more."

While I lingered with Morgana and Daniel, Jin Yeong made an irritated sort of clicking noise in the back of his throat from the foot of the bed, then jerked his head toward the door when I looked at him.

"All right, all right," I complained. "It's not like you didn't take your time this morning."

"The result," he said coldly, so that we could all understand, "was worth it."

I didn't know whether he was talking about his looks or my annoyance, so I just said, "If you say so," and brushed past him and out into the corridor.

He was still muttering to himself as he followed me down the stairs, so he must have been talking about his looks. I ignored the muttering and joined Zero, who was standing by Athelas' chair amidst wary looks from the werewolves.

"Right," I said, as Jin Yeong passed fastidiously between a werewolf and Zero. "We going off to see if this bloke's okay?"

Zero shook his head. "No. That is for yourself and Jin Yeong— Athelas, too, if he should choose to go. I have another errand."

"Another errand?"

"There is someone who might be able to clear up a few things about the investigation before we dig too deeply," he said.

"You, come with me, then," said Jin Yeong, and sauntered away again.

"You don't know where you're going!" I called after him, but he must have filched the address from Zero's pocket when he skirted around us, because he fluttered it at me over his shoulder mockingly. Of Athelas, I asked, "You going with Zero?"

"And miss the delight of your interactions with Jin Yeong?" he enquired, rising at once. "I think not. I shall accompany you. My lord does not require me."

We caught up with Jin Yeong outside, me at a trot and Athelas at a smooth stroll that didn't look nearly quick enough to catch up with anyone.

"Are we to walk through the entire human neighbourhood?" Athelas asked mildly, as we passed through the gate. If there was a barb to his question, I didn't know what it was.

"Yes," said Jin Yeong, with a dark, liquid glance at Athelas that made me very aware that there had, in fact, been a barb. "I shall walk in the human world if I wish to do so. The world Between is boring and dirty."

I rolled my eyes a bit, but there was nothing new here: Jin Yeong was always annoyed when he got dirty. A bit ironic for a vampire who likes tearing out throats and draining the blood of his enemies in a glorious, arterial spray, but everyone has their quirks, after all. Jin Yeong just has more of them than most...people.

Halfway down the street, I pinched the address from between Jin Yeong's fingers, prompting a small snarl.

"What?" I asked. "Who knows this place better, you or me?"

His lips pursed but he didn't try to take the paper back. He did look pretty sour when I badgered him and Athelas onto a bus, though; probably because of the pungent smell of pee to the seats.

"What?" I asked, once again. "It's halfway across town. You said you didn't want to take a short cut—look, Athelas isn't complaining."

"Please don't confuse my bewilderment at my surroundings as approval, Pet," mildly said Athelas. "I don't particularly like this mode of transport, myself."

"Well, if you lot don't drive, you've gotta expect to take a bus or two," I told him. The same went for not going Between when they could—but I left that bit unsaid because sometimes it's more fun when you know you don't have to say the annoying thing aloud to have it heard.

CHAPTER THREE

IT WASN'T THAT I WASN'T EXPECTING A RUN-DOWN LITTLE place stuffed between heritage houses.

I was. I just wasn't expecting it to be *quite* so rundown. I expected windows, you know—at the least, a bit of glass or something. I didn't expect it to look quite as modern as it looked, either. Built from the weird yellow-tan brick that looked more like a façade than real bricks, it was wedged into the space made by the back walls of three heritage houses, just barely visible from the road and the boxiness of it coloured outside the lines; untidy.

The whole place was a wreck. Garbage bags on the front lawn, half a car slowly rusting away near the letterbox, and lawn that was nearly hip high and probably full of snakes. Even kids who were there to tag stuff would know better than to be wading through *that* grass. Actually, the grass itself was a bit surprising— most of the grass around here wasn't long grass: it was crab grass.

"Hang on," I said suspiciously, looking at the whole a bit closer. My eyes tried to skate away over the filth, and I made them concentrate. "Someone's put a glamour on this place!"

"Well done, Pet!" said Athelas. "Although I suspect you've had a great deal of practise seeing these since you learned what they are."

"Oi! Don't take back your praise! I did a good job!"

"Perhaps you could add to your good work and fetch out this human for us?"

I grinned at him. "No need to get carried away. So do we go in?"

"I don't see why not," Athelas said, after a moment.

"Won't the person who made the glamour know we're here?"

"Perhaps," he said. "But I don't sense an alarm spell attached to the glamour. Besides, it seems likely that the person who made the glamour is the occupant, and we're in search of the occupant of the house, so it seems worth the risk."

"It's not like they're gunna come running *for* us, I suppose," I agreed.

"Indeed," Athelas said. "And that is why Jin Yeong will go around the back."

Jin Yeong raised a brow, but when we stepped through the gate he melted away and around the back of the house so quickly that I almost didn't see him go.

"Lot of windows between here and there," I pointed out, but it wasn't like he could do anything about it anyway. If there was someone in the house and they tried to make a run for it after their glamour was breached, Jin Yeong was bound to be quicker than they were.

He was also *really good* at following a scent.

The door was pretty hard to get through for a door that wasn't locked and that was hanging off its hinges. It wasn't that it was hard to open so much as it seemed hard just to step through the thing.

Even Athelas hesitated as he stepped over the threshold, and that must have bothered him because he looked a bit more thoughtful as I struggled to follow him into the main room. It was almost like being pushed against by a very strong wind, but once

I'd forced my way through it and joined Athelas in the house, everything was back to normal.

Proper normal, that is; not glamoured normal. It looked like a regular place on the inside. The kitchen was empty and in need of an update from the grungy tiles on the splashback, not to mention the fake-marble laminate bench tops, but it was a normal kind of outdated. A couple of dishes were in the drying rack over the sink, and the window had a few streaks that showed it needed cleaning again soon, unlike the sharp, broken-edged version outside. Even the door looked normal, from here.

And that was a bad kind of weird.

"Don't reckon he's here," I said, opening and shutting the empty fridge, then heading down the hall toward potential bedrooms.

"That was rather the point of us coming out here, wasn't it?" gently enquired Athelas, but he followed me without investigating any further.

"Nah, I mean, I don't think he was ever here," I said. I checked in the second bedroom, just to be sure, but that was it: the whole house. Empty and unremarkable. "This place isn't set out for someone cerebral palsy—or even with a *cane*. It's not connected to the internet, either: there's a modem plugged in out in the living room, but no lights on. I don't think the power's on, actually."

"A front?" he mused. "The whole house is a front?"

"Reckon. *And* it's a front that's covered by a glamour. They probably didn't want anyone in the neighbourhood to see that it wasn't really occupied."

"Then where," asked Jin Yeong, prowling into the room from the direction of the laundry room with a cobweb clinging to one shoulder, "is the human? *Is* he human? And why did he guard the place so well? And why did the dog not notice this?"

"*Daniel*," I said pointedly, "is a werewolf, not born Behindkind, and he says he's not much good with magic. He probably couldn't tell it was a glamour; he could only tell that there was no one at home. Reckon he could have gotten in through that door?"

"It gave me pause," said Athelas, as if that should answer my question.

Maybe it did.

"So all he would have been able to do is check through the windows, and I'm betting he just saw a mess. What do we do now? No one's lived here in a while, by the looks."

"Lived, perhaps not," Athelas said, stooping to pick up the rubbish bin that was sitting beneath the desk in the bedroom we'd ended up in. "But I rather fancy someone has been here, for all that. A human someone, by all appearances."

"There is a human smell," agreed Jin Yeong, looking around narrowly. "It is *familiar*, but there is no blood to tell by."

"Heck," I said, impressed, as Athelas emptied the bin on top of the desk. I wouldn't have thought to look in the bin. Like everything else around the place, it looked a normal sort of messy; the sort of messy your gaze slides right past without having to have a glamour on it.

I helped him separate the rubbish, and added, "You're right," as a waxed cardboard box scuttled away beneath my hand. I picked it up and brandished it at him. "This is a pie that just came out a month ago at Maccas. It hasn't been here longer than that. D'you reckon it was our missing bloke, or someone else?"

"I would question how someone else could get in," pointed out Athelas. "Considering the fact that it's glamoured and this area is almost entirely comprised of humans. It would be some feat. I very much doubt our quarry is himself, human."

"Then how did the stuff get here, and why does Jin Yeong smell human?" I asked, homing in on the small scrap of material that I could see beneath the bed. I left the rubbish where it was, and ducked down to pull it from beneath the bed, but instead of being a scrap, it was an entire sleeping bag, dirty and rumpled, but still whole.

I waved it at Athelas and JinYeong, and JinYeong plucked it out of my hand.

"Oi," I protested, but he gave the whole thing one thorough sniff.

Distastefully, he said in Korean with the edge of Between to make himself understood, "This is dirty and human and also familiar."

"Reckon you can follow the scent?" I asked him.

"Of course."

"You go," Athelas said, making a small, elegant shoo-ing gesture at us. "I will remain here to see what else I might find. I trust you can interrogate any human you find without my assistance."

"*Ne*," said JinYeong, purringly confident.

It's *so* flamin' annoying; he reckons he's irresistible, and when it comes to humans, he's pretty nearly right. I shouldn't complain, not when it makes investigating so much easier, but *heck* it's annoying!

Lean and taut and focused only on the scent, JinYeong paced rapidly down the hall and through the wall at the end of it.

"Yikes," I said, and hurried after him. Into the sudden, soft mossiness of silence, I called, "You sure you should be going Between when you're chasing scents?"

"The scent comes this way," he answered, without turning or stopping.

"Zero says that humans can't get Between by themselves."

"Yes," said JinYeong. "But the scent came here."

"Well," I said, "I s'pose that means that either Zero's wrong or your sniffer is broken."

"*You* are here," he pointed out, and this time he did stop. He turned back to me and said accusingly, "You know this."

"Yeah," I said, "but I figured you'd just got it wrong and Athelas is right that it's not a human we're after."

He shrugged. "It is possible. But I think it is a human."

"Okay," I said. "But if it is, they're probably about as loopy as the old mad bloke, and we're gunna have a bit of trouble trying to talk to them."

"I won't have trouble," he said, far too smugly.

"What if they're like me?" I asked him, grinning.

Jin Yeong paused for a moment before he said, "Then it will be trouble *for everyone*," and kept on his way.

"Rude!" I said, hurrying after him through a hallway that wasn't quite a hallway anymore but wasn't really the cleft between hills that it was pretending to be, either. "Oi, where's this? Did we go too far?"

"We are still Between," he said. "Here is a piece that touches on fae land, so there is more of grass and flowers."

His voice was somewhat fastidious, as though Jin Yeong didn't care much for nature—or maybe just fae nature.

"Don't like getting stuff on your shoes, do you?" I asked him, but there was no sharpness to my voice. I touched the grass that grew up a steep embankment on either side of us, and found that it felt very real despite the fact that it looked more like 3-d wallpaper.

I looked ahead again just in time to see Jin Yeong turning back around, and there was a sharp curve to his cheek as though he'd turned to grin at me and was still doing so. That was weird and also surprising, so I was glad to have missed it.

Maybe I'd have to be sharp again. Couldn't have Jin Yeong feeling friendly enough to grin at me without the dark look to his eyes that suggests it's all a ruse to get you close enough to bite you. It's a lot safer when you remember there's a bite at the end of the grin.

I'd caught up with him by the time the cleft in the hill opened out and gave us enough space to walk together instead of in file. When I looked up, the sky was still human sky—or did Behind sky look like human sky? I wasn't sure—and it was off-putting to tilt my chin back down and find myself looking at the confusing reality that was Between. Here and there, brick and mortar pushed out of a hill, or a foggy, slick window gave a dim view into someone's house, but for the most part, it was pretty mossy and grassy, with steep hills all around us and windy ways between them.

"What would you see if you climbed to the top of that?" I asked, pointing to the closest hill. I was already pretty sure that all you would see was a creepy continuity of sharp hilltops, right to the horizon. It felt like a maze here without actually being one, and I didn't appreciate the sense of confinement it gave me.

"That way," said JinYeong, pointing without hesitation, "is a canton we should not be near. That way is another. There is *bog* over there, and—"

"Lemme guess, over there is another canton we shouldn't be near?"

"*Maja*," he said, spinning on the balls of his feet, his eyes sharp and searching.

"What?" I asked, but he padded from one end of the small valley to the other without answering, his nostrils flaring.

To himself, he muttered, "*Isanghae*."

"What's up? What's gone weird this time?"

"Too many scents," he said, frowning. "Why are there so many scents? And I do not think a human should be coming here."

"Yeah, what with all the cantons we shouldn't be going to—"

"And *bog*."

"Yeah, and the bog—hang on, bogs aren't worse than cantons in fae."

"Yes," he said flatly. "They are worse."

"Anyway, it's no use saying they shouldn't have come here, because they did. Where did they go from here?"

"There is no scent."

"You just said there are too many."

"There is no human scent now," he said, narrowing his eyes at me. "And too many other scents. Ah! What is this!"

"What's what?" I asked, as he stalked toward one of the hills that looked as though it might have a similar cleft in it to the one we'd come from.

He stopped short of the actual spot, and for a moment I thought I'd been mistaken. Then I saw the way he'd stiffened, his head turned and his focus intent on the passage between hills. Again, he turned on the balls of his feet, lightly, decisively, and this time he was grinning, his eyes dark and joyful.

"*Noh—chunbi dwesso?*"

"Ready for what? What have you gotten us into?"

"*Ssawoyahae.*"

"Hang on, we've gotta fight? Who've we gotta fight *now*—oh. Ah, flamin' heck."

A good half of the things that attack me Between aren't identifiable, but the three four-armed men who bounded into the valley were pretty flamin' familiar. I'd seen a few of these particular fae flunkies—usually when some important fae was annoyed about where I was and determined that I shouldn't be there.

"Lemme guess," I said, looking around with narrow eyes for something I could fight with. "These blokes belong to one of the cantons we shouldn't be near?"

It's always a matter of how you see stuff when it comes to bringing things out of Between—or out of the human world when you're in Between. You have to know where to look for a weapon, for a start, and then you need to know how to turn it into a weapon when it's Between.

Lucky for me, I've had a fair bit of practise at this sort of thing, now.

As JinYeong stepped forward to meet the four-armed men, snarling, I relaxed my sight a bit and let my eyes rest on the bits of the world around me that were definitely human instead of Behind. Human windows, human garden ornaments—was that gnome solid concrete or was it just trying to keep its head down? —the handlebars of a human bike—and there! There it was!

I don't know if there was someone playing with the cricket set, but just then, it seemed more important to save my own life than it did to worry about someone's cricket stumps disappearing mid-game. I grabbed the middle- and off-stumps and brought them up to meet the sword-flashing attack of a four-armed man who was far too close for comfort.

I didn't have to think about that, either; the guard was there in my reflexive memory, and so was the swift, left-circling spin away that made the flunky step back hurriedly to get out of reach of cricket stumps that were now long, lean swords with edges sharp enough to cut light.

"These ones are *mine*," said Jin Yeong's voice near my ear, as we passed back to back for a brief moment.

"Greedy," I said, but I wasn't complaining. I'd be lucky if I could deal with one of these blokes—I mean, they had four arms and I had two. The dark, bloody shadow that was Jin Yeong flickered and scuffled somewhere to my right, dark against the green hills, and I still circled left, as wary of the four-armed man as he was of me.

He feinted from his left upper arm as if to slash from my neck right down through my body, but I'd already seen the way his feet were positioned; the tiniest shuffle back instead of forward. So instead of circling to the left and having my head cut off when he changed his stroke, I came in fast and low and ran him through with what had been middle stump.

I didn't move quickly enough to avoid the flopping arms that thumped down on my back as he died, but I wasn't slow enough to cop the full weight of his body bearing down on me, either. I sprawled in the churned-up grass and dirt, half covered by a four-armed madman and felt my wrist twinge with the strain.

"Ow," I said, crawling out from under the mess and very glad that I didn't have to worry about the two others that Jin Yeong was looking after.

My sword didn't want to come out of the bloke, and I nearly

left it where it was because when it did come out, the feeling was pretty much the same as it had been going in, and I didn't particularly want to experience it again.

Still, you never know when you're going to need a weapon when you're between, so I gritted my teeth and did it anyway. By the time I was free and it was free, there was a second body on the ground and Jin Yeong was on the last Behindkind.

Literally on him.

Thumping the last one's head into the rocky ground for every word, he said in a cold rage, "You. Have. Ruined. My. Clothes."

They *were* pretty mucky: the jeans I'd bought him were soaked through with blood at the knees and spattered pretty much everywhere else, and the jumper had a gaping tear on one side with yellow, woollen loose ends floating on the breeze.

The tear framed an equally bad gash in Jin Yeong's torso, from the back of his hip and curving toward the front just below his breastbone. That was gunna bother him a bit later.

I grimaced and said to him, pointing at the four-armed man, "Think he's dead."

"I *know*," he snarled, throwing the head away from him in one last flash of temper. "You, what do you want? Why are you staring at me?"

"You've got a pretty big hole in your rib cage," I said. "You okay? Gunna need blood, or what?"

Jin Yeong twisted to inspect himself, *tch*-ing in annoyance, and said something in Korean that I was pretty sure was rude. "It will heal."

"Then I'm pretty sure we should be leaving now," I said. "Yanno. If you don't need blood and we can't find the trail again and there's nothing nearby but unfriendly cantons and bogs."

Jin Yeong's eyes were just a little bit more liquid when he looked back at me. "I do not need blood," he said. "This place is boring and dirty. We will go home."

"Yeah, we probably better not go out there looking like this, though," I said, gesturing at my own bloody appearance and then at his. "Got a better way home?"

"There is no other way home but through the bog," Jin Yeong said flatly.

"Better than the unfriendly cantons, though, don't ya reckon?"

Jin Yeong opened his mouth, closed it again, then said, "My clothes are ruined *already*," and stomped away toward what I assumed was the bog.

I followed him, grinning, and soon found myself wading knee-deep in a mixture of mud and moss that was too loose to be called mud. Jin Yeong, without a word, grimly waded ahead of me, and by the time we pushed back into the human world just a bit short of the kitchen wall, we were both pretty well splashed up to the waist.

Jin Yeong pushed through the kitchen wall without bothering to go the few steps around the house that would have led to the front door instead. He sploshed past Athelas and Zero, who were eating pizza from the box at the kitchen island, and went right for the bathroom without a word. He seems to think it's fine to walk around in just a towel and a scowl afterward, but Athelas tells me that if I weren't here he wouldn't even bother with that, so he and Zero probably count their blessings these days.

"Well," I said to Athelas and Zero, throwing the swords down on the kitchen tiles, where they splattered blood and grass and turned back into cricket stumps, "we had fun. How'd your arvo go?"

I called Morgana just long enough after we got back that I wasn't still panting from a mixture of exhaustion and adrenaline, and I reckon she must have been expecting what I said, because she didn't sound surprised.

"Daniel couldn't see anything, either," she said. "But I'm glad you could get in there, at least. What will you do now?"

"Don't know yet," I said. "I haven't talked it over with them. We had a bit of a lead but it went um, cold. Zero might have an idea where to start again, but we haven't discussed it yet. I gotta have a shower first."

"How messy was it?" she demanded, her voice astonished. "Daniel said it was mucky, but I didn't expect you to have to have a shower afterward. Sorry."

"Just a bit of mud and um, stuff," I said. "Nothing to worry about. But if Blackpoint hasn't been living there, it's probably gunna be a bit difficult to find him again, especially if you don't have another address."

"I'll work on it," she said. "He could have thought someone was going to come looking for him and managed to lace in a bogus address, but if so, he was really thinking ahead. I couldn't trace him back directly; there were too many bounce points. I just went with his name and found him in the police system."

"Pretty sure that's just as illegal," I remarked.

"Yeah, but in this case it was quicker and easier," she said. "He's too good at hiding his trail. All right, I'll try the old-fashioned way, but it'll take ages and probably won't come up with anything anyway. Oh. I don't know if it's important or not, but someone tried to breach my firewall again while you were gone."

"That same creepy bloke again? Zero visited him, though."

That had been a surprise to hear while I was getting coffee for myself—and by default, everyone—because although Zero had taken the address, I hadn't expected him to go and see the bloke today.

"That's why I told you," said Morgana. "If he was busy with Zero, I don't see that he'd have the time for the kind of sophisticated attack that came on after you left. I don't think he'd have the guts, either."

"Yeah," I said. "Zero made him think again about bothering kids on the internet."

That was reading between the lines. What Zero had actually

said was, *He peed himself on the carpet.* Athelas, smiling faintly, had said, *I take it that he annoyed you somewhat, my lord?*

I wasn't exactly sure what Zero had said after that, because I was too busy trying to pinch a piece of pizza while neither of them were paying attention, but I think it was, *He was already busy when I got there.*

"Was he an old bloke?" she asked.

"Bit younger," I said. That was reading between the lines, too. Zero had described him as just barely having a beard, which could have meant he was just weedy but probably meant he was youngish as well. "Don't think you have to worry about him anymore: Zero scared him a bit, I reckon."

"Yeah, but if it wasn't him making the attack on my firewall, who was it?"

"Good question," I said. "I'll let ya know when I figure it out."

Since someone had brought pizza home, I didn't have to get lunch for anyone, which was a nice change. For a little while when a snarly Jin Yeong came out of the shower, it looked like he might leave the house to look for a snack of his own, but Zero didn't tell him not to go, which helped. If Jin Yeong went out looking as cranky as he did, I pitied the human who came into contact with him.

"I will eat pizza," he said at last.

"'S'pose it's the right colour at least," I said. I had already been scoffing pepperoni for the last ten minutes without bothering to take the shower now it was empty. If I left while there was still pizza hanging around, I could be sure there'd be none when I got back. "Oi, Zero; the place we went to was empty."

"So Athelas tells me. What does your friend want us to do?"

"She reckons she's gunna try to track him the old-fashioned way. I told her we'd try on our side. What about your bloke?"

"He trawls the game for playmates," said Zero. "He didn't know Blackpoint except by name."

"You sure about that?" I asked. "'Cos—"

"I am *very sure.*"

"Oh." I looked across at him and saw the ice in his eyes. "All right, then. What do we do next? If the bloke's hidden himself away it's gunna be a bit hard to check on him and see if he's all right."

"You lost your track somewhere Between, I take it."

"The trail led somewhere Between that was better not to go," Jin Yeong said, looking up from his pizza at last. "And the trail was human."

Zero's brows went up. "I see. You think it wasn't our quarry?"

"Pretty certain," I said. "There was a glamour on the place to look like it was derelict, but when we got inside it was pretty normal—it was just empty there. And it can't have been our bloke because the power wasn't on, and no computer. Someone had been squatting, so we followed their trail 'cos we didn't have any other leads."

"I see," Zero said again.

"So interesting, isn't it, my lord?" Athelas said. "We don't know whether or not our quarry is human, but a human was squatting in the house and led a trail Between. Certainly we are living in er, *changing* times."

"Yes," said Zero, a faint crease between his brows. "That's exactly what worries me. More, it worries me that there are apparently humans using magic willy-nilly."

"I'm more worried that there are still people around saying stuff like *willy-nilly,*" I told him. "How old are you, anyway?"

"Perhaps something we should follow up alongside our interest in the case," Athelas suggested. To me, it looked like he was trying to hide a smile. "The crown will certainly be interested if they find out about it."

"Yes," said Zero, and it seemed to me that he said it heavily.

Something he'd rather not acknowledge, or just something he was worried about? I'm pretty sure he sometimes refuses to acknowledge stuff he just doesn't want to deal with, whether or not it's a bad thing.

I asked Athelas, "You didn't find anything else there?"

"The amount of refuse in the house was not conducive to finding anything useful," he said. "I left shortly after you did. Your young human friend will have to try a little harder to find something with her skills."

I didn't like the way he said *your young human friend*. With anyone else it might just have been a statement of fact, but coming from Athelas it sounded like every one of those descriptors was in peril of being changed without notice. It's a skill he has.

"She said she would," I reminded him.

"I'll start some enquiries from our end," Zero said abruptly, surprising me.

I'd expected him to say much the same as Athelas—that Morgana would have to help herself a bit more.

He caught my surprised glance, and looked away. "Whether or not we find him our way, it won't hurt to have her collecting as much data as she can manage; we still don't know whether he's human or fae."

"Someone's still having a go at her over the internet, too," I said. "And we already know it's not the bloke you visited today."

"Agreed," he said, with a certain gleam to his eyes. "I don't despair of your friend finding a little more on her own, but I have my own sources of information."

"Yeah? Don't s'pose you're going to tell me what they are?"

"Not just yet," he said, after a slight pause. "I know this is your case, but I have some things I'd like to be sure of before I go too far with what information I give."

"There's a change," I said, grinning; but I wasn't really upset.

"Perhaps you could employ your mouth with pizza instead of

verbal jabs," Athelas suggested. "Otherwise I could feel that it was a waste to get that pepperoni especially for you."

I grinned at him and grabbed another piece to show my willingness to comply with demands that were reasonable, and it wasn't until later when I was up in my room to get myself some fresh clothes that the thought occurred to me. If Athelas had left around the same time JinYeong and I did, and he was only just starting to eat pizza he had brought back home with him when we got back after fighting and slopping our way Between, that meant he hadn't gone home straight away.

I wondered where he'd been. He would probably just lift his nose at me and point to the pizza if I asked, but I knew exactly how far away that pizza place was—which was not far. I also knew that he could order it on his phone, which would have left him a good hour or so to himself between all of us leaving the house and picking up the pizza for himself and Zero.

He doesn't like me to talk about it, but I'm pretty sure Athelas goes off and does his own thing half the time when he gets bored with us. I'm pretty sure Zero knows about it, too, so I don't bother to say anything.

Puzzles, I thought. That was all there was these days: puzzles and riddles and stuff I couldn't remember. Athelas wasn't the only thing that left me wondering. There was a bottle-top in my pocket that shouldn't have been able to find its way into my room, a vampire downstairs who had been acting downright *weird* for the last week at least, and secrets hidden inside this room itself, not to mention the mysteries that had clung to me since my parents' deaths.

I took out the bottle-top absently, and let it tumble through my fingers. Somehow or other that made my feet wander as well, and when I looked up, I was standing in front of the place where I had hidden treasures of a different kind.

Ah yes. One of my other puzzles.

I put the bottle-cap back in my pocket and sifted through the bowl of marbles that was on display to make sure that the familiar, rectangular slice of glass was still where it was supposed to be.

It was, and that left me feeling a bit more secure about everything.

It didn't look like anything special: it was a USB drive but it looked more like a slide of glass that you used to get in those old chemistry sets, just a bit thinner and shorter, with a tiny gold chip in one end. Tiny and all but invisible when nestled in my bowl of marbles, it waited.

With it, I had bargained for help for humans, freedom for myself, and a chance at shaping the world instead of letting it shape me. It was pretty small for something so powerful. I still didn't know exactly what was on it, but I did know I wanted to find out before I handed it off to Zero, if possible.

I kept another USB in a tiny chest of drawers that was meant to hold jewellery but instead held all of my baby teeth: that USB was less showy and more frustrating. Red and a little bit soft, it had far more easily accessible files on it than the glass USB. Far more easily accessible, but just as incomprehensible.

Perhaps it was time to see if the incomprehensible could be made comprehensible. Or maybe it was just time to see if I could get rid of one of the puzzles that beleaguered my life.

CHAPTER FOUR

I slipped the red USB into my pocket and left the house after the bathroom had aired out enough from Jin Yeong's cologne for me to be able to shower without being gassed out. I had a friend I wanted to see.

My friendship with Five Four One isn't the longest, but it's a pretty close relationship despite that. You get pretty close with a leprechaun after you've fought off dropbears together with an old umbrella sword, a bow made from fibreglass and twine, and the leprechaun's wooden leg.

It helps if you give the wooden leg back at the end.

The thing you probably don't know about leprechauns is that they're *scary good* at chasing up records—especially if those records have anything to do with where money is, or where money ought to have been and mysteriously isn't anymore.

The stuff I wanted him to check out was only tangentially involved with money, but I was hoping that would be enough. Well, that and the fact that I would pay him in cash to find out what I wanted to know. Turns out that leprechauns don't just have a nose for following money trails—they really love smelling actual money.

When I first met him, Five was black-carded and locked out of the world Behind; he now had an apartment in the human world and a small but rapidly growing bit of money in the bank due to discovering he had a nose for following the stocks as well. I'd only known him about a week, but that had been long enough to find out he'd do anything for a twenty no matter how much he had in the bank, 'cos you can't smell the money you have in the bank.

Also he likes me, so he'll do stuff for me.

I was hoping he'd be able to make some sense of the stuff on my little red USB. Detective Tuatu had given it to me a little while ago: it was a copy of all the stuff Athelas had asked him to find in the police system. He'd owed Athelas a favour and hadn't been able to refuse, but he had made a copy of what he'd found to give to me.

Turns out that Detective Tuatu doesn't like not having a choice in what he has to do, and he's pretty creative about making sure he gets a word in edgewise. Athelas probably would have approved, in fact, but since I didn't particularly want him to know that I was checking up on what he was up to, I didn't think it wise to tell him.

I just took the USB and went to the tumble-down old block of flats where Five was living. For a place as tumble-down as it was, it still had a pretty well functioning communication system—by which I mean when you pressed the 'talk' button for any particular flat, the screen only flickered once or twice, and you had a pretty good chance of being connected to the right unit first time around.

Or second, at a pinch; and you don't always get a wild-eyed bloke in his pyjamas, either. Sometimes it's a night worker with half her makeup still on and a pleasant kind of sleepy face.

This time, though, it connected me straight away.

It connected me to a grim, bearded face with sharp eyes and a very loud silence that jutted out every bit as much as its beard. Fortunately, it was a silence I knew.

I said, "Gunna let me in?"

"Oh, it's *you*," he said grumpily, as if he hadn't already been able to see me.

But if you think he was annoyed to see me, you'd be wrong. When Five is actually annoyed by something, his little peg leg starts tapping sharply against the floor, and he sorta stares at you with a dead expression on his face and his small beard fairly bristling with hostility. From Five, grumpiness is tantamount to welcome.

But the biggest sign that he likes me is that he pressed the button to open the grubby sliding door to let me into the lobby.

As usual, the elevator wasn't working, so I took the stairs two at a time and had to slow down by the third floor because I was already panting. So much for all my training: give me one too many flights of stairs and I'm coughing like a seal at the beach.

I was still puffing a bit when I got to the sixth floor. You could say that Five has a penthouse apartment if you're going by the fact that it's the top one and his is the only one up there, but the reality of it is that it's the only one at the top of an old building that should have been demolished about twenty years ago, and it's the only one with a tenant because the other ones are all missing a roof, a window, or half a wall.

"Told ya you should've moved in with us," I told him, when he opened the door and the number on the front fell onto the concrete hallway floor with a tinkle.

"Guff!" he told me, in a small, gruff explosion of speech. "Not with those three! No, thank you!"

"Yeah, well," I said, but I was grinning. It wasn't like I didn't know that Zero had absolutely refused to let Five live with us anyway. I would have fought for it if I'd had to, but Five had remained just as certain that he didn't want to be nearer to my three psychos than he strictly had to be.

"What's the problem, kid?" he asked me. His sharp old eyes

grew a bit sharper under the wild eyebrows. "Those three giving you trouble?"

"About the same," I said, and added happily, "Brought you some bikkies!"

They were store-bought instead of home-made, but I hadn't had the time today for baking.

The eyebrows drew together slightly. "How many?"

"Exactly forty-eight," I said. He doesn't need exactly forty-eight, but he prefers even numbers and he loves twos and lots of twos.

"You'd better come in, then," he said. "And if you're going to ask me to do something, there better be more than a biscuit or two."

"Or forty-eight," I said, grinning. "Got you a twenty, as well."

"Well, there's something," he said. He still sounded grumpy, but now it sounded as though he was trying very hard for it. "Don't worry about trying to shut the door; it won't close properly when the number's off."

"That doesn't make sense."

"You're telling me, kid! Nothing makes sense since I've—well, nothing makes sense. Where does the hot water come from? Mystery! No magic in there!"

"That's the bit of paper you have to pay a hundred and fifty bucks every quarter for," I told him, trying not to grin more. "I told you about the water bill and electricity."

"And the cold blower won't blow cold anymore."

"You probably need to change the batteries in the remote."

"Listen kid, I've *been* in batteries, and I'm telling you—"

"Heck," I said. "*I'll* make the tea; you sit down and I'll fix the electronics later, okay?"

"This time, explain it better," he said, scowling at me.

"Yeah, like I'm the one who doesn't understand!" I said cheekily.

That made him grin, which must have annoyed him, so I pretended I hadn't seen it and went off into the kitchen to boil the jug and dump my packages of biscuits. He followed me in, but that wasn't surprising: Five doesn't have any living room furniture at the moment—I mean, he barely has a living room at the moment—and the couple times I've visited, we've sat at the kitchen table to talk.

Well, as much as a taciturn old leprechaun talks, that is.

"What is it you want?"

"Got a bit of paperwork for you," I said, as the jug bubbled away in the background. It was more than a bit of paperwork: hopefully the library still had some paper now that I'd been through and printed out everything on the USB.

I dumped the plastic bag of it on the table with a thump, and pointed at it.

"What's this?" Five demanded. "I don't do paperwork. Where's my console display?"

"You don't know how to use a human computer," I objected. "Thought you just needed to see the stuff!"

"Where's my twenty?"

I grinned, and passed it over. I was almost sure he would have done it without the money, but he likes to pretend he's a grumpy old man and what's the point in stopping people having fun? Anyway, it was Zero paying for it, and that was a bit of fun for me.

"What is it?"

"Dunno," I said. "Figured you'd be able to tell me that."

"Typical!" he said, but he couldn't hide the gleam in his eye. He'd caught sight of the top paper—a water bill—and there was already a scent of the game in it for him. "You want me to follow the money?"

"Maybe? Dunno. It's a whole lot of stuff that someone gathered from police files and databases, and I want to know why. Why he wanted it; what it all leads to, that sorta stuff. Reckon you can find some meaning to it?"

"I can tell you where the money goes," he said. "That's all I promise."

"That'll do," I said cheerfully. It was more than I'd had that morning. "When d'you reckon you'll have answers for me?"

"Hard to say," he said. At first, I thought he was just being grumpy for the sake of being grumpy, but his face was serious. "I follow it where it goes, but I have to find a pattern first. And I'm not used to dealing with hard copies. If I had my portal and console, I could do a bit more."

Disappointing, but it wasn't like I really knew what to expect from this mixed lot, after all. I could wait as long as it took. And try to forget the implication that Five would be able to access human data from a Behind interface.

"All right," I said. "You figured out how to use the phone?"

"Green and gold! You showed me last time: do you think I've forgotten since then?"

"You press the buttons in the same order as the number."

He glowered at me over the top of his mug. "I knew that. And then I press the red button—"

"Green."

"Yes, I press the green button and then wait."

"You got it. Call me when you know anything, all right? I'll bring you some more biscuits later."

I got home just as Jin Yeong did: we met on the doorstep and eyed each other with suspicion. He probably wanted to know where I'd been, and I definitely wanted to know where he'd been —and just as definitely didn't want to be talking about where *I'd* been, so I said accusatorily, "You don't come through the front door! What are you up to?"

"Humans are watching," he said, his eyes flicking back toward the road, where a human couple were out walking their dog. "And *hyeong* said we should be more careful these days."

I opened the door and stepped through ahead of him. "Since when do you obey Zero?"

"I obey needful things."

"Yeah," I said, narrowing my eyes at him. "I remember."

Jin Yeong said something in a snarl of Korean that was unintelligible despite the fact that I could usually understand him now, and said bitingly, "You are a *bother* to me."

"Yeah, you've said that before," I said. "It's my flamin' pleasure!"

One of his eyebrows went up and he grinned, suddenly and startlingly.

"Pet," said Zero, cold and commanding, "stop needling Jin Yeong. He has some information we need, and I'd like to get it before the end of the day."

"Right, sorry!" I called, and left the still-grinning Jin Yeong in the hallway. "You lot want tea and coffee? Dinner won't be until later if you're still sorting out boxes."

"Biscuits, too," said Zero forbiddingly, but honestly even a fae lord can't entirely pull off the forbidding thing when he's requesting biscuits. Especially the pretty little shortbreads I get.

I popped up into the kitchen to start the jug boiling, feeling as though today was one round of tea and coffee after another, then hung around in the doorway so I could see what it was that Jin Yeong had been sent out about. To my surprise, they had all decamped to the upstairs living room, and by the time I got up there with my tray of drinks and bikkies they were gathered around the computer, looking perplexed.

Turns out it hadn't been for information gathering so much as game gathering.

"You been buying computer games?" I asked Jin Yeong in astonishment, as Zero turned over a rectangular package between his hands.

"*Aniyo*," said Jin Yeong, looking far too pleased with himself. "I did not buy it."

"Yeah, that's being *real* careful," I mocked. "Zero will be *real* happy when you're pulled up for shoplifting!"

"I will not be stopped; I am too charming."

"Yeah?" I said. "'Cos I know one human detective and one human pet who are both pretty flamin' immune to your mojo."

"You are both defective."

"It's *detective*—"

"*Pet*," said Zero, on a sigh. "You're spilling biscuits on the keyboard."

"Look at you, learning what stuff's called!" I said admiringly, picking up the couple of biscuits that had slipped off the side of the plate. "Five second rule. They're fine. Want me to put the game in and start it up?"

"Yes," Zero said. He still looked faintly disturbed, but whether that was because he had to accept help from me or because of the biscuits, I wasn't quite sure.

"You look after the tray, then," I said. It was nice to be able to give orders now and then, especially now that I wasn't a pet for a little while. Didn't mean my orders would be obeyed, of course, but I could give them.

Zero accepted the tray with the same rather bemused air, and shifted minutely to allow me to sit on the chair in front of the computer. I saw ghostly reflections of my three psychos in the computer screen as I turned it on, each one helping himself to his own drink from the tray. I was pretty sure that Zero slipped a few biscuits into his front pockets, too.

Lucky for me, it was an easy game to load—either that, or we had a good computer. I haven't played computer games since I was a kid, and they were pretty different then. I was also pretty impressed that JinYeong had managed to get the game in the right format, until I remembered that he had probably just talked the game shop owner into giving him the right thing.

Open world, Morgana had said. That was true; before we got to it, though, there was a whole range of choices and about half an hour of cut scenes and tiny interactions to teach us how to use the keyboard commands.

I went through it all impatiently, but for my three psychos, it seemed to be a lot more interesting. They hung over my shoulder —or at least, Jin Yeong and Zero did; even Athelas, who had sat down elegantly after drawing up a chair close to me, leaned forward to gaze at the screen—and watched avidly through the entire length of the cut scenes and exposition.

That made me pay more attention, and as I watched, it occurred to me that if I knew the names of the fae families and factions, this could almost be a primer for Behind as it pertained to the fae. Zero and Athelas at least seemed very familiar with the names; Zero frowned a bit more each time a family or faction was named, and Athelas, a soft reflection in the screen where it was darkest, smiled.

There wasn't much in it about any other Behindkind, despite the Characters you could choose from. I wondered if that was being kept for the next game, and I wasn't entirely surprised when, at the beginning of the gameplay itself, Athelas sat back and crossed one leg over the other, still very much amused.

"How interesting!" he said, sipping his tea. "Is it a Behindkind plant, do you think, or is there a game writer out there who knows just a little bit too much for their own good? Those names are...very nearly correct."

"I'm not sure yet," Zero said, frowning. "It will be difficult in either case."

"That mean you're gunna drop the case?" I asked, rather anxiously.

He shook his head. "We have an interim agreement. I can't renege."

"You say that as though you would have reneged if you could," Athelas said, apparently to himself.

Zero looked across at him coldly.

"I do beg your pardon if I spoke out of turn, my lord."

"Do you."

"I was merely indicating to the pet that the way I would act is at odds with the way you conduct yourself."

"Don't think he believes that, either," I warned Athelas. "Oi. Zero, what do you mean that it'll be difficult either way?"

"If it's an unauthorised Behindkind enterprise, we'll be running up against Behindkind law enforcement unless we're very careful. If it's a human who knows more than they should...that is something of a problem for you."

"Oh," I said. "I see."

And I did see. I already had a good idea of what was expected to happen to a human who knew too much: it hadn't happened to me, but it had been threatened a couple of times. Zero was telling me that if it came to a human who knew more than they should, he would adhere to Behindkind guidelines, despite any objections I might have.

If that was the case, it was indeed my problem, and I would have to think about how I was going to handle it when the time came.

"In the meantime, try to remember that you'll be referred to as *pet* and that you should so refer to yourself: if we come into contact with Behindkind Enforcers it will be...advisable. We've also taken on a job from the Enforcers—"

"Job?" I sat up straight. We were already full up with the murder and now Morgana, and— Wait. Was this job one of *those* ones? The ones that had to do with helping humans? "What job?"

"—and it would be best for everyone concerned if people still think you're the pet."

Zero hesitated, and I could fairly *see* him struggling to make himself say more. Close-mouthed is one thing: Zero is an air-tight vault hermetically sealed in a room that's part of a safe-house stashed inside a flamin' mountain.

I gave him an encouraging smile, but that only seemed to annoy him, so I asked again, "What job? Is it one of the ones that golden git brought us?"

"His name is—"

"Jin Yeong already told me," I said. "It sounds like a sneeze and I can't pronounce it. It's easier to call him the golden git."

Zero's gaze took on a slight frosting of ice. "If you call him anything of the sort to his face—"

"Yeah, you'll trounce me," I said gloomily.

"I think my lord was more worried about having to clean up a body," Athelas said.

"Oh. Well, at least I can fight these days," I offered. If I couldn't, I was still pretty good at running away, and I could nip behind Zero quickly enough at a pinch.

"Not your body," said Zero briefly.

"I would advise learning how to pronounce that particular sneeze," Athelas said. "But after all, I shouldn't wish to interfere with that charming insouciance of yours, so consider yourself free to ignore my advice."

I gazed at him for a few moments, then said, "Don't you threaten me with the consequences of my actions."

Athelas sputtered into his teacup, and I turned back to Zero.

"Yeah, anyway: what's the job?"

"The job is the same one your little friend brought us, though from a slightly different angle."

"Oh," I said, a bit glumly. Of course Zero had taken on the job from Morgana; he'd known that it had something to do with Behindkind. Had he already taken it on from the Enforcers before he spoke with her? "When did you learn about that?"

"When your friend told me about it," he said. "I made some further enquiries this afternoon, since it seemed like a familiar sort of setup. The crown occasionally uses such plants to gauge the response of humans to the existence of Behindkind—or to scout for potentially useful employees. However, this is an unauthorised testing, if test it is. We've been tasked with finding the source of the game and apprehending them; the crown believes that humans are likely to be injured by this sort of setup."

I heard the very faint edge of sarcasm in his voice, and although it made me grin, I still felt comforted. As things stood, it didn't look too bad. If Blackpoint really was human, it would be worse, but if he was Behindkind, then at least humans were going to be looked after no matter what the outcome was.

"Reckon I should tell Morgana to stop playing the game?" I asked. Giving Behindkind of any sort information about human choices and reactions was bad enough, but people were disappearing. I didn't want that to happen to Morgana.

"I've already warned her to do so," Zero said. "I called her for further information earlier."

"How'd you get her number?" My voice was sharp, because I didn't like them having her number. When I was the only one with Morgana's number, it felt like I was able to be more of a buffer between her and the psychos, as if I could stop the Between and Behind worlds from affecting her more than they already had.

"It was written on the second piece of paper," Zero said. He hesitated for a moment, and added slightly stiffly, "I wouldn't have called her if she hadn't written it there: I would have kept you as our go-between."

"Thanks," I said, a bit mollified. It wasn't that I didn't trust them, but I didn't trust the kind of trouble that came along with them—or even the trouble that came along with me by default these days.

"This is your case," said Zero, looking away. "There's no need to thank me. Of course you're the point of entry."

That was nice, too. It meant that I was being taken seriously as a part of the team, at least when it came to the cases I brought to the psychos.

"That holds up until there's fae involvement," he added. "Then, if there should be a misalignment of purposes—"

"I know," I said grimly. "You'll go with fae law. I've already seen it."

I still remembered it, too. A whole office full of Behind-allied humans who were trading in bodies and souls; judged, sentenced, and put to death in one day. I wasn't likely to forget. Behind law dealt severely with lawbreakers when it caught up with them, whether those lawbreakers were human or Behindkind. And when you deal in bodies and souls, you have to expect to pay in the same coin.

I already knew that was what I'd signed up for, and so long as it protected humans who hadn't done anything wrong, I was willing to go along with it. Especially if it was the only protection humans would get.

I left the three of them to get on with their exploration of the computer world, but by the time I was cooking dinner they'd either finished with it, or, as I suspected from the looks of annoyance on the faces of both Zero and JinYeong, run into a problem in-game that they couldn't solve with their limited knowledge of computer games.

I nearly grinned and asked them if they needed a bit of help with it, but I remembered in time that they were actually being proactive and co-operative in the investigation and managed to close my mouth instead.

Athelas murmured, "That must have been difficult, Pet!" as he passed me the tray from upstairs.

I choked on a giggle and took the tray. "Dinner'll be ready in ten," I said, so I didn't have to answer him.

Athelas came in later, while I was doing the washing up, and sat down at the kitchen island with his teacup in one hand. I poured him a refill, careful to keep my sud-dripping to the counter and not his teacup, then went back to washing up.

I was pretty sure he was here to say something, but if it came to information being given, I wasn't prepared to exchange for it. He would have to either tell me or not tell me, whichever one he wanted.

"Perhaps, Pet," he said at last, "you're not quite aware of exactly who the golden fae and his entourage are."

"Yeah," I said. "They're the cobbers that come through the linen closet. What's wrong with 'em, by the way? Why can't they use the front door now that they've found us?"

Athelas sipped his tea. "Someone took the liberty of attaching a particularly specific strain of poison to the front door when we first arrived. It will have no effect upon humans and most fae, but the golden fae would find himself made very uncomfortable by it."

"Very uncomfortable, or very dead?"

"In life, I find it's not so much about people being dead, as *wishing* they were dead."

"Yeah, that doesn't surprise me," I said. "But d'you reckon you could be a bit more specific?"

"Let us say, very uncomfortable and then very dead," he replied.

"Well, it wasn't me that did it, so I'm gunna go out on a limb and say it must have been you," I told him.

"You may say exactly as you choose," he said placidly. "However, it would behove you to remember that that particular fae is allied with the Family, as are we now, by some bizarre and wholly unfortunate circumstance—"

"You better not be talking about me this time," I warned him. "If you are, I won't give you the butter cookies I made."

"I can't help thinking sometimes," he said reflectively, "that you're far too perceptive for your own good."

"That means yes, doesn't it?"

"We are, it seems, once more allied with the Family in a tenuous manner; we are also now, Pet, allied with the King Behind in a manner far less tenuous. The Enforcers are his officers, even if they're allied more closely to the Family and Zero's father than the king would like. Should there be unpleasantness between us and our liaison, no matter the outcome, it would bring us into greater scrutiny here than most of us would find…comfortable."

"Is it anything like scrutiny from Zero's dad?" I asked. I'd already experienced that particular scrutiny, and I would very much rather never face anything like it again.

Mind you, given my current status in the household, and the likelihood of meeting Zero's dad again now that we were a bit more officially connected, I was probably likely to face at least the Behindkind again.

And I understood, faintly, why Zero might say that it was safer for me if I maintained my outward appearance of being a pet, even if I wasn't one at the moment. Like Morgana's game, the fae tended to think of humans as the lowest of the low, and servants just barely higher; they expected little of me and would likewise suspect little of me.

"Considerably worse," said Athelas. "But scrutiny from my lord's father is far more likely at the present, and we're better equipped to deal with it."

"Hang on, is Zero's dad likely to come to the house?"

"I rather think my lord would have something to say about that," murmured Athelas, gazing into the reflection of his tea. "But after all, there's no saying that there wouldn't be an attempt."

"He better not be growing grass and flowers and stuff all over my carpet if he comes here," I said, scowling. As if I'd be able to stop him doing it. As if I'd dare to scowl at him if he did. "I don't wanna have to start weeding the hallways—and that reminds me; which one of you lot has been making dust bunnies come alive in the hallways? They're chewing on the skirting-boards and leaving the bits everywhere."

"I rather fancy the banshees have been busy," Athelas said. "Perhaps you could do something about that when you have a spare moment. They do bother Jin Yeong so."

He left his teacup on the counter and got up to go as he said it, before I could say more than a startled, "Oi! What am I supposed to do about 'em?"

I didn't want to do anything to help Jin Yeong, either, if it came to that. Maybe I could talk the banshees into moving into his room and setting the dust-bunnies free in there. That was a thought.

I came back out into the downstairs living room after I'd finished the washing up, but they'd gone back to their own case by then, Zero now poring over the files in one of the boxes while Athelas contemplated the ceiling with his cup of tea in hand. Jin Yeong was back to sniffing stuff and tasting stuff, his eyes far away and bloody, so there must have been some interesting scents in his boxes. I've seen his eyes like that before: dunno what he's seeing, but it's like watching an almost-human computer process information.

That meant I was on my own tonight when it came to Morgana's case, and I didn't have a clue where I was supposed to start. I could always ask Detective Tuatu to do some digging, but if Morgana and her scary good computer skills couldn't produce a useful address, I wasn't sure the police department could do it. They were meant to do things by the law—and they restricted themselves to government systems.

Not to mention the fact that there was still a pretty big Behindkind finger in the police pie around here. No, it would be safer if I didn't go to Detective Tuatu about this. Safer for him, too, most likely.

Zero must have seen me squirming and guessed the reason for it, because when I brought out the hot drinks and biscuits by way of dessert later on, he said, "I've made some enquiries about your case: we could have an address as early as tomorrow. Don't...fidget."

I took that as a warning not to go off and do anything stupid, but despite my annoyance at the implied insult I felt a little bit warmer. It was nice to know I wasn't on my own anymore.

I just had to make sure I didn't trust that warmth too much.

CHAPTER FIVE

I'VE GOTTEN USED TO FAE POPPING THROUGH THE LINEN CLOSET by now, but it's still a bit of an annoyance to have them popping in after dinner. I never know whether or not to offer them dessert. Even if I do offer it, not all of them will take it. Once upon a time there was a mix-up with Jin Yeong's blood snacks and the regular food, and it turns out that fae really don't like biting into little blood bubbles in pastry. Who would have guessed? A real shame, that.

Still, sometimes it's fun to offer just to see how horrified they look—or amused, depending on which fae it is.

But when someone knocked at the linen closet door after dinner the next day, the sound was sharp and bright. A nice business-like knock that sounded patient rather than imperious.

So I yelled into the living room, "I've got it!" and went to open the door. I was pretty sure I knew who it was. Sure enough, when I opened the door, I didn't cop a sight of highly armoured, highly supercilious fae captain. Instead, I found myself grinning at a female fae who was just as golden and just as highly armoured, but a lot more fun to be around.

"Let you out on your own, did he?" I asked.

If her captain was an idiot with a name like a sneeze—and, unfortunately, our point of contact with the Behind legal system —this fae was tough, had a surprising sense of humour, and the ability to stand her ground even in the face of Zero's icy glare, which was something I didn't get to see too often.

"I'm here to assist Lord Sero with a particular enquiry," she said, a line of amusement deepening along the lower edge of her cheek. "My captain couldn't make the journey today."

"What a shame," I said insincerely. This was an interesting new development. "Oi, they didn't tell me your name."

There was the briefest of pauses, while I wondered if she was going to tell me I could refer to her by her rank, before she said, "You can call me Palomena."

"Right," I said. "Want something to eat, Palomena? You're just in time for dessert."

"Is there blood in it?"

I grinned. "Not for you."

"In that case, yes."

"Coming up!" I said cheerfully. "You might as well head into the living room; they're all in there, plus a banshee or two, I reckon."

I ignored Jin Yeong's startled *mwoh*? from the living room, and went back to the kitchen. Palomena was another tea-lover, which rounded out the usual three coffee drinkers to one tea drinker a bit, so all I needed to do was put out another cup for her and hope Athelas wouldn't mind sharing his pot.

I hurried, because if this was about Morgana's case, I wanted to be there when the discussions began. I could already hear Zero's voice from the kitchen, cold and hard and carrying. "Why are you here?"

"Orders, my lord," said Palomena. She didn't say it cheerfully, but she said it without hesitation or undue worry. "As I should suppose you would know, since my captain informed you of it when you spoke with him earlier."

"And I should suppose that your captain remembered me telling him I didn't require assistance from the Enforcers," Zero said, his voice sinking into a deeper rumble. Not so much ice now as hard, craggy rock.

"I couldn't say, my lord," she said, as I put a few more biscuits and a bit more fruit and cheese on the tray, grinning. "I have my orders from my captain, and that's all."

"Your orders—"

"Here we go!" I said cheerfully, before things could get more exciting. In general, I like a bit of excitement, but not when it means the coffee and biscuits are going to get messed up. I pointed with my chin at the soft cheese, and said to the lieutenant, "You'd better get in on the brie before this lot gets at it, or you won't get a look-in."

"Don't feed her biscuits and cheese!" Zero said in exasperation.

"Well, you can't just put her in a corner, and it's rude to eat cheese and biscuits without giving any to your guests."

"She's not a guest," he retorted.

"You just want to eat all the cheese," I said.

Zero very visibly took in a breath, and turned to the lieutenant. "Have you at least brought information with you?"

"I have a potential address," she said. "We've been keeping an eye on *City Fae* for a month or two now, but we've only just been able to pin down the source of those problems within the game and the human world when it comes to usable intelligence."

"You've been looking for Blackpoint, too?" I asked, frowning. "And you found where you think he's living?"

"Just recently," she nodded. "Like I said, we'd already had our eye on *City Fae*, but it took us some time to figure out how to interact with it enough to get usable intelligence. The players seem to develop pretty rabid fascination with the game, and we wanted to be sure that *consequences* weren't going to spill over into the human world."

"Yeah, can't have humans learning about stuff," I said, before I could stop myself.

Palomena's eyes fell on me. They weren't annoyed or exasperated, just a bit considering. "It's certainly not safe," she said. "But after all, life isn't safe. My job is to make sure that life is kept as...*safe* as possible for the greatest amount of people."

"With a bias toward Behindkind?"

Heck. I was really gunna have to try not to antagonise people when they were being nice to me.

To my surprise, she answered me swiftly and honestly. "Yes. Behindkind are always the first priority. But although there's a hierarchy, humans are still given consideration. It's the best I can do."

"S'pose so," I said. And since she seemed sincere about doing her best, I pushed the biscuits toward her. "Here, have a chocky one. They're the best."

"I'll accompany your team for the investigation of the address I have provided," she said, taking a biscuit. "If needed, I'll assist, but please consider me to be an observer only for the time being."

Zero didn't say anything, a crushing silence that grew heavier by the moment. Maybe Palomena was used to that, because she let it stretch out and bit into her biscuit as though she didn't have anything else to be doing. I mean, they were good biscuits, so that probably helped.

When she had finished her biscuit and was delicately brushing the crumbs from her fingers, Zero finally said, "An observer *only*. We'll visit the address tomorrow."

Maybe he was hoping she would leave and we could slip out early before she got back, because I've never known night time to be a barrier to any of them going out and getting things done that should usually be done in daylight hours. None of 'em sleep as much as a human—I'm not sure they even *need* to sleep, though they do sleep a few hours here and there—and they seem to like to take advantage of every hour when they're on a case.

Palomena must have had the same thought, because she said, "There's no need to wait on my account. I'm ready to accompany you at any time: I don't see the necessity of leaving things so long."

"We need to recharge," Zero said coldly.

"I see. That's different, of course. Shall we plan on tomorrow morning, in that case?"

He gave a very small nod. "Certainly. I hope you'll excuse us from inviting you along while we recharge."

"Of course!" she said. "I'm quite fresh, as it happens. You can leave me alone here in the house with perfect impunity."

Good grief! She was actually winning tricks here! This is what happens when you're powerful enough to stand up to a fae lord: you get to have fun without worrying that it's gunna get you throttled one day.

Zero gazed at her meditatively for a few moments before he said, "The pet will remain. You should know that I've made it impervious to fae Command."

Ha! I was impervious to it all by myself, and if we were going back to calling me *it*, I was gunna—

"I don't foresee the need to Command such a well-trained pet," said Palomena equably.

"And I don't care to have my property damaged."

Was he talking about the house, or about me?

Palomena didn't seem to have any difficulty in deciding which one. She said, "I'm not in the habit of interfering with other peoples' pets, and I'm well aware that humans are usually sleeping at this hour."

Zero nodded shortly. He probably didn't have any other choice, but I had the feeling he could have made another choice available to himself despite the expert rounding up Palomena had just performed. If he'd really wanted to, that is.

He must have been reasonably sure she wasn't going to cause problems or kill me in my sleep or anything, because he didn't ask

Jin Yeong to stay behind, either. That meant he trusted her to a certain extent—or maybe he just wanted to get Jin Yeong to do something else while she was here with me. It wasn't like Jin Yeong needed to recharge, after all.

Jin Yeong, who knew that just as well as I or Zero, shot a narrow-eyed look at Zero, and for the briefest moment I thought he was going to complain. I saw Palomena watching them with the faintest hint of amusement in her eyes, and it occurred to me, far too late, that Palomena should also be very well aware of the fact that Jin Yeong didn't need to recharge.

She didn't object, either, and that interested me. Cutting her losses, or not worried about what they were up to? More worrying, was it because she was more interested in anything that could be around the house?

"Go to bed, Pet," said Zero. "You'll need to be fresh tomorrow morning, early."

"Right," I said. So I wasn't supposed to poke my nose into whether or not Palomena was poking *her* nose into what was around the house. And since it seemed like Zero was waiting for me to go upstairs, I trailed away toward the stairs without trying to clear up the dessert things. "See you lot tomorrow, then."

"Yes," said Zero, and if it sounded like a threat, at least it didn't seem like it was directed at me. That was nice for a change.

I went to bed as I was told, because even if I'm not a pet anymore, I still know when to do what's good for me.

I woke to the sticky silence of a house that was nearly empty, but not quite. The sheets were damp and hot under my back, and the air seemed to hum. The hum bent itself around a solid shape a few steps away from the bed, sending a stab of fear right through my heart, and I tried to get up.

It was no use, of course. The nightmare's always the same: for those first few seconds of terror, I can't move.

I struggled against it, the breath caught in my throat; struggled vainly. Then the force that lashed me to the bed vanished as that solid figure leapt for me, a gleam of metal glistening in the moonlight. A scream tore from my throat and I threw myself sideways. Something thudded against the wall; me or that black figure, I wasn't sure which, because I was reaching through space or Between or something else in a frantic search for a weapon—any weapon.

My hand found a hilt and I slashed in a wide, awkward back-handed stroke, my weapon too heavy and unfamiliar to use properly. I was used to light twin blades, not the heavy two-handed sword that was in my hand and should have been downstairs in the hall-stand, pretending to be a yellow umbrella.

The slash passed through the black figure without making contact, even though it was still so much of a presence that I could hear its breath, and the sword buried itself in the wall, leaving a long gash. It stuck there, too, so I reached out with my other hand and slapped it over the light switch, flooding the room with brightness.

Gone.

It was always gone by the time I turned on the light.

Panting, I reefed the sword out of the wall and became dimly aware that someone was shouting my name. A female someone.

"Pet! Pet! Answer me!"

There were no women in this house. Who was—

Palomena. It was Palomena's voice.

"Pet, you have to tell me how to get in. I can hear you, but I can't get in. If you need me, you have to let me in."

"I'm okay!" I yelled back, but my voice cracked, and I was pretty sure I wasn't fooling anyone.

"I'd like to see that to make sure," she said. "How do I open the door?"

Heck. The sword was still a sword, and Palomena definitely shouldn't see it like that.

"Go back!" I whispered to it, too muddled and shaking to focus like I usually had to in order to make things do what I wanted them to do. "Go back! You're not meant to be a sword where she can see you!"

Palomena must have figured out the trick by herself, or maybe the house decided to let her in, because the door swung open, whispering heavily across the carpet. In the opposing light that opening brought, the flaps of a furled umbrella made odd shadows against the far wall and I breathed a small, shaking sigh of relief.

"Pet?"

Maybe it was because I had stopped screaming that she hung back in the doorway—waiting for permission to come in? Maybe it was because she saw what she wasn't expecting to see that she just stood there.

It must have looked pretty weird. There I was on the bed with my knees slightly bent to allow for the bounce of the mattress, brandishing a yellow umbrella in one hand and staring wildly in all directions.

"What?"

"What are you fighting?"

"Nightmare," I said, trying not to pant. My heart was still beating far too quickly, and it seemed like everything in the corners of my eyes was crawling with movement and shadow that shouldn't have been there.

Palomena's eyes fell to the umbrella, and she asked quietly, "How did that get up here? Wasn't it in the hallstand?"

"Nah," I lied. "The banshees've been making nests in everything, so I've been bringing stuff up here to clean out and banshee-proof."

I mean, I'd planned to do something like that, so it was a half-truth.

"You'll have to teach me that trick," she said, walking deliberately across the room as if picking her steps carefully. Maybe there were a few too many shadows for her liking, too. Still, as she walked across the floor, they seemed to settle down. "There's always a problem in the barracks with those little beasts."

"Yeah," I said, climbing down from the bed with my fingers wrapped tightly around the umbrella's handle. Now that the room had stopped moving in the shadows, I could do it without feeling like I was going to step into a roiling pit of vermin or living shadow. "I'll do that."

She ran her hand along the cut I'd made in the wall and said, "You'd better come downstairs. No wonder you're having night-mares—I would if I had to sleep in a little tomb like this, too."

"It's not a tomb!" I said, hunching my shoulders. "It's safe. Well, when there aren't any figments of my imagination hanging around, that is."

"Figments?" Palomena, already at the doorway again, half-turned. "I thought you said it was a nightmare?"

"Yeah," I said, wondering if my brain was still scrambled, or if this was a missing step in understanding between the Behind and human worlds. "Nightmare. Figment of my imagination."

"It may or may not be real, but whatever it is, it's certainly not a figment of your imagination," she said, and left the room.

I scrambled after her. "What do you mean, it may be real?"

"Nightmares don't happen in a vacuum," she said.

"Well yeah, but—"

"Nor do they take form in a house this closely intertwined with Between without having more substance than even a normal nightmare."

"Thanks," I said, a bit sourly. "That's sure to make it less terri-fying next time."

"You should be terrified," she said. "Life between two worlds will always be dangerous, and the more frightened you are, the more likely you are to stay alive."

Disgruntled, I asked, "Call that living?"

She laughed softly and said, "We're all frightened. And it's a discussion that is as often had Behind as it is here, but that's beside the point. You shouldn't be at ease with Behindkind in the house."

It was funny though. Following her down the stairs, with the floor solid beneath her feet and her wiry shoulders square against the hallway light, I didn't feel afraid. I felt as though I could rest for a little while without worrying about something nasty showing up and making off with me.

"You remind me of someone," I said, trotting down the last couple of steps. Maybe it was habit; I kept on going into the kitchen. "You want pancakes?"

"Don't you need more sleep? I remember humans being more fragile."

"I'll go back to sleep later," I told her. "I want to cook something right now."

"I like pancakes," she said.

She knew better than to hover in the kitchen, which was nice; I heard her moving around in the living room, pacing back and forth, and wasn't quite sure if that was her being nice. I hadn't heard fae make that much noise walking before. It felt like she was moving around just enough so that I could have the comfort of someone else in the house, just living.

It was nice.

It was also very convenient, since my phone started buzzing in my pocket while the first lot of pancakes were cooking.

"Yeah?"

I heard muttering in the background, then a loud *crack* and someone swearing.

"Kid? Kid, are you there! Gold perish it, what's this contraption doing now!"

"Five?" I said, grinning. I'd know that cranky old voice anywhere. "You really managed to call!"

"Hello? Hello?" bawled his voice, tinnily. "*Is someone there? For all that's green and gold will you behave yourself?*"

"You gotta hold it up to your ear!" I yelled, giving up on the hope of not being overheard. "And stop yelling; my ears can only take so much!"

"Right!" he said, still far too loud. "I can talk to you here!"

In the living room, the sound of Palomena pacing ceased.

"Yes, but do you have to yell?"

"You said there were buttons," he said sourly, at a slightly more bearable level of decibels. "There are no buttons; just little flat circles."

"Those are the buttons on a touch screen device," I told him. "Anyway, congratulations on learning how to use a mobile phone; I'm so proud."

"I found a few interesting things in your paperwork," he said. "But it's going to take a lot longer than I thought, because everything's twisty like a rope and I'm at least eighty percent sure that it'll end up making one whole."

"Twisty, I get," I said. "But what do you mean, it's likely to make one whole?"

"Rope, I said!"

"Yeah, but—oh! You mean you think it's all connected."

"No. It's not connected. Not yet. But it's twining round and around, and I'll be very much surprised if it doesn't turn out to be all one rope of information."

I gave up on trying to make that mesh with his first statement. "Okay. Does that mean you know where it all leads?"

"Not the faintest gleam! Early indicators say that it'll all lead back to one source, but that's the last step of all. At the moment I'm just trying to trace all the strands back to a general direction. I'm following the money, but it's a faint trail because it's not about the money."

"Right. So you're pretty sure it's all going in one direction but you're not a hundred percent sure yet and you want to be. You also don't know exactly what direction it's all pointing in."

"Got it in one, kid! We already have one connection—the person who was trying to collate all of this. Who was that?"

"Can't tell you just yet," I said apologetically. It felt too much like betraying Athelas. "If it looks like that's an important thing, I'll let you know."

I already knew it was important to a certain extent: if Athelas was trying to find information on human websites, it was because it was needed. He also knew who had asked him to do it, since I very much doubted he was doing it off his own bat. And if he *was* doing it off his own bat, it could only be to protect or help someone.

All of those things were important to know.

And yet, I couldn't bring myself to tell Five as much.

"Green and gold," muttered Five. "Well, let me know when you're a bit less sensitive, and I'll be able to be more useful. How do I stop this thing chirruping at me?"

"I'll hang up first," I said, grinning. "Talk to you later, yeah?"

I hung up, but I'm pretty sure he spent the next five minutes bawling at his phone, trying to find out if I'd really hung up. In the living room, I heard Palomena begin walking again, and went back to my pancakes. I was just in time to flip them before they got a decent coating of charcoal.

If Athelas was protecting someone, it could only be Zero; Zero was the only one he would take so much time and trouble to protect or help, as far as I could see. If he was doing it on orders, there were only two choices: Zero, and Zero's father. If it came down to a choice between the two, I would have picked Zero for the win. Zero's father, Athelas seemed to obey from a toxic mix of fear and long servitude—and perhaps some misplaced loyalty—but if I wasn't completely mad, Athelas served Zero from a sense of loyalty that had more than a decent amount of fondness to it. He probably wouldn't admit that, not when he knew what being fond of people opened himself up to, but I was still pretty sure about it.

Zero was the most likely person for everything to point at, and I would need to remember that.

· · ·

I DIDN'T EXACTLY EXPECT ZERO AND THE OTHERS TO ARRIVE when they'd said they would, but I didn't expect the screaming in the background when he called me, either. The call came just a bit after I woke up on the couch, startling me into grabbing the phone before I was properly awake.

"We won't be home until later," he said, his voice rumbling below the cacophony. "Go to see your friend and let her know where we are in the investigation; make sure you're back in a couple of hours."

"Heck!" I said, sitting up with wild hair and one missing sock. "Is that—is someone being murdered over there?"

Palomena sat up straight in her chair, a sudden golden ray of movement.

"Not yet," said Zero, and hung up.

"They've got a real communication problem," I said to Palomena, who was looking bright and alert. I was pretty sure she was itching for a fight, and since I liked to think that Zero hadn't given me more information because he didn't want Palomena there with them rather than because he'd forgotten he was supposed to be sharing stuff with me these days, I told her, "They're fine. They'll be back later, he said."

"So I gathered," she said. "I'm inclined to go there myself and see what's happening."

I looked at her for a bit before I said, "Reckon you'd already have gone if you were allowed to go by yourself."

She grinned. "You're cheeky, for a pet."

"That's what I've been told. So how come you're not allowed to go around by yourself? You do something naughty?"

"My captain prefers for me to be under command at all times," she said, looking away.

She had definitely done something bad. Mind you, something bad to Behindkind could be either something good by human standards *or* something unspeakably horrible.

"All right," I said, since it wasn't like we were sharing everything with her, after all. "You want some breakfast before I go?"

Her eyes came to rest on me again. "The pancakes were enough, and I'm not entirely sure I like the idea of you going off on your own after receiving a call from your owner."

"Just liaising between Zero and a human," I said.

"I see," she said.

She didn't sound convinced, and since I was pretty sure she'd try to come along with me if I didn't do anything, I said, "You can use one of those truth spells on me or something. True blue; all I'm doing is going off to visit a human who's been giving us a bit of info on the bloke we're after from this side."

I wanted to say more, but the more you say the more trouble you can get in around this place, so I stopped talking despite the urge.

"I just did," she said.

Well. That explained tiny twitch in the back of my mind that had been trying to make my tongue talk more than it should a moment ago.

"Rude," I said. "Right, then; can I go?"

"I'm not your master," she said. "But I won't trail along, if that's what you really want to know."

Maybe it was rude, but it had to be said. "Don't reckon he wants you alone in the house."

"Possibly not," she agreed. "I'm not sure the house would let me stay, if it comes to that. It's pretty protective, for a human's house."

"What can I say? It's just too easy to get fond of humans," I said, shrugging.

"Yes," she said, her eyes faintly amused. "So I've come to believe. I'll sit outside."

"Gotcha," I said and saluted.

I ushered her out in front of me as I left, and I think that might have amused her, too, because she was smiling as she sat down on the bench on the patio. At least I wouldn't have to worry about Zero being annoyed at me for leaving her in the house, though.

I couldn't help wondering what had kept them away as I walked to Morgana's house. I don't like not knowing stuff; I was also pretty sure that outside of being suddenly attacked, the thing most likely to keep the psychos away was discovering another murder. I had seen enough of the crime scenes the murderer left behind him to know that it was just as likely for a fight to break out there between fae enforcers and Zero, as it was for them to be attacked for a completely unrelated reason.

Technically speaking, it was none of my business if there was another murder: that was their investigation. But there had been a body outside my window the morning that started all of this, and I'd managed to wrinkle out of the psychos the fact that my parents had been killed by the same person. It was kinda personal.

Still, there wasn't much I could do about it now, and if it they weren't coming home because they were being attacked and I went calling Zero back while it was happening, I wouldn't exactly be flavour of the month.

So I pushed it to the back of my mind and concentrated on Morgana. I was aware that I could have called her to touch base, but since Zero had distinctly told me to go and see her, I figured he didn't want Palomena knowing more about the human side of things than she needed to. He didn't have to hint twice about that: it was bad enough that Morgana was friends with me and Daniel. She didn't need more danger in her life.

Daniel waved at me from the top of the house as I came through the gate, which was pretty brave of him, considering there were about seven mischievous kids up there who liked to play dangerous games. He was there to meet me at the bottom of the stairs once I got inside the house, though, safe and sound.

If he'd been looking cheerful when I saw him first, he was

looking pretty cranky now. There was also a good bit of green and black moss in a huge smear across his denimed left hip and butt cheek.

I grinned at him. "What happened? The kids try to murder you again?"

It was a joke, but the kids were pretty scary. I still don't know where they came from or how they got into Morgana's house to visit her, but I was beginning to think they really did camp out on top of the house.

"I gave 'em dessert last night!" he said in exasperation. "They liked you after you gave them dessert! They tried to send me over the edge of the roof just now!"

"You ever wonder if we should have a word with 'em?" I asked. "They've gotta learn that stuff like that's actually dangerous."

"*You* try to have a word with them," Daniel said. "They won't come out for me! Not unless they're trying to push me down the stairs or off the roof! Morgana says they like to play, but this is a bit much, Pet!"

"I'll see if I can have a word with 'em in a bit," I promised. "I'll take 'em some food or something."

Daniel huffed out a breath and nodded. "All right. Thanks. You get anywhere with Morgana's friend? I figured you would have called if you'd found him or if you had any news, but—"

"Nothing yet," I said. "But we've got another lead; I'm just waiting for that lot to get back home. Looks like someone Behind has had their eye on *City Fae* for a while: they've given us an address to try. We don't know if it's his place or not, though."

He whistled softly. "That's not good."

"Yeah, you're telling me. Oi, I don't suppose Morgana's friend could be Behindkind, could he?"

"It's the internet. Anyone could be anyone."

"Yeah, I know, but..." I let that trail away.

"I don't like the fact that someone in the Family already had their eye on him—if it is him. I don't like the idea that they've been keeping an eye on the game, either."

"Yeah. Zero already told her to stay away from the game, but it might be an idea to keep away from the friends she's made in-game, too."

He nodded. "You staying for a bit with her?"

"Yeah—I'll go see the kids first, though. I'll make a bit of fairy-bread and try to bribe 'em. If *someone* had a coffee waiting for me when I got into the room, that'd be nice."

"There'll be macarons as well," he said, grinning. "A nice healthy breakfast for you. One of the boys found out that Morgana likes 'em and now it's macarons every second day."

"They're getting pretty comfortable, aren't they?" I said suspiciously. "They know they don't have to like someone just 'cos you do, right?"

He stiffened. "What's that supposed to mean?"

"What?" I stared at him. "You're getting sensitive again, you know that? You got a new werewolf turning, or something?"

"Just—oh never mind! I'll have coffee for you when you get in."

"Catch you later; won't be long."

I let him go up ahead of me and stopped in the kitchen to make a bit of fairy-bread for the kids. They're always better behaved when it comes to food. I took it up with me, shedding little hundreds-and-thousands everywhere in my care not to be too loud. Morgana would already have seen me on her little network of mirrors, but I didn't want to disturb her parents. Her mother was an author and her dad did something with stocks and trading, and I was pretty sure that noise in general would be annoying for either one of those professions. They were also pretty much reclusive; I'd only ever seen Morgana's mum once, and I'd never seen her dad. Daniel hadn't seen either of them.

The kids must have heard me coming just as I got to the top of the house, though, because I heard a sudden scurrying and saw the brief flutter of material as the whole crowd of them scarpered off to hide.

They weren't quite quick enough: I saw the last two of them diving for the cupboard that ran across the covered section of the roof-top, and heard the door squeak shut behind them.

"Come out of there," I called, taking the last few steps up to the roof and sauntering over to the cupboard.

There were a few giggles and a sharp bang from somewhere inside, but no one answered.

"I saw you all go in," I told them, tapping against the door with the toe of my boot. "C'mmon. What are you hiding in there for? It stinks."

It didn't exactly stink—it was more that it looked as though it *should* stink. It was a long, built-in cupboard with dirty marks and old nail holes all around it, and a layer of grime that could have been scratched away with a fingernail if you felt like you could comfortably bleach your hands afterward.

It ended too suddenly, too; maybe there had once been a wall where it ended, and it had been demolished years ago to make this long, weird half-room. Whatever it was about the place, it was odd, uncomfortable, and looked as though it should smell. A glamour without being a glamour: you can see the same thing in any bogan area around Tasmania.

"Not coming out!" yelled a voice.

"Well, I'm not going in there."

That shouldn't have worked, but the closest cupboard door actually cracked open with a scattering of grime.

"Hurry up, then," I said encouragingly. "I made you lot some fairy-bread."

There was a shout from within the cupboard and the fair, curly-haired little boy tumbled out, bringing with him two other kids with the sheer force of his exit. He dived on the plate of fairy-bread, and that was enough to bring the other four out of hiding. It's weird: when they're playing tricks on Daniel or running around the place upstairs while you're downstairs, it feels like there could be at least twenty of the little beggars. There's only seven, though.

The rest struggled out, eager to pounce on the fairy-bread before it disappeared, and I waited until they were all sitting around the plate and munching before I said, "You really gotta stop trying to push Daniel off the roof and dropping stuff on him from the top of the stairs."

"We don't like him," said one of the kids, through a mouthful of bread.

"Yeah, I guessed that."

"You're nice, though."

"Thanks. Look, do you think you could try not to kill him for a bit? He's nice when you get to know him. And it makes Morgana happy to have him around the house—*and* he hasn't told on you. He could have made things pretty hot for you with Morgana after all you've done to him."

There was a pregnant sort of pause while they all crunched on their fairy-bread. They were kids, so I didn't expect them to follow the logic enough to actually like Daniel, but it would be enough if they thought there was a possibility of annoying Morgana and getting into trouble with her. They put up with me, but they really seemed to love her.

"Anyway," I said. "The stuff you're doing is pretty flamin' dangerous. You could kill him, you know?"

"If he's scared, he should go away," muttered one of the kids.

Must be the Jin Yeong one.

"Yeah, but Morgana likes him," I said, pushing that point a bit more. That was actually the problem, as far as I could see: Morgana liked Daniel, and the kids weren't used to her liking anyone but them. They just needed to see it in a slightly less selfish way. "And you're always doing stuff for her beccause you like her and want her to be happy. So why not look after Daniel instead of trying to mess with him? He makes her happy."

Seven young faces scowled at me with a pretty varied mix of resentment, annoyance, and wariness.

"All right, all right," I said. "Just think about it, okay? And don't eat hundreds-and-thousands off the floor. If they drop, just let 'em stay there—someone's gotta feed the ants."

They were still picking up hundreds-and-thousands from the rooftop when I went back down to Morgana's suite; probably picked up a couple of ants while they were at it, but it was extra protein, after all.

"There you are!" said Morgana as I came in, bouncing as much as she could. "What *took* you so long!"

"Been feeding the kids," I said. "Took 'em some fairy-bread."

"I thought you came to see me," she said, her eyes big and tragic. It's the dark eyeliner that does it. She grinned a second later, and then a second after that, she was serious again. "Did you find out anything about Blackpoint yet?"

"Nope," I said, taking the coffee Daniel offered me. She already knew that: Daniel would have told her while I was up with the kids. "We've got another address to try, but we don't know yet if it's your friend or just someone kinda...connected."

"I'll keep digging, too," she said. She was glum, but not exactly discouraged.

"How much do you really know about your friend? He's clever, right?"

She nodded. "*So* clever, Pet! I'm pretty sure he's not just a gamer; I think he's a programmer as well. He knew the mechanics of the game too well—even if you're a really good gamer, you have to learn how to do some stuff new with each game. He did it like it was instinct; like he knew every scenario and line of code in the thing."

"And he's good with the same hacking thing you do?"

Morgana took in a thoughtful breath. "He knows his way around a computer—maybe even better than me—but I don't know how he does it. His style is different, and he's not predictable: I've got the feeling he might have taught himself."

"Good to know," I said. "I'll let Zero know. Oi."

"What?"

"He ever say anything...weird?"

"He said a lot of weird things. He was a conspiracy theorist."

"Oh. Well, anything *really* out there? Like the world being run by leprechauns or something?"

"Nah, he was more of a bloke for the mysterious *they*. You know: *they*'re out to get you and if you're not careful you're giving *them* information 'cos *they*'ve wriggled their way into everything."

"Bit of a fruit loop, huh?"

"He was pretty sound everywhere else, though," she said. "It was just that thing. Most people who spend their whole lives in a room are a bit weird. After twenty years or so, you just—"

She saw me looking at her and rolled her eyes. "Yeah, I know. I'm talking about myself here as well, you know."

"And when I told you that makeup wasn't normal—"

"Shut up, Pet," she said, grinning. "You're the last person who can talk about normality."

"Rude!" I said. "What's that supposed to mean?"

"You live with three strange men and help the police on cases. That's not the standard for normality, you know. Cool, but not normal."

"Blackpoint talk to you much about his theories?"

"No: I think he could tell I wasn't into them. He'd say something every now and then, but it was kinda hard to tell when he was talking about the game and when he was talking about real life, honestly. I think he couldn't tell the difference himself, sometimes."

That, I thought later, as I was walking down the stairs to head home, was a bit worrying. How much had Blackpoint known about Behind? Because if he'd been saying those kind of things to Morgana and he had disappeared, it was pretty likely that he'd been talking about Behindkind when he said *they*. And like the old mad bloke, it sounded like he had been skating on the edges of reality for a while.

I was still frowning when I shut the front door behind me and stepped out into the fresh morning again. I could see why Zero had been interested in this thing. There were more layers to it than I'd thought at first.

A familiar, holey t-shirt fluttered in my peripheral, disrupting my thoughts. I looked to the left, and found that the bird's nest in the bushes out the front was actually the old mad bloke's beard. An eyebrow wriggled at me between leaves, then the bushes rustled and he was off.

What was that? An invitation?

I trotted to the front gate and peered around the bushes, and sure enough, the mad old coot was still just within sight, pouncing on a leaf he had chased down. Yep, he wanted me to follow him.

Heck, why not? It wasn't like I didn't have an hour or so on my hands.

I turned out into the street and followed the old mad bloke.

<hr>

CHAPTER SIX

<hr>

TECHNICALLY, IT WAS A STUPID IDEA TO FOLLOW THE OLD MAD bloke. Technically; because following anyone who had anything to with Behind was usually either trouble, or brought trouble with them. Not to mention the small fact that anyone who thought it worth his while to follow me *technically* couldn't really be trusted.

I did it anyway, remembering that *technically*. Because in reality the old mad bloke had never done me a bit of harm. He'd just run around trying not to die and following me until I gave him food; that sort of thing. In a way, it seemed like he needed me, and I wasn't about to refuse help to someone who needed it.

Besides, back when I was younger, before I'd forgotten about him and remembered him again, the old mad bloke had led me on more than one adventure: a sort of white rabbit to follow, though hopefully not into Wonderland. Or Behind, if it came to that. The old mad bloke was a bit too much inclined to weave in and out of Between in a way that I was told wasn't possible.

And yeah, I do the same thing, but at least I'm sane and I don't have holes in my shirt, you know?

So I followed him. It must have made him happy, because he

cackled to himself and slowed down a bit to make sure I didn't lose him.

I followed him further up toward the older streets nearer the base of Mount Wellington, where the hills got steeper and curvier, panting a bit. For an old bloke, he could set a decent pace. It wasn't until we got to the empty computer repair place that jutted out into the street like a ship's bow that he started to slow down. He didn't stop, mind you, but as we were passing through the ye olde houses and streets, he made sure I didn't lose him.

By the time I saw the first bottle-cap, I was already intrigued. The old bloke didn't stop as we passed it, but I saw it there sitting at the bottom of the telephone pole, plastic and ratty and the same colour as the one that had been on my windowsill and was now in my pocket. I saw the second when we turned up a path between two houses, tumbled down in the long grass beside the stile that was meant to slow cyclists down before they plunged on down the path.

Heck. How had the dodgy old beggar gotten into my room to leave it?

I spotted another as we came back out onto the open road, but the old bloke didn't go back onto the road. Instead, he turned left and vanished between the fronds of a huge weeping willow that hung over someone's front fence.

I looked through that curtain of willow and thought I saw a flicker of movement that wasn't just willow frond, dark and swift. Even the close-set leaves on the fronds seemed to curl with something that wasn't the breeze and was almost definitely the smudging of Between touching the world.

Oh, this was definitely a bad idea. Almost instinctively, I took my phone out of my pocket and looked at it, as if for inspiration. Should I call Zero? Then I saw the time and realised I'd already been gone two hours.

Time to go home.

There was no way I was going to be following anyone through

that particular area; there was especially no way I was going to do it when I had already run out of time. I could just see Zero's face if I managed to get myself killed.

Nope. I was going home, and I was going to jog while I was about it, because Zero's glares are murder, too.

Despite my jogging, I got home a bit late, after all.

Zero was looming near the hallway when I got back, probably wondering why I was still out of the house when he'd told me to talk to Morgana a couple of hours ago. Athelas was in his usual chair, too, and although I couldn't see Jin Yeong, I could smell him. Palomena was back, too.

"Heck," I said. "You lot waiting for me or something?"

Palomena pointed at me. "Do you know that your pet is having nightmares?"

"Of course." Was it my imagination, or had Zero become just *slightly* stiffer than usual?

"The house was warping around her," Palomena added. "You should find a way to deal with it before it becomes attached."

"I'll remember that," Zero said, and he was definitely stiffer this time. "I'm capable of keeping one pet and a house in check, thank you."

I noticed he didn't tell her that the house had already tried to follow me over to another house, but that could be considered as common sense rather than pride, after all. There was no need for Palomena to know all of our business, as much as I thought she was nice, for a fae.

"Are you quite refreshed?" she asked Zero, and she managed not to sound ironic at all, which was pretty flamin' impressive.

"We're ready to go," he said. He and Athelas looked about as bright and brilliant as they usually did when they went to recharge, so they must have done as they said they would, but when Jin Yeong came out of the kitchen, sucking on a blood-bag, he didn't look particularly refreshed.

In fact, he looked bad enough that when we were on our way

out of the house, I poked him in the ribs and hissed, "You look flamin' awful!"

"I am *very hungry*," he said, biting down harder on his blood bag.

I looked from him to Zero and back again. "Hang on, Zero wouldn't let you fight someone?" I took another look at him. "No, you're a mess. You fought with someone and he made you stop?"

"I am *very hungry*," he growled.

"Drink up, then. You can fight some people later."

That left me still very curious about where they'd all been when they weren't recharging—because they'd certainly been up to more than just recharging. I couldn't ask, of course; not with Palomena there, so I followed the others through the softening of Between around the front door, jumping to grab Zero's sleeve when he commanded it.

Heck. It had been a while since I'd had to hold onto him to get Between, and I'd nearly forgotten that me being able to get there myself wasn't something Zero wanted widely broadcast. I was going to have to be more careful now that we had a watcher.

WE CAME OUT SOMEWHERE HALFWAY BETWEEN HOBART AND Sandy Bay, right at the waterfront. Zero and Palomena first, me tumbling after them and through the bushes out onto a private, bitumened road. Athelas followed seamlessly with Jin Yeong at his side, and I think we were all pretty surprised, because no one said anything for a good fifteen seconds as we looked up at the house.

"Are you quite sure this is the address?" Zero said at length.

Palomena said, "Absolutely," but she looked down once at something that flickered with magic or Between in her fingers, and I saw the quirk of surprise that curled her lips for a moment.

Because there was no way a kid owned this place. Well, there was no way a *normal* nineteen-year-old kid owned this place.

"D'you reckon his parents are loaded, or d'you think he's a

grown adult playing games with teenaged girls? Morgana would have said if she'd got a creepy vibe of him, but she might not have known."

"Now this is becoming quite the mystery!" said Athelas. He almost purred it, which meant that he was enjoying the mystery. The more catlike Athelas becomes, the more you have to watch out. "We have yet to ascertain the true age of Morgana's friend, I would suggest."

"Morgana said his records put him at nineteen," I said. "But it's anyone's guess, on the internet."

"And how much would you like to guess a house in this location would sell for—or rent, as the case may be?"

"A flamin' lot," I said. I didn't know the exact amount, but I knew that houses along the waterfront in Hobart were priced in the millions. I couldn't imagine how expensive they were to rent.

"As you say, Pet," agreed Athelas. "A...er, *flaming lot*. This property, I believe, sold a few years ago for five million. I am wondering exactly how a human who spends his time ill, and playing a computer game, affords such a spectacular domicile. Whatever his age, it's an unlikely scenario."

"Yeah," I said gloomily. "Flamin' dodge."

"You do not speak English," Jin Yeong said, with conviction.

I stuck out my tongue at him and said to Athelas and Zero, "Unless he's a heck of a lot older than we think or has really rich parents, there's no way this place belongs to Blackpoint. Not if he's a normal human, anyway."

Palomena, her brow troubled by a faint frown, said, "I think we can assume he is not a normal human, if human at all. This is as worrying as I feared it would be."

Zero sent her a keen look. "Is there any reason you were already inclined to think that he's not human? Your captain didn't seem to want to divulge exactly why this address was a possible candidate for the person we're looking for."

She didn't quite meet his eyes. Interesting. She was keeping stuff back, but it looked like she was feeling bad about it.

"I was told," she said carefully, "that it was a person from a family which would be very annoyed to have a member accused of something against Behindkind law. I was told that we should be very careful when we question the owner of this house. If he is the person we're looking for, it's unlikely that he's more than partially human."

"Is there anything else we ought to know before we go in?"

"I've told you all I was told," she said. "I'll do a circuit of the house before we go in; there's something about the place that's bothering me."

I expected Zero to go with her, or to send one of us with her, but he let her go without comment. In a low voice, he asked Jin Yeong, "What do you smell?"

"Humans," said Jin Yeong. "One or two. Behindkind: many Behindkind."

"Could he be vampire, perhaps?" asked Athelas. "His appearance would remain youthful, and from our own experience we can say that his maturity level wouldn't much advance through the years, either. It would be easy for such a person to pass as an older teenager, especially in an online setting. Less easy for most Behindkind to pass as human, juvenile or otherwise."

Jin Yeong sent a very small snarl in his direction, but it wasn't like it wasn't the truth. I'd only known Jin Yeong for about half a year, and I already knew that he had the emotional maturity of a teenager.

He must have known I was about to say something, because Jin Yeong turned a smouldering, narrow-eyed look on me and said, "You. Don't even dare to say it. A person who is emotionally stunted should not talk about the maturity of vampires."

I gazed at him in shock. "What? *I'm* emotionally stunted? Look who's flamin' talking!"

"I," he said, sounding far too pleased with himself, "am not stunted. I have *very much* emotion."

"Okay, that's a fair point, but it's nothing to brag about!" I told him. "And it doesn't mean that I'm emotionally stunted, it just means you have all the mood swings of a hormonal teenager!"

"I don't think any of us here can make a claim to normality, do you?" suggested Athelas.

"Speak for yourself!" I protested. "I'm a normal person!"

Athelas let his eyes dwell on me for a few moments.

"But I am!" I said, with slightly less assurance than before.

"Your parents were murdered," Zero said. "I think there are very few humans who would have remained in the house after something like that. Certainly not normal ones."

"It's *my* house!"

"You've said that," he told me, his eyes steady on me. "It's not a good enough reason."

"You can't tell me what's a good enough reason!" I protested. "You're only half human; you don't even deal with your own emotions!"

"You obviously crave companionship, and yet you remained there, hidden away, while the world passed you by."

"Yeah, and that turned out *real* well for me," I muttered. "It's not like I asked you lot to move in with me, you know. I don't—I don't crave companionship. I was fine by myself."

"I may not want to work with humanity, but I know something of it," added Zero. "And I know that they generally take care of their own. Yet you hid yourself away when the police came calling."

Quietly, I said, "I didn't know if they were going to kill me or not. I was scared out of my brain."

"No," said Athelas thoughtfully. "I think you were very sane, Pet. But you weren't normal, human-type sane."

"That's rude, too," I said. "You lot need to learn about not insulting humans."

"A worthy study, I'm sure," said Athelas, his grey eyes laughing at me. "And as for companionship, Pet, well—considering your distaste for JinYeong's cologne, it has always surprised me that you allow him to share a seat with you. Or, for that matter," he added gently, "constantly to remain by your side."

I hunched away from JinYeong and glared at him for good measure. He was always taking up too much space and coming over into my half of the couch, and right now he was standing next to me, too. JinYeong met the glare with a particularly pleased, mocking smile that he turned on Athelas, too.

"You try and chuck him off the couch when he wants to sit on it," I said to Athelas sourly. "See if that works out for you."

"I've yet to learn that you have to descend to such levels, Pet," said Athelas. "I'd formed the impression that you're far more subtle in your machinations."

"I thought at first that it could have something to do with you not remembering anything," Zero said, and it took me far too long to switch my mind back to what he was saying. "But you remember too much for that. No, there's something far short of normal when it comes to you."

"Is it 'cos I'm supposed to be one of those heirlings?" I asked, cautiously.

"No," Zero said, sharply and with finality. "You are not an heirling."

I saw the look that Athelas slid him; enquiring and maybe a little bit amused. "There is certainly somewhat to be said for Pet *not* being an heirling," he said.

"Yes," said Zero deliberately. "There is a lot to be said against it."

"I have no objections, my lord."

"That suits me!" I said frankly. I had no desire to be an heirling. "I've heard what you lot have to say about how healthy it is to be an heirling: I'm fine being a weird human."

"Oh, I shouldn't think that's likely to change, Pet."

"Thanks," I said, sourly. "We gunna be doing any investigating, or are you lot just gunna sling insults at me for a bit longer?"

"We might as well go in," Zero said. "The lieutenant can follow us in. I have a few questions and a few suspicions: I'll know if they're likely to be answered when we breach the place, and I'd rather have a moment to look around before she gets back."

"Yeah, that's not at all worrying," I muttered, but I followed the three of them when they melted through the stone security wall by dipping into Between.

I followed them through the wall of the house, too, and that was much weirder than the wall around the property. When I went through the stone wall, I had felt as though I was doing it myself; the stuccoed wall, on the other hand, felt as though it simply opened itself to me without effort, the light meringue peaks of the stucco softly brushing against my skin as they turned to massive petals.

I passed through giant, perfumed fronds of flowers and into a living room that moved around me as it tried to tell my eyes that it was a huge, marble chamber with vaulted ceilings and windows everywhere, and at the same time tried to tell me that it *could* possibly be an airy, sunken clearing set somewhere in a lightly forested area that somehow managed to have young bamboo growing around one side.

"Heck," I said, gazing around. "This is weird. It is weird, right? It's not just Behindkind weird?"

"This is...an unusual setup," said Zero, frowning around the massive living room.

"What's up?" I asked. "I mean, more than usual. I can tell it's pretty flamin' connected with Behind, but why was it so easy for me to get through without half trying?"

"It's plugged into Behind," Zero said. "The whole property, I suspect; it's a complete Between portal that exists in both the Behind and Human worlds. But it's still connected in all the human ways as well: security, power, and internet access."

I'd been in a house a bit like that a while ago. "You mean like Janna Snotnose—"

"Whiteleaf," said Zero, pinching his nose. "Janna Whiteleaf."

"Yeah. Like her place? Only instead of the magic being backed up by the electricity, it's all working together? Does that mean humans can get Between here?"

"Yes," said Zero. "Something that is not only ill-advised but illegal by Behind law."

"Yeah, we seem to be coming across a bit of that around Tassie at the moment," I said. "You reckon it's the bad guys again?"

"I'm afraid you'll have to be more specific, Pet," Athelas said. "When you say *bad guys*, whom can we assume you are referring to?"

"That's a good point," I observed. "Could be you blokes—"

"*Ya!*"

A sigh from Athelas. "Really, I should have expected as much."

"I'm surprised you didn't," Zero said, and I could have sworn that his left brow twitched up just a little bit. From him, that's about as good as an eye roll, which meant he probably believed that Athelas was taken by surprise as little as I believed it.

"Could be you blokes, could be Upper Management, could be the Family—"

"Yes, yes," Pet," Athelas said hastily. "Spare us a list of all the people you could potentially have been referring to under the heading of *bad guys* and tell us precisely to whom you were referring."

"Upper Management," I said. I explained, "Well, they're usually the ones involved when there's the human world connected to the world Behind in a way that makes it possible for humans to be interacting with it. They're the ones who have human resources, after all, right?"

"It seems likely," Zero said heavily.

"He could be working alone," Athelas said. "It's not unknown, after all! And if the Family and the king are just beginning to find out about it now, it does seem likely that it's a lone wolf rather than a big movement."

"The Family doesn't know nearly enough about Upper Management, either," Zero pointed out. "In fact, the only reason they do know about Upper Management as anything other than a nebulous force in the dark is because we've been interacting with them."

I opened my mouth to say that they must have known a bit more about Upper Management than that, given that the Family had not only sent a whole squadron of killer fae into the house over the road to kill everyone there, but had magically collapsed the house in on itself to get rid of the pocket of Upper Management that was living there, but was cut off.

"I rather fancy that the Family know a little more than they allow you to know that they know," suggested Athelas, before I could. "Even if the king does not."

"And that lot with Five Four One," I said instead. "They weren't Upper Management; they were just another lot who figured out a profitable way of making humans work for them. They were only contracted to get rid of me—they didn't know why they were doing it."

"It's a bit too soon to be making assumptions," said Zero, as if agreeing.

It took me a while to realise that he said it that way because he was agreeing that he wouldn't jump to conclusions too quickly, either. That was a bit of a weird feeling. I wasn't used to being listened to properly: not as if my opinion and reasoning were actually reason—or actually mattered.

It gave me a bit of a shock, and a moment of uncertainty: what if what I'd been arguing was just nonsense, and I was edging the investigation in a way that wasn't right? Maybe I should be trying to listen to the psychos more and do a bit less of my own reasoning.

Or maybe they were listening to me because I actually had a good idea every now and then. That would be a nice thought.

The wall behind me bulged a little with an excess of Between pushing into the human space, interrupting my flow of thought, and a rather exasperated voice said, "I thought you were going to wait!"

"I didn't say we'd wait," Zero said, unmoved. "You said you were going to satisfy your own curiosity, so we came on ahead. You're here as an observer: if you can't keep up, that's your own affair."

Palomena's brows went up briefly, and she said, "I'll remember that. Why is this place plugged into Between, do you suppose? Any human could wander in here. I don't like it."

"The king won't like it, either," said Zero. "But as for humans, the human security measures should be enough to keep out the humans he wants kept out."

"What about the ones he wants in—no, actually, why does he want humans wandering in at all?" she asked. The frown was back on her forehead, wrinkling the alabaster. "This is—good never comes of allowing humans to wander into other realms."

Not to mention that the last time we'd seen something like this, it had been for the specific purpose of allowing human minions to work around the place; even Janna Whiteleaf hadn't gone to the same extent for her private residence. Which made it harder to know whether this bloke was actually a human who knew about Behindkind or a Behindkind using humans.

And if I was thinking that, you could bet the psychos were thinking it, too. They hadn't said so aloud, so I didn't, either. I liked Palomena, but Zero had made it very clear that she wasn't part of the group. I would ignore that for the purposes of feeding everyone without exception, but I wouldn't ignore it when it came to the sharing of information.

"Agreed," said Zero. "Athelas, take Pet around the other side of the stairs. I've the feeling we're already too late, but if there's anyone there and they try to run for cover, I want to make sure we've blocked their exits."

"I'll go to the back," said Jin Yeong, his eyes gleaming in the soft, green darkness of the Between room. "I think there is a way out there."

"That's another thing," said Palomena, her eyes flicking toward me as Jin Yeong vanished into the gloom. "Why did you bring your pet? This sort of situation isn't particularly...safe for pets."

"The pet can fight," Zero said, starting up the stairs without waiting for her. "And its human instincts are often useful."

Well hooray for me. I mean, I knew he was saying it because he didn't want people to know I was around as anything other than a pet, but it still stung a bit.

I found that Athelas was already making a move for the other side of the grand staircase that approached the upper floor from both directions in a sweeping half-circle on either side, and started after him. Palomena and Zero climbed into the gloom opposite us, a distant, hard-to-see presence, and I found myself walking a bit closer to Athelas. Zero is a comforting person to have by your side because you know he's capable of shielding you from pretty much everything so long as you stay behind him; Athelas is comforting because he's a shadowy figure that is somehow more deadly and frightening than anything else out there.

"You lot trying to wear out Palomena's patience?" I asked Athelas quietly. I wasn't sure how good Palomena's hearing was, and I *knew* how good Zero's was. "Or were you just having a really good time at the waterfall? You took your time getting back."

"Nothing of the kind, Pet," murmured Athelas. "We are entirely at the disposal of the Enforcers."

"Yeah, I bet."

"We merely happened to be so unfortunate as to meet with a

few mercenaries who thought it would be a good idea to try and rid the world of Lord Sero while he was recharging."

"Is that why Jin Yeong's all bloody and disgruntled?"

"Jin Yeong was looking forward to a fight that he was not allowed to continue," Athelas explained. "It tends to make him... dissatisfied with life."

"What else?"

"How very suspicious you seem to be these days, Pet! Why should you assume there's more?"

"Because I don't see Zero letting blokes that attack him to kill, live," I said frankly. "Which means something else happened that was important enough to make him drop what he was doing—and make Jin Yeong drop what he was doing, too. What was it?"

"A very conveniently placed body," he said.

"Heck, one of yours?"

Athelas, for once entirely startled, stopped short and asked blankly, "I beg your pardon?"

"One of the ones you and Zero are looking for, I mean? The ones that are disembowelled and strung up."

"I see. What a...quaint way you have of expressing yourself at times. Yes, it was one of those—a peripheral body, we're inclined to think."

"One of the ones that wasn't an important murder, you mean?"

"That," said Athelas, stepping silently up onto the landing, "is a matter of opinion."

No one ran from the darkness of the hall up ahead to try and make a run for it down either side of the grand stairs; there wasn't a movement or the wail of alarms going off, and that was *weird*.

"Don't reckon there's anyone here," I said, when we met up with Zero and Palomena again.

I could see Jin Yeong prowling out of the shadows down the hall now, stalking quick and hungry and angry; he hadn't found anyone to fight up here, either. I took a quick peek in the room closest to me: it was an upstairs bathroom, and it was empty but for a bubble bath that had been drawn so long ago that the bubbles had made a scummy etching all around the tub where the water met the porcelain.

As I came back out, Jin Yeong said, "There is human smell, but no human. Fae smell, but no fae. This is a *very annoying* day."

"I don't sense anyone in the house at all," Palomena said. "Human nor Behindkind. Nothing living. Well, I certainly won't put myself to the trouble of searching every room. I've nothing more to do here; you'll report any findings of your investigation as it pertains to the owner of this house, I suppose."

Zero looked at her a little grimly. "You think he's dead? I wonder how you know that."

"I don't know it," she said, meeting the look without flinching. "But if he's not here and he's been meddling with Behindkind without being one...yes. I should imagine he's dead. If he's Behindkind and meddling with humans and not here then my conclusion is also that he's dead."

"I see," said Zero. "Yes, the king always did have more of a soft spot for dead problems than live ones."

"A person can't be questioned if he's dead—nor can his family be dragged through the mud," she said, as if she was agreeing. "I do trust you'll keep us informed?"

"I'll keep you informed," said Zero, after a very brief moment.

I had the impression that they were both speaking in code, and when I looked up at Athelas he was wearing that faint smile of his, so I must have been right. He likes that kind of stuff. I'd like it a lot more if I could understand it, I suppose.

"Any security spells that have recordings..." she added, and left it lingering.

"There's nothing here," Zero said. "I've already checked for recording spells in the security batched spells downstairs. Unless he's far better with fae magic than I am, or unless he deals in a completely arcane form of it, there are no spells for recording."

"What about security cameras?" I asked. I'd already seen the cameras as we came up the stairs: they were small, elegant, and unobtrusive, but they were there. "There should be a security room around here somewhere, right? Reckon it'll be downstairs: most of the wires I can see are running downward."

Palomena looked impressed, which was both laughable and warming at the same time. "I see why you bring her with you," she said.

"The pet has many qualities that are useful on the field, but those don't include pointing out the obvious," said Zero, with a flat look at me that suggested I *did* point out the obvious, but it wasn't very useful.

"Don't say you'd already thought of it," Palomena said, on her way back down the stairs. "I very much doubt any of us will believe you."

Zero sighed slightly, and pinched the bridge of his nose.

Delighted to see how very nearly she'd gotten a rise out of him, I said, grinning, "Should we have a look around, then?"

"Jin Yeong and I will check the rooms before we come down," he told me, piercing me with a look. "Take Athelas and find the security room; we'll join you when we've secured the place properly."

"Gotcha," I said, pleased to be the one listed first for once. To Athelas, I said, grinning, "C'mmon. The boss says you're with me."

"I wonder if you aren't being just the smallest bit...unwise," suggested Athelas, as he followed me.

There was a threat to his voice, soft and chiding, but when I looked back, I was pretty sure I could still see the amusement in his eyes, so I said, "That only works if I can't see your face."

I'd swear his foot faltered for the slightest moment before he said calmly, "I should very much advise against judging by appearances, Pet. It wouldn't be wise to forget how...very easily I killed you."

"Don't worry, don't reckon I'm gunna forget that," I said, but I wasn't sure if he was warning me or himself. There was a tired look to his grey eyes that worried me a bit, so I waited for him to drop down another step and slipped my hand into his.

And yeah, I know we were supposed to be working and I *know* he's a psycho, but sometimes even psychos need their hands held. I hadn't done anything like this since Dad was alive, and I was surprised at how much it comforted me, too.

I thought he might try to pull his hand away—and he did. But he didn't pull away until after we'd gotten back downstairs, and then it was to usher me ahead of him down the hall with a polite command to tell him which room was the security room.

It took us a while to find it, since my only directional clue had been that it would be somewhere downstairs, and there were a *lot* of doors along the hall in the lower half of the house. The light wasn't great, either; maybe Behindkind liked that kind of soft, mossy light, and maybe I might have liked it if it was in the forest, but inside a house it made things pretty flamin' hard to see.

We found the security room despite that: it was one of the middle ones on the left, and when I found it at last, Athelas hovered by the door while I turned on the electric lights and gave the computers a bit of a look over.

"This is a bit higher end than the sort of stuff I usually use," I said doubtfully. Not only were the cameras really good quality, they ran with a good enough rate of frames per second to present a smooth feed. I also didn't recognise the operating system. The last time I'd gotten anything off a security feed was when Jin Yeong and I had been trying to get into the latest iteration of Upper Management. That had been nice and easy to use: this had far too many screens and far too many monitors for my liking.

"This is a bit much for me," I said to Zero, when he appeared in the doorway ten minutes later. "What about you two?"

"Whoever and whatever he is, he's been gone for roughly a couple of weeks," Zero said. "I can trace a heat signature through the place that seems to be pretty well combined with the house, but it ends at the computer upstairs; I can't trace it back further. He must have spent a lot of time at that computer."

"What do you mean when you say it's pretty well combined with the house? And how do you know it's the bloke we're after?"

"I know it's the bl—the man we're after because it's combined with the house," said Zero. "When a person lives in a house for long enough, they create recognisable patterns around the place that stay where they are and sink into the house. Even if it's not a house that's particularly inclined to Between, it's something we can pick up on with the right spells. I can see that, but there's very little left of any other trace. The kind of trace that would be useful to show us his last hours tends to fade beyond a couple weeks."

"Oh well, at least that fits in with our timeline," I said.

"There is no scent of humans in the bathroom upstairs," JinYeong added, slipping through the door and making a quick prowl around the room. "Or in the main rooms. Here, there is human scent. I am *hungry*."

Heck. It was definitely looking like Morgana's human gamer friend wasn't so human after all. At least I wouldn't have to worry about a human being in too deep, I supposed.

I sighed, and tilted my head toward the computer. "I dunno how this lot works; it's gunna take me a while to look over it and make sure I don't do something wrong."

"Will your detective friend have a better idea?" inquired Athelas.

I wasn't sure if he was asking because he really thought Detective Tuatu would be any use, or if he was asking because he still had things he wanted to ask the detective to do. Knowing Athelas, it was likely to be both.

"Yeah," I said. "Reckon he'll know how to use this lot. Want me to give him a call?"

"Do it," said Zero. "And make some coffee before JinYeong bites someone."

. . .

BELIEVE IT OR NOT, THERE WAS NO COFFEE IN THE KITCHEN, only some weird herbal supplement that smelled like dirty washing powder—and I only found that out after Detective Tuatu was already with us.

"I see you're still breaking and entering," he said, when I opened the front door for him. "Who lives here? *Are* they still living?"

"That's rude," I said. "I don't go around killing people willy-nilly—heck, it's catching. I've been around Zero too long. I don't just go around killing people, you know."

"Good to know," he said, and he grinned a bit. "Where's this security system you need me to look at?"

"Through here," I said, and took him down the hall. While he familiarised himself with the computers and looked suspiciously over his shoulder at Jin Yeong, who was glaring at him, I hung around in the doorway and said, "There's no coffee or tea in the kitchen. If we're gunna be here for a while, I'll get us some from a café."

"Don't go far," said Zero, without looking around.

Right. They'd found an unexpected body on their way home before, and Zero probably thought the murderer was likely to still be around in Hobart.

"Just up the street," I said. I pointed, just to be sure they knew which direction I meant. I didn't particularly want to be murdered today. I was wearing my good jeans.

Jin Yeong gave me a bit of a narrow look as I left, but he'd been weird for a while now, so I let that go. Look at me, maturing and stuff. Just yesterday I would have stuck out my tongue at him.

It would have been sensible if I'd gone to a chain coffee store: there was one pretty nearby. If I'd gone southward when I got out of the house instead of northward, I would have been able to walk to one of the chain stores in about five minutes.

But I wanted a walk, and I wanted a particular type of coffee, so I turned up toward North Hobart and took a fifteen-minute walk instead. It had been a week since I'd been here last, so at least I was holding out a bit longer than I really felt like.

They make *really* good coffee at that café.

Besides, there's a regular there who smiles at me every time I go in, and for some reason that smile is as addictive as coffee.

It's funny how a smile can make you warm right from your toes to your nose. Mind you, it helps if the smiler is a brown-eyed Italian bloke with careless, curly hair and smells like coffee when you pass by his wheelchair.

I try not to look at him too much. Just long enough to see that he's smiling, and to smile back—not long enough to start going as red as I find myself once I'm safe outside again. Only it seems like every time it happens, it's just a little bit longer that the look lasts; and, just like the dead bodies, it seems like it's just a *little* bit different each time.

Except instead of blood on the outside, it's the blood on the inside that's making trouble.

This time when I got into the café, he was sitting at the same table he usually sat at, but he had a laptop out on the table in front of him. He had been caught up in what he was doing, but when I pushed open the door he looked up as if he knew exactly who it was that he would see, and for the briefest of moments I looked directly into his sun-kissed face and wondered if it would be as warm to the touch as it looked.

Maybe I looked at him for too long, because the smile curved up a little more, and his eyes widened just a fraction. I looked away hastily and kept walking with just the smallest stutter to my steps and a slightly bigger one to my heart.

I waited at the counter for my drinks, like I always did. Somehow, I'd managed to come here for the last month on the same day every week; first to buy coffee for Morgana and Daniel, and now for my three psychos.

It certainly wasn't something I should be encouraging myself to do, I thought, as I turned with my drinks. He looked up and smiled at me again as I turned, which meant that it wasn't until after I got out of the café, feeling red and flushed as usual, that I was able to return to the problem I'd been thinking about.

I stepped out into a refreshingly cool breeze and paused for a moment to enjoy it while the door closed behind me.

The problem was—well, there were two problems, actually. The first was that I knew a little something about Between these days, and I was pretty sure that the bloke in the wheelchair was doing something very clever and sneaky with his computer that involved Between today. Which meant that he was probably one of us—if by *one of us* I actually meant Behindkind—and that he might not be as nice as he looked. Still, there was Palomena and North, so I knew it was possible for Behindkind to be nice.

Possible, but not exactly normal; which made it a very bad idea to be visiting a particular coffee shop just to smile at him and be smiled at in return.

Heck, I lived with three otherworldly blokes who routinely killed people; who was I kidding?

The second and most pressing problem, however, was that as I stood outside of the coffee shop, a bit redder and more flustered than normal, there was a narrow-eyed vampire watching me from across the road.

Flaming heck! How long had he been standing there?

Beside him was a massive figure that I really should have seen first—would have seen first if Jin Yeong's glare hadn't been quite so hot and liquid—Zero, which made three problems.

I marched across the road toward them, instinct kicking in to attack first.

"What, you lot can't do without me for five minutes?" I demanded.

Jin Yeong took his coffee and waggled it at me. "You who need coffee every five minutes?"

"It's the stressful life I live," I told him. To Zero, I said, "If I didn't know better, I'd think you had another body around here somewhere."

Zero's eyes went faintly bluer. "The detective is working on the computers and I thought I'd like to get another look at the new body before the police discover it."

"You mean you still haven't told the detective?"

"He'll find it soon enough," Zero said briefly. "And we need him where he is right now; more than we need him walking around and disturbing our body."

"Don't reckon he's going to see it that way," I said. "Anything special about this body?"

"It's Behindkind," he said. "Nothing you need to be worried about. Go back to Blackpoint's house and help the detective."

Technically speaking, I could have demanded to go with them. Technically speaking, I had a right to go along and see everything these days, until we signed a contract again.

But there are only so many dead bodies you can see in a few months without being glad to skip the ones you can skip, so to Zero's lightly-etched relief, I said, "Reckon I'll look at that footage for a bit, then. Catch you blokes back at the house."

What did I tell you? I'm maturing.

CHAPTER SEVEN

WHEN YOU'VE BEEN A PET FOR ABOUT THE LAST HALF YEAR OF your life, you tend to get used to curling up and falling asleep on the couch, no matter whose house you're in. Even your own. When your owners are fae and vampire and don't spend a lot of time sleeping, they don't tend to worry about keeping regular hours.

And then there's the nightmare, which apparently might be more real than I'd like to think, and which always seems to be scared away by Zero; so by and large I like to be downstairs with him when I sleep, these days.

And yeah, I know I'm like part of the furniture around the house, but I didn't expect to wake up covered in paper and sticky notes after falling asleep on an unfamiliar couch.

"Oi," I protested weakly, instinctively shying away from the rustling of paper that had woken me. "Heck, I'm drowning in paper."

"Don't wriggle, Pet," said Athelas. "I'd appreciate it if you didn't send my file somewhere down the back of the couch; it was very cleverly mislabelled and a labour of love to find. I daresay we'd never get it back."

"Boy have I got some exciting news for you about detachable couch cushions," I said crankily, sitting up very, very carefully. By the look of the light coming in through the small forest outside the glass wall in the sunken lounge, it was late afternoon; golden hour. "Heck. Did you bring this lot over from our house? And how come this sticky note says *kill under cover of darkness?* You fallen off the wagon, or is this someone else's to-do list?"

"Your statement would seem to assume both that I have ceased killing for some time, and that there was a problem with the execution of that service."

"Of that *what?*"

"I must therefore assume that you are either being facetious or don't know what the position of steward entails," he added, ignoring that. "I'm inclined to believe it's both. That note, my dear Pet, is attached to the file I do not wish to lose. Our murders are reasonably evenly split between those that occur under cover of darkness, and those that are enacted under the full glare of the light."

"That sounds like a pretty stupid way to murder Behindkind, so I'm gunna go ahead and guess that the thing about Seelie and Unseelie being light and darkness is true."

"Well done, Pet. The Unseelie do not cope well with light; to them, it stuns, dazzles, and crawls with the unexpected."

"S'pose they sleep in the day as well," I said, stretching. "Like really big bats."

Something hit me in the head: a cushion thrown by Jin Yeong.

"Oi!" I said. "I wasn't talking about you this time!"

Maybe he didn't believe me; he scowled at me, eyes dark and stormy, and stalked away in the direction of the palatial kitchen.

"There's nothing good to eat in there anyway!" I called. Mind you, maybe someone had brought back blood bags from the house, along with the box of files Athelas was methodically working his way through.

I pointed at JinYeong's retreating back and asked Athelas, "What's with him? Why's he still spoiling for a fight?"

Athelas looked at me curiously. "I really believe you don't know."

"That's why I ask questions," I said. "I don't just do it for the fun of it, you know; that sorta thing is bad for your health around here."

"Asking questions for the fun of it should not be sneered at," he said, reaching forward to remove a photograph from the file that had been tangled in my hair when I woke. A young boy, his eyes wide and his hair messy, looked briefly at me before vanishing into the pile beside Athelas' chair.

"Would have thought that was an expensive sort of way to have fun," I said. "But that's just me. Who's the kid?"

"Expensive, but *very* good for practise; and less expensive the more practise you get. The boy is the son of a couple of murder victims we've recently discovered. The parents were torn apart in their own living room; their bodies and parts strewn over the carpet. The boy was never found."

I sat up just a bit straighter. "His parents were killed like mine instead of hung? Where'd you get this one from?"

"It's a Queensland case, I believe."

"Can I have a look?"

"It will be here for some time, I believe. Peruse at your leisure —but *not*, Pet," he added, when I reached for it, "while I am doing so. I am trying to establish a connection between this case from the past and our current rash of murders, tangential and primary."

I stuck my tongue out at him, but the file wasn't going anywhere, after all. I would have to look at it when my psychos were doing something else.

"We gunna be doing anything on Morgana's case today?" I called down the hall to the broad shoulder I could just see protruding from the doorway of the security room. It was a bit worrisome that even while we were here, supposedly working on her case, they had brought over case files and evidence for the murders they were also working on.

The shoulder emerged, bringing the rest of Zero with it, and he came back into the living area with a file already in one hand.

"I'm busy," he said briefly. "I've already seen the security footage that the detective has brought up so far. If you wish to look at it yourself, he's still in there; I think he's asleep."

I looked at him suspiciously, but it occurred to me that instead of this being Zero trying to keep me away from his investigation, it might actually be Zero asking for help in the most oblique way possible. It wasn't possible for them to do all the things all at the same time; divide and conquer would have to work, even if part of the division was human.

"I'll look at it," I said. "I suppose he hasn't made copies or anything?"

"He says," said Zero, with very blue eyes, "that it would be illegal for him to make copies of someone else's footage without their permission, but that should someone happen to accidently overhear him talking about how he would do it if he could, he wouldn't be responsible for that person's actions."

I grinned. "All right. I'll go have a word with him and see what I can do."

I would have liked to take it to Morgana, who loved to have an active part in investigations, but it was too likely that there would be something otherworldly on there that she wasn't used to seeing outside the *City Fae* game. It would have to be a long, boring job for me—but at least it was *my* long boring job.

I stood up, ready to make a start before dinner, but Zero said peremptorily, "Practise first."

"Thought you were busy," I said suspiciously.

"I am," he said, confirming those suspicions. "You'll work with Jin Yeong."

"Ah heck. But he *wants* to fight!"

"I am," said Jin Yeong, stalking back into the room with liquid eyes, "*very hungry.*"

Obviously not much had changed since early this morning. I headed for the backyard, hoping it was as palatial and private as the rest of the house, and said over my shoulder, "Well, I'm not a snack and you can't bite me."

"I can bite you," he said, following me. "But you may not bite me."

"That sounds fair, coming from the vampire," I muttered.

Totally fine for the vampire to bite me; I wouldn't turn unless I bit him back and got a pretty big mouthful of blood, apparently. Oh well, I suppose it's better than werewolves. They bite you and it's all over, red rover; you're pretty much sure to be dead or a werewolf by the end of a week or two.

Ask me how I know.

Still, sparring with Jin Yeong isn't all bad. He's not as powerful as Zero, even if he's faster, and he doesn't usually make me scramble to find weapons like Zero does. After fighting Jin Yeong I'm always left with the feeling that maybe one day, if I work hard enough, I might be able to be as good as he is. It's probably an illusion, but it feels possible.

With Zero, you're just left with the thought that no matter how good you get, he'll always be able to crush you like a bug. It makes you feel safe when he's fighting someone else, but it's not that comforting when you're the one diving across the lawn and getting grass burns to avoid him until you can find a weapon, any weapon. A weapon which probably won't mean too much in the long run because he's still about four times your size and twenty times as deadly, and you can't get in a good hit and are nearly too scared to do it even if you could.

I definitely couldn't get away with threatening to cut off his tie, for example.

"Do not look at my tie," said Jin Yeong coldly. He loosened it with firm fingers, then stripped it off completely, glaring at me. Carefully, he laid it over a bean trellis. "This is my favourite tie."

"All right, but no murdering me because you wanted to fight someone else and Zero wouldn't let you," I told him. I knew that restless, dark look to his eyes. Jin Yeong with that look in his eyes was Jin Yeong spoiling for a fight no matter the consequences; the most dangerous Jin Yeong.

Luckily for us, the whole backyard wasn't just spacious, but well tree-lined, and I was pretty sure that not much sound was getting out, either, because not much was getting in. Even in here, we should have heard some traffic noise.

We split up without a word to find something we could use as weapons. The rules of training start with the fact that you have to find your own weapon first: scrambling or coolly and calmly, you have to bring something over from Behind and through Between for it to count as training. Otherwise, it's just fun for the vampire and a waste of time for me because Zero's sure to send me back out for another session.

I found a couple of sticks with a great curve to them that didn't even take a moment to turn into two sweeping blades that were a tad longer than what I was used to these days. Yeah, that's right, I have my own weapons; I'm just not allowed to start with those ones. Dunno why I've even got them, if it comes to that.

Jin Yeong came back double-bladed as well. Zero and Athelas had decided that double-bladed was the best way for me to learn —apparently I go a bit blind and mad when I'm really fighting, and having two blades as a whirlwind is more effective than having just the one.

Goodness knew where Jin Yeong had gotten his from: they looked like they were pretty sure about being blades, and it was hard to imagine that they could have started their lives as sticks, like mine had done.

"Time to play," he said, and attacked.

I guarded without thinking about it, curling into the right as I followed the guard with a low thrust toward his stomach with my left blade. Jin Yeong deflected but I could have sworn the thrust separated the lower half of one belt-loop from the waist of his perfectly pressed trousers, and that made me grin as he danced back and came in again for the attack.

It must have annoyed him, because he was swift and relentless in the attack that followed, and after a short flurry of swords, my left-hand sword went flying. I drew back to slightly higher ground, my guard altering to make up for the loss on my left hand.

Heck. Whirlwind I might be in a real fight scenario, but when it was against one of my psychos, I seemed to keep most of my senses about me—great for learning, but not so great when you lose one sword and need to make up for it in madcap fury.

A quick dive to the left, I could snatch up a training stake from the garden; to the right, if I timed myself well, I could go for the garden shed. Jin Yeong followed my eyes both ways, and I saw him weighing up which way he thought I'd go, and how he could stop it.

But this time I wanted to try something different. Instead of bringing weapons into the human world from some potential Between, I wanted to turn a couple of weapons into something that looked more suitable for the human world.

I'd done it once before—pulled a paperweight from the Behind world through Between and turned it into a gun on the way. Zero says that it must always have been a gun, and that I just showed its human world appearance, but I've never been sure about that.

It was time to test my suspicions.

Quickly, too; Jin Yeong, a whirl of sword and teeth and fluid movement that was too fast and too strong to hold a defence against, forced me back across the yard through the garden beds and toward the house.

Usually when I changed things back into their human world counterparts, or whatever it was that I was doing, I had to talk to them. *You're a gun. You're a stick.* That sort of thing. But I very much wanted to take Jin Yeong by surprise, and I very much wanted to learn how to use this skill in my fighting. I couldn't be talking at my enemies' weapons all the time. Berserker mad is one thing: actual mad is another.

So this time I just looked at Jin Yeong's blades as I circled at the intersection of garden paths, trying to keep my distance for long enough to see things in *just* the right way. And if I squinted at them a bit, with the green and brown reflection of the trees around reflecting in them, his swords did almost look like sticks.

Nice, curved sticks that I would have played with as a kid, pretending to be a knight fighting dragon dad.

Nice, curved sticks that were going to annoy the vampire when he realised what they were, because they were definitely not swords anymore.

I grinned in delighted victory, and Jin Yeong, feeling the difference in weight, or maybe in feeling, looked down at the sticks in his hands. I saw his head tip to one side as he considered them, but I didn't give him time to think: I slashed riverso and circled to the right with it, freeing myself from the confines of the area he'd driven me into and demolishing his sticks in one swift, slashing twist.

Jin Yeong looked down at the ruined sticks once more, his eyes dancing.

Was he *laughing*? I had just disarmed him. Why was he laughing?

I held my guard and we stared at each other for a good ten seconds; then Jin Yeong tossed the sticks aside and took one swift step forward.

Ah heck. I forgot he doesn't need a weapon.

He *is* the weapon.

Laughing, he sprang, and I made another clumsy riverso, cutting sharp and fast; but it was too high and he was too fast. A suitful of vampire collided with me, knocking my sword right out of my hand and somewhere out of reach, and the world tumbled painfully around me. I tasted grass, then blood.

When the world stopped moving, the suitful of vampire that had knocked me to the ground pulled away, allowing me to suck in a welcome breath of air and swipe the back of one hand across my mouth to get rid of the tiny wetness of blood there.

JinYeong, looking far too pleased with himself, settled back on his haunches. That left my legs pinned between his knees, and with no tie in easy reach I just puffed a grassy huff of air at him and didn't bother to try and wriggle away.

I'd fought cleverly, but I hadn't fought cleverly enough, and the win was his. I mean, they usually were, but every now and then I managed to fight cleverly enough to get in an actual hit.

"Fine," I said to him, hitching myself up on my elbows. "You win."

"You forgot that I am not human," he said. "That was stupid."

"That's us humans," I said. "Stupid! Didn't you know? You should ask Zero about that."

He grinned. "Did I not tell you that my body is a weapon?"

"All right, all right, no need to rub it in," I complained.

I wriggled my legs to let him know that I wanted to get up, but his knees pinched in, stifling the movement. I rolled my eyes, and reached forward to poke him in the ribs. "All right, I said you win. You can get off me now."

He leaned forward at the hips, which startled me enough to send me flopping onto my back in the grass. "And if I do not wish to do so?"

The blue sky above us was too clear; dizzyingly clear. I focused on JinYeong's face instead, but that didn't make it much better.

It was funny. His face was much the same tone as the man from the coffee shop—maybe even a touch deeper with honey instead of sunlight—but it didn't give me the immediate sensation of warmth that the face of the man from the coffee shop did every time I saw it.

I reached up to cup his cheek in one hand, curious to know what it might have felt like to touch the other cheek that looked as though it ought to be warm, and Jin Yeong's head tilted to the side, following my hand.

Funny, though. His face wasn't warm.

Jin Yeong didn't move, his head still tilted to one side, but he did ask softly, curiously, "*Mwoh hanun koya?*"

"Your face is cold," I said accusingly. I'd expected his cheek to feel warm beneath my hand; he's always warm when he sits next to me. Was it because he was a vampire?

I took my hand away thoughtfully, which left Jin Yeong blinking down at me. He shifted a bit, dipping forward as though he was using the momentum to get up, but instead he reached down and took my hand. He brought it back up to his cheek; and this time, it was warm.

"Oi!" I said in surprise, gazing up at him. "How'd you do that? That's not a normal bloke thing, right? That's a vampire thing?"

"I am warm when I wish to be warm," he said.

The hand that held mine to his face was warm, too; both together, it was a surfeit that made me feel too hot. I tugged my hand away and pushed him from me as I sat up, but he didn't seem inclined to do more than lean back on his haunches again to accommodate me, which still left my legs trapped.

"Oi," I said again, and he raised his brows at me.

"*Wae?*

"Jin Yeong," sighed Athelas' voice. "Do you suppose you could refrain from encouraging the pet in bad behaviour? I had the impression that you were meant to be teaching her—"

"I am," he said, rising in a single, fluid movement. "I am teaching her what happens when she forgets that my body is a weapon."

"Yeah, I'll be sure to remember that," I said. Next time I would remember that I needed to incapacitate him, not just disarm him. I would have to remember that armed or unarmed,

Jin Yeong was still dangerous, and I couldn't let my mental guard down any more than I could let my physical guard down. My physical guard had been up, but I hadn't expected him to attack and it had taken far too long for me to respond.

I rose beside him with the same suppleness and speed as he had done, and then realised that it wasn't just blood flowing through my veins. I felt fast. I felt *good*.

And something small and warm was trickling down my neck and into the hollow of my left collarbone.

"Oi!" I said. "You *bit* me!"

I hadn't even felt it; I remembered a brief, messy moment when his head tucked into my neck as we tumbled, but I hadn't felt his teeth go in—or come out if it comes to that.

"I was hungry," he said, in deep satisfaction.

"Yeah? Well, I reckon you're going to regret that," I said. "'Cos I'm feeling pretty flamin' good and that tie of yours is closer to me than it is to you."

"Do not touch my tie!" howled Jin Yeong, leaping for the strip of green and gold fabric that he'd left over a far-too-nearby trellis.

He was swift; but with vampire spit and a head-start, I was swifter. I flicked the tie up and into motion over Jin Yeong's head as his leap sent both of us through two cucumber frames and bowled over a wheelbarrow. I hardly felt it, rolling tight and fast and using Jin Yeong as ballast to offset the speed of our tumble.

Vampire spit doesn't just give you extra speed; it gives you a *really great* sense of balance and timing.

This time I was enough in control of the fall to bring it to a stop with me perched on Jin Yeong's ribcage, one foot skidding across the mossy flagstones of the garden path to stop our wild tumble.

Jin Yeong's tie was within easy reach once again—but it didn't look like a tie anymore. He turned his head, homing in on it with all the precision of a vampire whose preternatural neatness has been forcibly challenged, and his hand twitched once before it became still.

"*You*," he said, through his teeth. "What did you do to my tie?"

Because as JinYeong looked at his tie, his tie looked back at him.

Then it croaked.

Then, with long, folded legs and an unlikely green-and-gold striped tail, it made a frog-like leap for the side of the closest garden bed.

"*Ya!*" gasped JinYeong, in disbelieving outrage, dislodging me and making a wild dive for it. "*Nae naektai!*"

"Not anymore, it's not," I said, collapsing with laughter into the wreckage of the wheelbarrow. "It's a frog now!"

We made enough noise that we woke Detective Tuatu, who stumbled out into the backyard, yawning, and then forgot to shut his mouth when the frog that had been a tie made a long-legged leap for freedom from JinYeong's darts and dives, and vanished into the house, its tail fluttering behind it.

"What the everlasting *oddness* was that?" he demanded, clinging to the door frame in his effort to avoid the tie frog. "Am I still sleeping? I've gotta stop doing all night stakeouts and then coming when you lot call me."

"Tie frog!" I said, still laughing so hard that I almost couldn't talk. "It's a tie frog!"

"What the—?" the detective stared at me. "Are you bleeding? Is she bleeding? Is that a *bite mark* on your neck?"

"Calm down," I wheezed. "It was just JinYeong fighting dirty —and I ruined his tie for it, so it serves him right. Zero says you've got an idea of how to copy some of that footage for us."

"I can't do it—"

"Yeah, yeah, you can't do it yourself because it's against the law. Feel like talking to yourself for a while, though?"

"I hate to mention it, Pet," said Athelas mildly, as JinYeong pushed past Tuatu to follow his tie, "but I'm quite sure that

Zero expected you to train for a little longer than twenty minutes."

"Lost my sparring partner," I said, recovering some of my breath but still grinning. From inside the house, I could hear shouting, swearing, and a very colourful vocabulary that I could follow if I paid attention. "Seems like he's a bit busy at the moment."

"So I gathered," Athelas agreed. "It occurred to me earlier that Jin Yeong has been somewhat distracted today, so I offered my services to my lord in case of accidents. It would seem that I arrived just in time."

"Don't look at me," said Detective Tuatu, meeting my eyes. "I've already achieved my daily quota of sneaky behaviour. You'd better patch that up before you keep fighting, hadn't you? It's bleeding a bit."

I dabbed at the bite with the cuff of my hoodie; the material was already grass-stained and probably had shards of glass in it, so it wasn't like I'd be able to keep it after this, anyway. What's one more contaminant?

"Weird," I said. "They usually don't bleed too much. The mosquito must have forgotten about his clotting agent or whatever it is he does when he licks stuff afterward."

"He usually *licks* you afterward?" asked Tuatu, appalled.

"We prefer our pet not to faint due to blood loss," explained Athelas. "You'd best fetch your weapons, Pet; I won't wait for you."

"Heck," I said, and left the doorway where I could hear the pleasing sounds of Jin Yeong still chasing his tie, to scramble after my weapons. After you've been killed about six times by a bloke, it's sensible to listen when he tells you to go for your weapons.

Maybe I should have tried to be nicer to Jin Yeong. By the time I was done with Athelas, I was sweaty, grass-rashed, and bruised up and down—and I mean, at least he didn't bite me, but he certainly hadn't gone easy on me, either.

Athelas, with the very faintest sheen of sweat at either temple, said mildly, "You're distracted today, Pet," and went back inside.

Tuatu got up from where he'd been sitting on the highly polished decking, and said, "You're a lot better than I remember you being."

"Thanks!" I said, meaning it. "When a few dropbears have a go at you and you don't know how to do anything except go mad, it gives you a flamin' good reason to try hard."

"There are *drop*—no, never mind, I don't think I want to know. Are you going to come in and listen to me talk to myself for a while?"

"All right," I said. "But you better talk slow: reckon Athelas has knocked a few of my brain cells out."

IT TOOK US A WHILE TO FINISH COPYING THE FOOTAGE— mostly because my muscles were shaking and so were my hands. It seems that as soon as I get used to one level of training and feel like I'm doing well, the psychos up the program so that I'm still gasping at the end of it.

Still, we got there in the end, and by the time Zero came in to check on us with a bit of magic clinging to his fingers like soap-bubbles, I was just packing up the copy I'd made.

"Finished?" Zero asked briefly.

"Yep," I said.

"Good. I'm getting nothing upstairs. It's been too long for the enchantments I used: I was right at the first. He's been gone at least two weeks."

"Nearly two and a half," said Detective Tuatu. He sounded very pleased with himself, and I didn't blame him. "I got sick of skipping back hour by hour so after I woke up, I started skipping back day by day and then refined it once I hit a day when there was a bit of life to the place. See this? This is probably when it all went down."

"Probably?" Zero's voice was a rumble of annoyance.

"You'll see," the detective said, grinning.

He set the footage running, and at first all we saw was the upstairs game room, empty of anyone and much neater than when we'd gotten there.

"Thought you said there was movement," I said, but it didn't need Detective Tuatu's hiss to make me shut my mouth. A moment later, a tall, thin bloke in a red jumper and blue jeans dashed through the door and hauled the filing cabinet across the door in one swift, mighty motion that was belied by his thinness.

"Not in a wheelchair or anything," I said dispassionately. "Or crutches. Doesn't mean he definitely hasn't got cerebral palsy, but the house isn't set up for something like that, either."

"I'm also inclined to think that he was able to lift that cabinet rather too easily," said Athelas, from the door.

Something croaked behind him, and JinYeong shouldered his way into the room, scowling. The tie frog was cupped in his hands: he threw it at me and I caught it, startled to find how cool and pleasant its fabricky skin felt.

"Change it back," he said, looming over my chair.

"In a bit," I told him, perching the tie-frog on my shoulder, where it clung quite happily. "Stop moving so suddenly; you're scaring it."

"It shouldn't," he said coldly, "*be* scared. It should be a *tie*."

"I don't even want to know," said Detective Tuatu, turning back to the computer screen.

I did the same, just in time to see the red-jumpered man sit down at his desk, his chest rising and falling obviously with breath that was too fast. The screen flickered, elongated, and went black.

"Oi!" I said. "What's that?"

Zero leaned forward in interest, and JinYeong pressed against the back of my chair to do the same, causing the tie frog to shuffle its cool little front pads onto my unprotected neck. The screen abruptly flashed into life again, and there was the room, just as it had been—except that there was no patch of red.

"Heck," I said. "He's gone. Did he jump out the window?"

"Those windows don't open," said Zero. "They're fixed. Replay it."

Detective Tuatu did as he was told, and the frames wound back until the brief interruption of blackness, then further back again until we saw the man dash through the door again.

"What about the door?" I asked. "How come he barricaded himse—hang on. Look at him—he heard something. He heard 'em downstairs, or maybe he saw 'em on his security system as they came through the front gate. Why'd he barricade himself in instead of running for it?"

"If he's human, he might have thought that a barricaded door would work against fae," suggested the detective.

"*Hotsori*," muttered Jin Yeong. "Any human would know better after meeting Behindkind. Even you know that."

"That's because three Behindkind walked through the walls of my interview room to rescue their pet," Detective Tuatu said. "I'm going to go out on a limb and say that my experiences are not reflective of the general population."

"Dunno," I said slowly. "If it's our bloke, he knew enough to be warning humans about Behindkind—and to have a place that's plugged into the Behind world, whether or not he knows how it works or who did it. And him just picking up a filing cabinet definitely isn't normal human stuff."

"On the other hand," Zero said, "he *did* use it to barricade the door, and any Behindkind would know how useless that is."

"Maybe," I said thoughtfully, "he just wants people to think he's human?"

"I'll let you four sort that out," said the detective. "I want to know what that is—the thing that happens just before he disappears."

"Power surge?"

He looked at me disbelievingly. "You really think that? After everything you've seen?"

"Nah," I said. "But I wanna know what you think it is."

"I think it's some sort of targeted attack to take out the human side of his security systems—just *listen* to me these days!"

I grinned at him sympathetically. "I don't reckon you're wrong, if that helps? Whoever it was that did it, I reckon they didn't want anyone seeing what happened to him—or who did it to him."

"Yes, but I don't know how they did it without blowing out the whole system entirely," said the detective. "The system comes back on again in less than five minutes. Something that took out the picture this well should have fried the whole system."

"Keep it rolling," Zero said.

I exchanged an amused look with Tuatu; hearing Zero say *keep it rolling* was nearly as funny as hearing him say something like *willy-nilly*.

"Watch the screen, Pet," said Zero, his voice cold. "You're here to be useful, not to smirk."

I'm pretty certain that just made me smirk a bit more, but I did pay attention to the screen again, and I was suitably rewarded for my good work ethic: the filing cabinet with which the man had barricaded his door went flying across the room and collided with a stand full of games.

"Typical," I muttered, because the fae that segued into the room didn't need to do anything so flamboyantly destructive. They had wanted to produce as much fear as possible, and they fully expected their quarry to be present in order to *be* afraid.

I couldn't help laughing at their expressions when they saw he wasn't there. A whole group of too-ordinary humans looking dazedly around the room like they didn't know how someone had managed to steal their own trick.

"Well," I said. "At least we know that they think he's human."

If I didn't know better, I'd have said that the group were

humans, too: they might not be able to hide their true selves from photos, but video feed is another matter. If it wasn't for the fact that I'd seen the way they came through the walls and burst through the door—if it wasn't for the slightly-too-ordinary sameness about all of them—I could have thought it.

But I did know better.

"A very good point," Zero said slowly, as the Behindkind on the screen recovered and began prowling around the room. "They didn't expect him to be able to remove himself from the room by any function of Between, at any rate. They thought they had him at a disadvantage."

"What about the house being keyed into Between?" I asked. "Wouldn't they expect him to at least use that?"

"The bit that's keyed in for humans is limited to the downstairs area," said Zero. "Up there, everything is as it ought to be."

"I'm inclined to agree with the pet that our quarry has been very careful to seem human," Athelas said. "He's given himself every minuscule advantage to be able to escape as lightly as possible."

"What I would like to know," said Detective Tuatu thoughtfully, "is why they didn't get rid of the security feed we're watching. They could at least have disabled the cameras if they didn't want to go to the trouble of finding the security room."

I grinned at Athelas and said, "You wanna tell him, or should I?"

"Behindkind do not typically trouble themselves with human security," Athelas said.

"They don't know how to use it, you mean," I said gleefully. "I'm surprised they knew enough to be able to knock out the camera, even briefly. They probably thought it worked perfectly, and it wouldn't have occurred to them to look. If it did, they would have figured that some local cops getting a look at their pretend human forms weren't worth worrying about."

"Sadly true," agreed Athelas, his grey eyes just slightly amused.

"However, Upper Management is certainly beginning to er, *worry about* humans, and I haven't noticed that you're particularly happy about that."

"Well," I said, "then I suppose the surprising thing is that this time Upper Management isn't involved. They would have handled the human connections a lot better—reckon they would have gotten rid of the footage, as well."

"The thing that interests me," said Zero, pointing back at the screen, "is that."

A lone figure had appeared on the screen. Detective Tuatu hadn't bothered to stop the playback, and it had played quietly by itself as the Behindkind group methodically threw over the room; searching behind and under everything that could be moved and strewing games and computer parts everywhere. After the froth and fury of that boiled away and the room was empty again, it had remained still for quite some time before the lone figure casually strolled in through the back wall.

"Now that," purred Athelas, "is *very* interesting!"

"Oi!" I said in surprise, at the same time. "It's the golden git!"

JinYeong laughed, a small chuckle at the back of his throat, and leaned over my shoulder. "This is not official, I think."

"Shall we say rather that it's not an officially *sanctioned* visit?" Athelas murmured. "I've no doubt that at least the Family knows about the visit, whether or not the king is cognisant."

I looked up at Zero in astonishment. "The Enforcers didn't do it, then? They're actually looking for him, too, just like they said?"

That was *not* what I had expected. Failing Upper Management, it had seemed obvious that the Family or the King Behind must have been involved.

"It just means they didn't do it officially," Zero said, echoing Athelas.

"If I wanted to look very good in the eyes of the public," said Athelas, in a reminiscing sort of way, "I would arrange the thing under cover of darkness, appear in my official capacity at a point well past the episode to show my lawful intentions toward the victim, when it was obvious that I could have had nothing to do with it. I would try to make sure that the investigations began in just less than two weeks' time after I appeared so that I could be observed in my blamelessness without being observed in my work. Then I would arrange to keep an eye on the secondary investigation that is happening to make sure it goes in the right direction."

"What about people like you?" I asked him. "You wouldn't fool those ones."

"Notoriety isn't a bad thing," he said. "In certain contexts, and with the right people. Of course, it's important that there be nothing to incriminate one, but it's likewise important to leave enough of a calling card to ensure repeat customers. Suspicions, after all, are not proof."

"Right. So we don't know whether or not the golden git is sucking up to the king or the Family by offing this bloke, or if it was the first lot who did away with him. Or if he got away."

"Unfortunately so," Zero said. Of Tuatu, he asked, "Is there anything else?"

"That's all I've found so far," the detective said. "There might be more, but that's the room just as it was when I saw it, so I doubt there's anything else. Pet has a hard copy of the feed from that room, plus copies of every other screen for a time bracket of a week before and two weeks after."

"There's gotta be something else," I said.

"There's too much footage," he said. "Unless you've got a specific time in mind, you'll be watching this for weeks to get anything useful out of it. And that's only if there's something to see."

"That's all right," I said. "So long as I've got a copy to look at when I get home. I'll look at it bit by bit."

"Take it and go home, then," said Zero.

I looked at him suspiciously. "Have you lot been camping out here with me and the detective 'cos you're worried about the—you-know-who being out on the streets?"

"We're expecting another incident," he said, without directly answering that.

"Who is *you-know-who*?" asked the detective.

"If you don't know, can't tell you," I said, grinning. Then the meaning of Zero's words sank in, and the grin vanished. "Hang on, you mean there's gunna be—"

"Another body," Zero agreed shortly. "Soon. And close."

Detective Tuatu looked alarmed. "What body? Why is there going to be another one?"

"*You*, come with me," Zero said to him. "I have something to show you. *You*, Pet; go home."

CHAPTER EIGHT

By the next morning, Zero hadn't come back home either with or without the detective, so I slipped out while Jin Yeong was showering and Athelas was going over his files, and visited Morgana.

"Pet!" she said when I walked in, brightening. "I didn't expect you again this soon! I was just going to call you!"

"You found something else?"

"You first," she said. "What were you doing yesterday?"

"We got a tipoff from someone and dropped by the address they gave us, but no one was home."

Morgana settled back against her pillows in disappointment, and said, "I suppose you can go back when they're home, then, if you've got an address."

"No, I mean, whoever it was had either done a runner or been spirited away," I said. "There was still a bubble bath in the bathroom and someone had gone through his computer room and scattered games everywhere."

Morgana's eyes sharpened on me straight away. "What was his setup like?"

"Fancy," I said, fishing out my phone. "Figured you'd want to see, so I took a photo or two."

I'd nearly gotten in trouble for it, too: I'd nipped upstairs and taken them after Zero told me to nick off home, which had let me in for one of his ice-king looks. I didn't tell Morgana that.

I just asked her, "Look familiar to you?"

"That's the setup he said he had," she said, nodding as she swiped through the pictures. "This is his place; you found Blackpoint."

"Found an empty house," I corrected her. "Still, we've got a couple more leads, and it's not like we saw him get murdered or anything."

Morgana smiled, black and brilliant, teeth white between the matte darkness of her lips. "He's pretty smart. If he wasn't there, he might be safe."

"He might be," I said. It probably wasn't useful right now to tell her that it was likely someone had just knocked out the cameras at the time he was kidnapped or killed. She was right: he could have gotten away. "Oi, giv'us me phone back!"

"Good grief, Pet!" she said, still swiping through my short stash of pictures. "Is that all you've got on there? There's one of Jin Yeong, but—"

"Think he checks his hair in my camera," I said gloomily, taking back the phone and deleting the picture of Jin Yeong's smug mug.

She looked at me with her mouth open. "What about selfies?"

"What the heck are selfies?"

"Exactly what the name says: pictures you take of yourself."

I stared at her. "Why would I do that? I can see myself in the mirror."

"How did you even get this far in life without my help?" Morgana shook her head in wonder. "Pet, I'm stuck inside and I *still* know what selfies are! You take pictures of yourself when you think you look nice and you post 'em online and stuff."

Oh. Was this more of that *normal* stuff? "Do you post yours online?"

Morgana's smile dropped a bit. "No. I don't like the way they come out. I keep thinking I'll be able to take a good one next time, but they all come out weird."

She pulled out her own phone and showed me.

"Heck," I said. She was right; in every selfie there was a flash-back that enveloped her face and gave it a glowing halo. "You ever reckon you're wearing too much foundation?"

"I *have* to wear that!" she said earnestly. "Otherwise I look terrible!"

"It's probably all the mirrors you have around the place," I said. "Catching the light and stuff."

"We should try," she began, sitting up a bit more in bed, "to get some selfies of you! I'll show you how and—"

"Next time," I said hastily. I had already been conned by her into trying out makeup and I hadn't particularly enjoyed the experience. That was probably because it didn't look much good on me, but it hadn't left me keen to try selfies. "Look, are you *sure* this is Blackpoint's setup? Can I tell Zero that this is definitely our bloke?"

"He told me how he built it, and he sent me a few pictures; I can see a few of the custom parts he told me he built it from in the photos, too."

"Yeah, but there wasn't the other sort of stuff there should be," I said.

Her eyes flickered to me. "What do you mean?"

"Your sort of stuff," I said. "Stuff to help him get around— wheelchairs, or bells, or stuff for physical therapy. It doesn't look like this bloke was disabled at all."

"I don't—I don't think he could have pretended about that," Morgana said quietly. "We talked a lot about that. I'll show you his messages."

She passed me her phone; it was open in a gaming chat app

with a long scroll of messages back and forth that I glanced down at initially, then took a closer look at.

Sometimes I feel like I can cut it out of me, but there wouldn't be enough of me left to think afterwards. Gotta keep thinking.

I hate this body. If I knew a way to get out of it, I would. How are you supposed to escape when it's your own body you're trapped in? I didn't choose this. At least if I did it, that'd be my choice.

I didn't ask what he meant by *if I did it*, because I was already pretty sure I knew what he meant. I'd had my own share of dark thoughts after my parents died, but contradictorily, I'd been too busy trying not to starve to be able to pay attention to the thoughts that told me I could take away the aching pain of loss if I just stepped in front of that car, or let myself drift off the side of the Tasman bridge.

"You feel like that?" I asked her. I mean, I know her makeup is dark, but there was such a zest for life in her—had been since I'd known her.

Morgana looked away. "Not now," she said. "But for a while I did. Sometimes it comes back, but I know how to deal with it these days. I don't think he was pretending that. I don't know what it was he had, but I know it was something that couldn't be fixed, and it was something that went really deep. It affected the whole way he interacted with the world."

But there hadn't been anything in the house to indicate that. Nothing on the security feed to show anything but a man who was, to all appearances, completely healthy. Completely healthy, and completely human. I had been coming to think that he was not as human as he was pretending, but the messages made me wonder.

It was very possible that he was a human who had been so much in contact with Behindkind and so much exposed to the constant barrage of insults and derision that he'd come to believe it all. It was funny how sick that made me feel, after everything else I'd seen fae and other Behindkind do. Every grisly murder had been done to the outside of a person, human or Behindkind; if I was right, this was more akin to murdering humans from the inside.

"You said you had something, too?" I said, pushing away the thought for now. I didn't know if it was true—there was still a lot of reason to think that Blackpoint was fae, and tricky into the bargain. It was more likely that he'd been lying to Morgana— especially since we'd seen him walking.

"Not something I found out so much as something weird happened."

"All right, what happened?"

"The attacks started again—the ones on my firewalls, I mean. Someone's been trying to get through all morning, but they stopped as soon as you came into the room. Literally as soon, which is—oh! The webcam!"

I followed her eyes to blink uneasily at the shiny eye of the webcam and felt as though it wouldn't take much for it to blink back at me. The green light built into it flicked on, and I said to Morgana, "Oi. That meant to be on?"

"Nope," she said tersely, and grabbed it off the top of the laptop. She turned it off and stuffed it under the pillow, too, for good measure. I noticed that the built-in camera on her laptop was already covered with tape. "How the heck did they get into my camera if they can't get past my firewall?"

"There was someone looking at us?"

"Someone turned it on remotely," she said, chewing on her black lips. "And I don't think they'd do that if they weren't planning on looking. I haven't had this happen before. I don't like the way all these attacks are happening at once—and I definitely don't like that it stopped as soon as they saw you."

"Creepy as all heck," I agreed. "Anything else you can do to stop people from getting into your computer?"

"I'll be working on it," said Morgana, her dark brows drawing together. "Trust me for that."

My phone bingled, and she added, "You get messages more these days."

"Yeah," I said. "It's a flamin' joy."

It was a text from Five. How in the *world* had he—no. I was wrong. It was a text to let me know that he'd left a message for me. Goodness knew what he'd done wrong this time: I hadn't even heard my phone ring.

"Hang on a tick," I said to Morgana, and played the message.

"For all that's gold and green what th—Pet! *Pet! Is that you?*"

I pulled the phone back from my ear a bit, wincing. "Heck."

"You need to come here!" bawled Five's voice. "I need my console and the least you could do is mark significant passages!"

There was a series of what sounded like the phone hitting several surfaces before it hit the floor, then a scrabble, and the message ended.

"You know a lot of interesting people," said Morgana, trying not to laugh. "Does this mean you've gotta go?"

"Yeah," I said reluctantly. I should be off to do that before Zero got back to the house and realised—

Right on cue, my phone rang.

"Heck," I said again. There was Zero's name on the display, all right. I was tempted not to answer, but he'd probably come out to check on me if I didn't, and I didn't particularly want him to know what I was up to.

I sighed, and answered the call.

"Pet," rumbled Zero's voice. I was pretty sure he was doing something to it to make it more threatening, because it rumbled right out of the phone and around the room. "You're not at the house."

"I know," I said. "I'm with Morgana. She was telling me that it's definitely Blackpoint's house. His computer system is exactly what he described to her."

"Come home," he said.

"Yeah, but I have to get something from Blackpoint's house first."

Hopefully they'd think I was looking for Jin Yeong's tie; I still had to go see Five before I could go back home.

There was a heavy, disapproving silence before Zero began, "Pet—"

Persuasively, I said, "You don't want me to come home without my walk."

"Pet—"

"There'll be accidents on the furniture," I pointed out. "You know what us pets are like."

Morgana did a very small snort-choke of laughter, and on the other end of the line, the silence drew out; but this time I was pretty sure Zero was trying not to laugh.

"Pet—"

"I'll be home within an hour," I promised, waving silently to Morgana on my way out of the room. "Don't worry, I don't wanna meet up with our friend out in the streets, either."

"Be careful," he said, and hung up as I closed the door.

Maybe the idea of meeting the murderer out on the street left me more uneasy than I thought, because when I left Morgana's room I could have sworn a dark shadow flitted up the hall from the direction of the stairs, heading for the roof.

"Flamin' heck!" I said, starting back against the closed door. Were the kids playing jokes again? It wasn't the time of day they were usually playing on the roof, and it'd been a while since I'd thought I'd seen shadows moving in Morgana's house. Those shadows had been the outline of my house trying to follow me through to Morgana's, and that wasn't likely to be happening again, at least.

Still, it left me jumpy enough that I followed the shadow up the hall and onto the roof. I don't like leaving creepy things alone —shadows in the hallway usually belong to people up to mischief, but with the oddness I'd brought to Morgana's house while I was living there, I thought I'd rather be sure it wasn't anything... Betweenish...instead.

It was more than a shadow but less than a person, and I was able to follow it all the way up the stairs and out into the light of the outside on the roof. It was much harder to see up there in the daylight; it might have been easier to see at the time I normally came up here—golden hour, when the light seemed to cling to everything—but as it was, I could barely see it flit across the roof. I caught sight of it again just as it vanished into the wall beside the cupboards under the overhang.

"Flamin' heck," I said again, this time more thoughtfully. There was no way I was going to be poking my nose in there, mysterious shadow or not. It would likely be just the last, lingering effects of my house on Morgana's house, and I wasn't about to give the kids a chance to spring a surprise on me. I'd seen them tumbling in and out of the cupboards any number of times and I was pretty sure they had booby traps on 'em just in case of strangers getting too nosey.

Besides, I didn't have time now. I had to go meet Five while Zero still didn't know what I was up to, *then* double back to Blackpoint's place so I could say I'd had a bit of a look around for Jin Yeong's tie.

"I'll come back to you later," I said, narrowing my eyes at the cupboard. I raised my voice and added, "And if it's you kids playing tricks, I'll tell Daniel to stop feeding you."

Still, it was lucky that they preferred to stay on the upper floors to play their tricks, away from the werewolves on the lower floors, even if it did make them mischievous. The werewolves weren't always careful about staying human when they were on the first floor—at least Daniel had made sure they stayed human when they were anywhere else in the house.

I left the shadow for another time and hurried off to meet Five. The leprechaun was tapping around irritatedly in the kitchen when I got there, with the door ajar for me to slip through, and as soon as he heard my step in the doorway, he turned around with a fierce grin.

"There you are! The little thingummy worked, then?"

"Yeah," I said slowly, looking around the room. The whole kitchen table and bench were covered with the hard copies of the contents of the red USB, messy piles here and there, and a few pens mingled with the lot. It was chaos. "The um, thingummy worked."

"There's something in here—" he muttered, flipping up the edges of papers. "You need to tell me about it."

I took a sticky-beak at the papers in front of me: I'd already looked through most of the things, but only quickly, and most of the documents hadn't meant a lot to me. But as I looked down at one particular scrap, it occurred to me that I was looking at something very familiar.

"Hang on," I said, frowning. "This one isn't—I mean, I know this address."

Five tried to look around me, failed, and gave up. He trotted around and slipped under my arm instead, his beard tickling my elbow.

"Oh, that one. I wasn't looking into that one. It's just one address in a set—the first one was obviously the important one. It's the one that fit into the pattern. The others can be discarded."

"Yeah?" I said slowly. "I dunno."

Because even if it didn't fit into Five's pattern, I had a very particular reason for thinking it fit into some other kind of pattern.

Because that address was Morgana's address.

"Oi," I said. "How would this lot of addresses all end up on the same page? They're not alphabetised."

"Depends on the system," said Five. "If it was a block entry system, all of them from a pre-set page would appear when you search one of them—a bit like a paper page. Turn to a page with one address and you get all of 'em, pre-sorted to the original enterer's guidelines. If it's a single-entry system, you'd have to do a search with parameters that you specifically wanted."

"Beggar me," I said grumpily.

"I told you," Five said, turning his head to glare up at me, "that I *need* my *console*."

Since it seemed like he was really offended by his failure to know things that couldn't reasonably be known, I said hastily, "It doesn't matter. I can figure it out another way; ask someone, if I've got enough to pay for the question. It's probably not important, like you said."

He stabbed a finger at the first address. "Can you tell me why this one's important?"

"Yeah," I said. "That's my address."

"Well, I suppose that's good to know," he said. "You couldn't have told me that before, could you? Green and Gold! I *need* parameters!"

"Didn't think it was important," I said. I didn't even know why Athelas would have searched for it: he already knew where I was living these days. He'd known that for quite some time, which meant that he had been searching for something else when it came up—parameters, like Five had said. "It's my address, yeah, but—"

He trundled around the table, his wooden leg scrabbling against the tiles, and fetched a highlighter, which he tossed at me. "Mark up anything that has something to do with you."

I stared at him. "With *me*? You reckon that's going to be useful?"

I'd known a bit of the paperwork was tangentially connected to me, but it hadn't occurred to me that I would be a useful common point in figuring out the whole of it; there was too much of it that wasn't connected to me.

"'Course it will! It's all information, isn't it? And if my suspicions are correct—well, never mind that. You just mark it up."

"What was it you wanted me to look at?" I asked, fiddling with the highlighter. "I can't mark these now; I need to get back home before Zero comes looking for me."

"All right," he said. "But first you can look at this and tell me why you think it's in this lot."

I took the half-piece of paper from him, and stared down at the face of the teenager copied there in black and white. In monochrome, her hair looked utterly white, but if it had been in colour, it would have been more of a platinum; and instead of making dark blots in her face, the eyes would have been luminous grey.

"It's my mum," I said roughly. I definitely hadn't seen that one in this lot before I handed it over to him; if I had, I would have kept it. "It's um—I mean, it's her license photo from when she was younger."

"Had a license, did she? What for?"

"Driving a car," I said. "You know, the beep-beep things out—"

"I know what a car is," said Five, huffily.

"You didn't flamin' know when you grabbed my arm the first day and tried to climb up my leg 'cos you thought it was coming for you," I said, my voice growing huskier as I spoke. I couldn't help that. Couldn't help the hot wetness in my eyes, either.

"I didn't—why are you crying? Stop it. Green and gold, kid, I didn't mean to—I'm sorry. I haven't had my tea and I'm cranky."

"You didn't do anything wrong," I said, dabbing at my eyes with the shoulder of my t shirt. "Sorry. It was just suddenly seeing her again. We didn't have photos lying around the place, so it's been a while."

"Good idea not to have photos," agreed Five. "Especially not on the human internet. Hard copies are bad enough; you never know what Behindkind can do with a photo if they've got a leprechaun and a money trail to match."

"I don't know what that means."

"It means that your parents were either criminals or on the

run," Five said bluntly. "Always knew there was something not on the level about you."

"My parents weren't criminals!" I said indignantly. "And we weren't running, either! Why should we? We didn't do anything wrong!"

"Not everyone who's on the run has done something wrong," he said. "Green and gold, what do you think happened to me?"

"That's no reason to say my parents were dodgy!" I protested. Memories rose, fast and troubling; an early friend looking at me open-mouthed when they found out that I had moved ten times by my ninth birthday, the boy next door who had refused to play with me or even look at me because he said I was a little ghost girl, me asking mum and dad about the kids on tv who went to school and whose parents worked at office jobs. Dad gently but firmly refusing to let me buy one of the new, retro-look polaroid cameras that came out when I was ten—saying, "That's not the sort of record we want to leave behind us. We live in the present."

It wasn't odd. Not everyone lived life the same way; we'd just been a bit different to the normal, boring people. And there was nothing wrong with wanting to see more of the country; what was the good staying in one place all the time?

Only we hadn't gone out that much, come to think of it; when we had, it was mostly out for a drive in the country—nowhere urban, nowhere with a lot of people. But still, that wasn't any reason for someone to suggest we'd been on the run, or that there was anything wrong with our way of life!

"Don't tell me you haven't thought the same thing," he said. "Gold perish it, kid, you must have noticed that life changed at some stage!"

"Life didn't change!" I shot back at him. "It was always the same, and then someone murdered them! They weren't dodgy, and they didn't do anything to deserve it!"

"Are you going to tell me you lived hidden away everywhere you were—like that little room you told me about?"

I glared at him. I told him about my room because I liked him and because it had come up in the conversation one day—I hadn't expected to have it used against me. "I liked hiding in small places. It felt safe!"

He grinned a bit, but it was a sad grin. "Safe from *what*, kid?"

"I gotta go," I said abruptly. I wheeled and went for the door, still clutching the piece of paper with my mother's black-and-white face on it. I heard muttering behind me, and the agitated shuffle of Five's peg leg, but to my relief he didn't try to follow me out.

What *rubbish*. The cheek of a Behindkind leprechaun, trying to tell me what was normal for a human! At least when Morgana told me I was weird, she was coming from a human point of view; it wasn't like Five knew what he was talking about when it came to humans. He'd only just come to the realisation that we weren't a slightly more intelligent form of cow.

And there was Morgana, too, I thought soberly, remembering that address. Five's feelings on my parents and our life together before they were murdered aside, there was a lot more here that I wanted to know.

I *very much* wanted to know what Athelas had been playing at. Why had he pulled up my mum's early license? Mum was dead, so even if he had been trying to do what Five suggested, there was no living person at the end of the trail. I also wanted to know exactly what else there was that connected me and Morgana—we both had nightmares, and now both of our addresses had turned up on one page of *someone*'s address book. Was it Athelas' parameters, or the original pre-sets of the person who had entered the addresses?

I had a feeling that if I knew who had originally entered the addresses in the police system, I would be one very large step closer to figuring out a lot of what I wanted to know. I wondered if Athelas knew exactly what he was searching for, and if he would answer my questions about it if he did.

Of course, Morgana's parents were alive and mine were dead, but that didn't mean I was seeing a pattern that wasn't really there. It just meant that I didn't have all of the pieces to the puzzle yet.

I still hadn't come to a satisfactory conclusion by the time I arrived at Blackpoint's house again, but at least getting there gave me something to do that didn't involve obsessively going over old memories. Those old memories inevitably led back to the same memory, and I didn't particularly want to go back there. It was kinda nice just to have to think about where I'd last seen JinYeong's stupid tie last.

Had it been in the security room? No; last time I'd seen it, it was heading up the stairs.

I went up the stairs, too, whistling here and there as if it would come at a whistle, and found myself wandering back into the computer room instead of looking into the other rooms.

"What a flamin' mess," I said to myself, trying not to shiver as I crossed the floor. It felt like there were prickles running up and down my back; probably just because I was alone when I usually had one of the three psychos at my back. It made my back feel a bit chilly. "They were really looking for something in here."

I really had to stop talking to myself.

I picked my way carefully between the game cases and other detritus, frowning. Behindkind and the golden fae had each made a good mess in here, and there was something not quite right about it. Now, if I could only figure out what it was.

While I tried to get my head around that, I wandered around to the other side of the desk and had a bit of a shuffle through the stuff there. It had already been gone over by the Behindkind who came through, and then again by the golden fae, but none of them had done more than take a quick look at some of the items and throw them down again.

The golden fae, I could understand—he had probably been planning on sending Zero in to investigate anyway, watched over by his lieutenant to make sure that Blackpoint was actually gone and not just hiding somewhere out of sight—but the Behindkind were surprisingly lackadaisical. Had Blackpoint not been important enough to try and track down, or had they seen another clue we hadn't? Or, I wondered suddenly, aimlessly picking up Blackpoint's desk diary while I was thinking, had they in fact done what Athelas suggested he would have done in the same situation. If Blackpoint was done away with in those five blank minutes on the security footage, and they had merely shown themselves afterward to throw persons unknown off the scent, they wouldn't need to search very carefully. They would have already known where he was.

If the Enforcers and the Family was interested in him, Upper Management was sure to have him on their radar, too. It wasn't too much of a stretch to think that other Behindkind might be interested in him. And if the golden git had arrived here because he had an idea something was going down, something else must have happened to make him think that. Had someone out there given someone—or a few someones—a nudge in the right direction at the right time?

I turned over the desk diary, and a business card slipped from between the stiffened pages and fell on the desk with a tiny *tik*. What the heck? Had he sticky-taped business cards into his diary? I went back to the stiffened pages, and sure enough; they were stiff because they each had about four business cards taped to them. The pages closed together with the cards meeting face-to-face, with a space for the one that had fallen out. I looked at them a bit closer and grinned, then picked up the one on the desk and looked at it—which made me grin a fair bit more. I marked the pages with the fallen card as a bookmark even though they were easy enough to find, and tucked it against my ribs.

Now I had a reason to have been out and about today! This would be something nice to take home with me.

I fired up Blackpoint's computer next. I didn't really expect much: it would be weird if he didn't have a password requirement. If he didn't, it was probably a trap. But it didn't matter if it was a trap. All I wanted to do was check a few of the addresses on the cards online, and at the worst he would have set his computer to melt down, which wouldn't matter much to me. It wasn't like I could get much off it anyway, and even if Morgana could have done it, it wasn't like I could take it to her.

It only took ten seconds for the password prompt to flash up —only it wasn't a password prompt.

It said, *Are you human?*

"Rude!" I said. I typed *yes* into the password space.

Prove it.

"Flamin' heck!" I said in amazement. "What do you want, a blood test?"

You first, I typed. *What's the meaning of life, the universe, and everything?*

All right, said the computer, *you win. 42. You'd better go before someone comes.*

Who's coming?

Never you mind. Take the game in the bright orange case. It's under the diary.

I hesitated a moment, and the computer prompted, *Hurry up. This isn't a safe place for you to stay.* Then it turned itself off again.

"All right, all right," I said. I grabbed the orange game case; it felt light so I opened it and found a voucher for game redemption instead of a physical copy. "That's weird, too."

I couldn't help stopping and turning to look around the room before I left, despite the computer's warning. As I did so, the hair on the back of my neck prickled for a brief moment and someone said, "*Mwoh hae?*"

I nearly jumped out of my skin.

"Flaming *heck*," I said, with very great emphasis. "What are you trying to do, frighten the life outta me?"

He grinned, and sauntered around me. "What are you doing here? *Hyeong* is annoyed because you're not home."

"Had some stuff I needed to do. Oi. You're all obsessive about stuff—how come the room looks different?"

One of his brows quirked up. "Different than what?"

"Dunno. Maybe the security footage?"

"Ah. That," he said, unsurprised. He stooped for a video game case and brandished it at me. "One of these little things is missing. From the wall over there; the one in a frame."

He was right, beggar it all. "How come you didn't say anything before?"

He shrugged. "The house is open. Humans could come in or out—more Behindkind could have moved it. You think it is important?"

"Dunno," I said again. "Maybe? Probably not. I'll have a look at the footage to see when it changed, anyway. Do what Detective Tuatu did and go through day by day until I find where it changes."

"Yes," said Jin Yeong, "but right now, come home."

Maybe they were all suspicious of what I'd been up to, because when we got home, the first thing Athelas said to me was, "You were gone for some time, Pet. May one trust that you were using your time profitably by regaining possession of Jin Yeong's...er, tie?"

"Nah," I said, waving the purloined book at him. "Stole the bloke's diary."

Athelas gazed at the book. "How very interesting!"

"Isn't it!" I agreed. "All the schedules and stuff are on his computer, I'll bet: a diary's a weird thing for him to have, don't you reckon?"

Zero said, after a brief pause, "Well done, Pet. What is in it?"

"Not much," I said. I'd checked out a few of the business cards on my phone as I strolled home with Jin Yeong, and now I was even more pleased about the discovery of the diary. "About eight business cards. No writing."

Zero's brow went up just slightly. *Not very useful*, that brow said, but he took the diary from me anyway and leafed through the first few pages to look at the business cards.

"Not many," he said. "And the addresses are local, so if we need to check them we can divide them up and cover them all pretty quickly."

"Yeah," I said, "but they're all—"

"Residential areas," said Athelas, picking up one of the cards. "And if I were to guess, I'd say that the business names—"

"Don't exist," I finished for him. "Nor do the business numbers. Nothing listed under them on the government ABN website, anyway. If they're real, I dunno what they're doing for taxes without a business number, and the government will probably be after them anyway."

JinYeong plucked another of the cards out of the book and flourished it at us.

"I thought that one might interest you all," I said, smiling sunnily. The card he'd taken was embossed with the business name *Blackpoint*. "That's why I brought it back with me."

"Well done, Pet," said Zero.

Warm with pleasure, I shrugged. "Found it by accident, anyway," I said. I wriggled the game case at them. "Oh, and the computer told me to take this."

"I beg your pardon, Pet?" Athelas said. "Did you say the *computer* told you to bring it home?"

"Yeah."

"Correct me if I'm wrong, but that seems like unusual behaviour on the part of the computer."

"Flamin' weird," I agreed.

"I'm relieved to hear you say it. Perhaps you could explain why you thought it good to follow the promptings of the computer, in that case?"

"Reckoned it was Blackpoint talking to me through the computer," I explained. I very much wondered about Morgana's webcam, too. I had no proof, but if it was Blackpoint talking to me on his computer, it seemed likely that it had been him then, too. "There was a kinda test thing to make sure I was human, but I reckon that was him, too. He's out there somewhere with access to a computer, and he wanted me to take this with me."

Zero and Athelas exchanged glances.

"I think, my lord, we can safely assume that he is alive, in that case."

Zero asked, "Do you know what the game does?"

"Not a clue!" I said. "Sorry. There's no physical game in the box, though; just a code for downloading the game."

"Ask your friend about it before you go playing around with our computer," Zero said. "Better still, have Athelas set up an enchantment around it when you're ready to begin downloading, just in case of...accidents. What else?"

"That's it," I said. "What about you lot? How'd the detective take the new body?"

"About as stoutly as usual," said Athelas, shooting an amused look at Zero. "He was somewhat...perturbed when we told him there would be another one soon in the immediate area."

"You said that before," I said. "Is it really that predictable?"

"At this stage in the cycle, yes," said Zero. "Athelas and I have been working on pinpointing potential victims given their proximity."

"Any luck?"

"We've got a pretty good idea," Zero said coolly. "We're expecting a death tomorrow night, and we've got it narrowed down to five potentials in the area."

"What makes a person potential?" I asked. "Thought you hadn't decided how this bloke picks his victims."

"We haven't," Athelas said. "But there are always certain markers that point to one person being more likely than another:

proximity to the original murder, a propensity to prefer to be alone, someone who is either estranged from or unknown to their neighbours, and so on."

"So we're looking for a weirdo loner who might be Behindkind or might be human, somewhere within a kilometre of the original murder?" I stared at them. "Not to sound harsh, but I'm pretty sure there's more than five weird loners in this area of town."

Zero's eyes glowed blue. "We were able to narrow it down based on a few other factors," he said. "And for your information, Pet, many of the houses in this area of town are either unoccupied, occupied by single mothers attending TAFE, or housing foreign students."

"That makes things much clearer, thanks," I said. "What, our murderer doesn't go for single mums or students?"

"Not in general," Athelas said. "We don't believe it to be a prejudice on his part; merely that the people he hunts are not engaged in such pursuits as a general rule."

"How are we gunna stop him getting to one of his type, then?" I asked. "If we don't know exactly where?"

"That's exactly why I brought in the detective. He's arranging eyes on all of the potentials."

"Sounds to me like it's a good way to get him killed," I pointed out. "Or the cops he sends out."

So that's why they'd wanted me back; they weren't suspicious about what I was up to, they thought there was more than a decent chance that the murderer would be out tonight or tomorrow night, and they didn't want me on the streets when he was likely to be there as well.

"I've given the detective...hints...about which of the officers he should put where," Athelas said.

"Heck! You mean there's Behindkind in the lower ranks, too? Thought we got rid of that when we kicked out Upper Management from the police station."

"They're unaffiliated, in general," said Athelas. "Which means they need to make a living."

"Black-carded?" That explained how it had been so easy to set up Five in his place. There were obviously more black-carded Behindkind around than I was aware of. Maybe they had an online group—I'd have to find out.

"Some of them. Others are more like refugees—either way, they're aware of things your normal human police officer wouldn't be."

"Bet they've got a few more talents, too," I said.

"Exactly so."

"Stay inside tonight, Pet," Zero said.

His eyes were on me, cold and commanding, which meant *no funny business or else.*

"'Course," I said. "I'm not dumb. I'm still hoping to live to my nineteenth birthday."

"Athelas and Jin Yeong will be with you," he said. "I'll be on patrol between the possible locations."

"Won't you need the other two as well?"

"The detective has the possibilities covered," he said briefly, "and we don't expect a murder until the third night. It's likely he'll have to recalibrate once he sees that the targets are guarded."

"I thought the idea of eyes on people was to stay out of sight," I said. "And what do you mean, recalibrate?"

"He'll have to plan to kill the watcher as well as the target," explained Zero. "It will take him longer. There's no likelihood at all that he won't see them there."

"Do they know they're out on a suicide mission?" I asked, shocked.

"I thought you were of the opinion that Behindkind should be looking after humans?" said Athelas blandly.

"No, I'm of the opinion that they shouldn't be killing humans in the first place," I said. "And if they are putting their lives on the line, I just wanna know they know they're doing it."

"They know," said Zero. He gazed at me for some time with his expression unreadable, before he added, "Apparently there are Behindkind who feel as you do, Pet."

"All right," I said. Now that I was faced with the reality of such Behindkind, I felt oddly bad about it all. It was one thing to be protesting that Behindkind, who were far stronger and more suped up than humans, should look after them—or at least make sure they didn't kill them—but it was another to know that Behindkind were out there, putting their lives in danger for the sake of humans. "Make sure they don't die, all right?"

"We shall do our best, Pet," said Athelas.

CHAPTER NINE

IT WAS TEN O'CLOCK AND WELL AND TRULY DARK BEFORE ZERO left the house. By that stage Jin Yeong was pacing back and forth with dark, bloody eyes, and Athelas was sitting in his chair with a cup of tea, one leg crossed over the other and very slightly swinging, meditating on nothing. Neither of them, apparently, were best pleased about having to stay home while Zero went out; neither of them protested, however. That was more than slightly unusual, but I had noticed they were more likely to do as they were told without protesting when it came to things that had to do with the murderer. Everything else seemed to be negotiable—or, in Jin Yeong's case, open to disobedience—but in that one case they obeyed religiously.

I gave Morgana a quick call to ask her about the game download, and Athelas must have been glad for something to do, because when I told him I was about to start on the computer, he headed upstairs without a word and spun something weird and clingy and strong all around the CPU. It let me sit down and turn on the computer, though, so it mustn't have been aimed at me; and when I started the download going, all it seemed to do was get a bit easier to see and maybe cling onto the computer a bit more.

I didn't think I was likely to get to sleep, so I ignored Athelas' suggestion that I go to my room as well as Jin Yeong's increasingly erratic pacing, and sprawled out on the couch, staring at the ceiling. There was some sort of psychedelic pattern swirling around up there like a kaleidoscope. The house did that sometimes, playing with what really was there and what could have been there. When I was younger I'd thought it was my eyes playing tricks on me; these days I knew it was the house playing tricks on me.

I fell asleep watching the movement of alternate reality on the ceiling, into which Jin Yeong's swift, soft footsteps also melted, and woke in the dark to see a dark shadow sitting in Athelas' chair, watching me.

I yelped and nearly fell off the couch. "What the heck?"

The figure in Athelas' chair said in Athelas' voice, "Calm yourself, Pet. It is only myself."

I sat up, shivering with the suddenness of my waking. I really must be on edge: I was used to waking up to seeing Athelas in his own chair. There was no need to be getting jumpy about it.

I looked around the room, aware of the sudden lack of restless movement to the whole house. "Where's Jin Yeong?"

"I'm sure I don't know," he said. "He left some time ago; I was not feeling similarly motivated, as you can see."

"Maybe he went out to help Zero?" I suggested, getting up. Now that I was awake, I didn't think I was likely to get back to sleep any time soon: might as well make some coffee and wait for the others to get home.

"Very likely," agreed Athelas. "Do you mind very much *not* turning on the light, Pet? I've just managed to achieve some semblance of peaceful rest and I'd very much rather not have it disturbed."

"All right," I said, drawing my hand away from the light

switch. It wasn't like I needed the lights on to make my way around the house in the dark, after all. Even if I hadn't been completely familiar with the layout, the house was easily navigable these days by the feeling of Between to the different areas. The kitchen, with its one little cracked tile, I could have found blindfolded.

"You getting old?" I asked as I stepped up into the kitchen and living room area. There was a nice bit of moonlight drifting in there to make sure there weren't any cockroaches hanging about where I was about to step, so that was nice. "You don't usually have to rest."

There was a soft laugh in the darkness. "I begin to wonder about that myself."

In fact, the last time I remembered him having to rest with any noticeability was the time he had died and then fought his way through far too many Behindkind in revenge for killing him—or maybe for making him kill me, I wasn't quite sure which one yet.

"You hurt or something?" I asked sharply, my hand moving toward the light switch again.

"Calm yourself, Pet," he said mildly. "I am not injured: I have done nothing extraordinary tonight and if you imagine I'm still healing from our previous joint encounter with the Behind world, you may rest easy. I am merely in need of peace and quiet presently."

"All right, but you need to work on your recharging," I called back to him, switching on the jug. "I don't think you charged enough last time."

"I'm touched by your concern."

I grinned at the tiles in the kitchen. Sarcastic old beggar. The tiles didn't exactly grin back, but they had a bit of a glow to them, and that was more lively of them than usual.

"The house is a bit excited, isn't it?" I called into the living room.

"I'm very much afraid that something has happened nearby," Athelas said. "Do make me a pot of tea while you're in there, won't you, Pet? I fancy it may be too late for me to regain my restful state of mind: perhaps I shall have a bath. No doubt Zero will be home soon."

It was JinYeong who arrived home first, though. He arrived a moment or two after Athelas stood in a small whisper of movement in the living room, segueing through the kitchen wall in an absolute *welter* of blood that turned his grim stalk into more of a slither. If the barely concealed rage in his eyes was anything to judge by, he had had an annoying time of it.

I got a look at him in the soft moonlight as he stopped to get his balance on the tiles, and asked, "What happened to you? You been rolling in blood again?"

There was a *lot* more blood on him than I would have expected, even if he had been finding bodies.

"There was a bomb," he said coldly, slipping and regaining his footing in one furious flailing of arms as he stepped down into the living room and into the cover of darkness.

"Flaming heck!" I said, cold right to my ears, taking a step toward the living room. "Is it—is it *your* blood? I thought— Heck. You'd better sit down—why are you standing up? Do you need blood?"

"The *body*," he said, with great precision, "exploded. And now there is blood everywhere and I cannot smell anything else. *Hyeong* sent me home."

I heard him crossing the darkness of the living room, moving more easily across the carpet, and from somewhere near the linen closet Athelas said sharply, "Do *not* sit in my chair, JinYeong."

I could have told him not to bother: JinYeong was in exactly the sort of mood to do the opposite of whatever he was asked to do. I saw his profile in shadow as he gazed challengingly at the shadow that was Athelas, then he continued to saunter across the room and dropped down into the chair. There was a very distinct *squish*.

"Oi!" I said indignantly, jumping up to switch on the light. "Get outta the chair you flamin' mosquito! You've put blood all over it!"

I heard the ghost of a laugh from Athelas, who must have given up on moody JinYeong, because he had vanished away into the bathroom, the smell of lavender wafting with him. Good grief, if it was bad enough for him to want a scented shower, he really must have a headache or something.

I narrowed my eyes at JinYeong. "I'm gunna have to clean that," I said.

"Did you want me to sit on our couch?"

"Okay, fair point." It would be slightly easier to clean blood from leather than it would be to clean it from fabric.

"*Hyeong* wants you," he said to me. His eyes, dark and bloody, fixed on the wall opposite him. "Not now; soon. He will send a message. Ah! I smell of *blood* and there is nowhere to *wash*."

"There's the hose in the back yard," I suggested, but I didn't really expect him to take the suggestion. "If you hadn't got blood all over Athelas' chair, maybe he would have let you go first."

"Now I will smell of lavender."

I nearly said, *"Better than how you usually smell"*, but left it just this once. "You want blood, or coffee?"

"Coffee," he said. "*And* blood."

I GOT A MESSAGE FROM ZERO JUST AFTER ATHELAS CAME BACK out of the bathroom in his shirt-sleeves with a steamy, lavender-scented towel draped around his neck and JinYeong took his place, carrying with him his coffee-and-blood cocktail.

"You coming with me?" I asked Athelas. I was a bit worried: I hadn't often seen him in a headachy way. "Zero didn't mention you in the text."

"Certainly I am coming," he said, abandoning the towel over the bloody arm of his chair and smoothing back his hair with his damp hands. "My lord will need me."

That was all well and good, but I wasn't sure why Zero needed *me*, even though it was me he'd texted. Maybe this was a form of reverse psychology? Call the person you don't want and make sure the person you didn't mention comes?

I was even less sure of it when we got to the house on Lefroy Street where Zero was waiting, because the first thing he asked was, "Did you ask your friend about the code?"

"Called her while you were out," I told him. I saw the quick glance he sent in Athelas' direction, and although he looked away again at once, I could have sworn I briefly saw a faint frown of concern. So Zero thought it was weird, too? I explained, "She says so long as we've got a good firewall, it'll tell us if there's a virus in the download. Pretty sure the people who set up the computer did a good job of it, so I reckon it'll be safe; I've got it downloading at the moment, but it reckons it'll take another twenty hours or something, and I'm pretty sure that's because what Athelas did is slowing it down. Did the body really explode?"

"One of the bodies exploded," Zero corrected, leading the way into the house.

"There were two?" I hesitated at the door, because I could already see the glow of blood red through the house. Zero had one of his non-electric lights going in the next room; they were enough light to see by but didn't tend to show through the curtains—a bit of magic I'd be glad to learn.

This time, I wasn't sure I wanted to see what it illuminated, however.

"We brought in the body to keep it out of sight of the neighbours," Zero said, keeping to a precise path across the kitchen that I followed as well. The less evidence left for Detective Tuatu to stress over, the better. "There was already a body in the living room when we came in. The body already on the inside was the one that exploded, but it took bits of our body with it. Oddly enough, the murder victim we're particularly interested in didn't live in the house; she was just strung outside it."

"Interesting," murmured Athelas. "Not unlike the situation with our Pet, then."

"What about the Behindkind who was meant to be watching her?" I asked.

"Alive," said Zero. There was nothing in his voice to indicate it, but I was pretty sure he was surprised. "And feeling rather grateful. Because the murderer got to her through the neighbour, our watcher saw nothing. He would have known not to worry about the neighbour being our man."

"Hang on, what do you mean *he got to her through the neighbour?*"

"Go look in the hall," Zero said briefly.

I gladly turned away from the red-tinged doorway before I could quite see through to the horrors beyond, slipping a little in the blood that Jin Yeong had left when he stalked home to have a shower. There was another doorway across from us that led into the hallway, and I stepped through it, looking first to my left down the dark, shadowed length of it, then right.

Dull, empty wells for eyes looked right back at me from something that might have been a face sitting on a tarry entity: scarred and multilayered in torn and bloody tatters, it swept right through me with a sob of despair and stumbled down the hallway without a sound.

I yelped and staggered backward, slipping on blood in a mad, silky scrabble until Athelas caught me by the arms and steadied me.

"What the *flaming heck* is that!"

"It's a shade," Athelas said.

"What does it want and why is it so flamin' ugly?"

"Some crimes create a soiled place in the world," he said. "If they're repeated often enough—or if they're violent enough—in the same place. If I had a guess, I would say that this hallway has seen a steady parade of bloody women being marched to their deaths, and with each one, another layer of grime has been added to this part of reality."

"It's a woman?" I asked, dazed and sickened. "That thing was a woman?"

"Not one woman: many," Zero said shortly, from the other doorway. "The dead body that was already here was a human serial murderer—he must have been luring women to their deaths here for ten years at least, and at a good, steady pace."

I felt a vicious stab of satisfaction. "I'm glad the murderer got him, then."

"An oddly satisfying justice, is it not?" said Athelas, amused. "No doubt the human thought he was the predator."

"Are there—"

"Yes," said Zero. "There are other bodies. The shade leads the way to them—and is another thing you shouldn't be able to see, by the way."

"That why you wanted me here? To test if I could see it?"

"Yes. If you want to go now, you can. Jin Yeong will be back soon; you can wait outside for him to take you home."

"I'm okay," I said, thickly. "Did this human kill the woman next door, then?"

"I'm not sure which one of them killed her, yet," Zero said, as Athelas and I rejoined him by the other door and carefully stepped into the room. "But our murderer certainly used this human to draw the woman in; the human would never have been careless enough to murder a woman so close to him after doing this successfully for ten or fifteen years, unless he had been persuaded to do so. Whichever one of them killed her, the murderer made his show with the body as usual."

I looked around at the room, wishing I couldn't smell the bloodiness of it all, then there was the *squish* of bloody carpet beneath my foot as I shifted, and suddenly I wasn't okay anymore.

"Gunna go out," I said, and headed back grimly through the

kitchen and outside into the cool darkness. Darkness that didn't smell like blood and didn't squish underneath my feet, reminding me too much of another time—another place—

"Lean over the flowerbed if you're going to throw up," said Zero, sitting down on the steps next to me. "We still have to come in and out and the detective won't thank you for the extra mess when we tell him about this."

"Not gunna throw up," I said. It was pretty close, but after I'd struggled with my stomach for a while, I asked him, "How did the body explode?"

"I'm more curious about why it exploded," said Zero.

"Yeah, makes a lot of difference," I said, swallowing hard. We hadn't been able to stop this one dying, either. All three of the psychos were here, working together, but we hadn't been able to stop this woman from dying. We'd known another death was coming; we'd known it would be in this area; we'd known it would be soon.

Maybe if they hadn't been busy trying to chase me up a little while ago, they could have been further along in their investigations. Maybe they could have found this girl before the murderer did. Before both of the murderers did.

"Do try to look not quite so sick, Pet," murmured Athelas, stepping between us and taking to the grass to wipe his shoes fastidiously. "And lest you should think that I feel even slightly culpable for failing to get here in time, let me assure you that I place no blame on myself for having been taken prisoner and distracting Zero from his search for the murderer for some time. A setback it may have been, but it couldn't be helped."

I looked up at him, not entirely sure what to make of that. If he felt no guilt, why was he protesting that he felt none? There was no other reason to say such a thing than because he did, somehow, feel just a bit guilty, just as I did.

Athelas looked down and met my eyes briefly. "A body," he said gently, "is not a bad thing. Each one brings us closer to our murderer."

"Don't you get weary of them, though?" I asked. I knew I would.

Weary wasn't the right word, of course: the right word was closer to *soul-crushing* or *numbing*. I wasn't sure they would understand either of those words, though, so I went with *weary*.

Athelas' eyes went beyond me, and he smiled once more, very faintly. "Weary? Perhaps."

Zero, as taciturn as ever, said only, "Yes."

From the gate, Jin Yeong said, "A body is better than the living dead," or at least that's what I *thought* he said. He said it to himself without translating it for me, and I was slow to do it myself from lack of practise. Maybe I'd gotten too used to him making himself understood.

"It's not human," added Zero, his words terse but welcome. He glanced at me, then looked back at the house.

It shouldn't have helped, but it did. Behindkind dying wasn't good, either, but they at least had more of a chance not to die when it comes to this weird, layered world. They also had more people looking out for their interests—more people, and more powerful people.

And today a human murderer who had preyed on human women had found himself prey instead of predator, which had to count for something, too.

"It will be quite difficult to get evidence that isn't contaminated," Athelas said.

"Leave it for the police, then," Jin Yeong said. "They will do the hard work."

"That's it, then?" I said flatly. "That's all we can do? We couldn't stop a murder under our own noses and we didn't even learn anything from it?"

Zero said, "Not at all. We learnt a great deal and we very

nearly caught our murderer in the act. I've not been so close to catching him since this all began and we were in the same room."

"How'd that happen?"

"A series of very dangerous events," said Athelas. He hesitated and added, "I hate to say it, my lord, but the stirrings of a possible harbinger who seems nearly impossible to kill and the flurry of trouble mixing humans with Behindkind points inescapably to the rise of new heirlings. I don't think we can close our eyes to it."

"We've had one suspected heirling murdered, but we haven't yet proven that any of the victims were murdered *because* they were heirlings," said Zero. "However, if Pet's old friend is indeed a new harbinger, as we suspect..."

"You reckon the king's gunna come for you?" I prompted.

"Me," he said. "And any other heirlings that bob up in the maelstrom. If it's truly begun, we should start seeing them appear soon."

"There is too much chaos," Jin Yeong said. The narrow-eyed look he turned on me suggested that that was, in some way, *my* fault. "I heard that the chaos bubbles everything to the surface. It always comes back to the body that was in front of your house. The man that should have been dead and wasn't: he is certainly a harbinger."

"If so, the heirlings won't be far behind," Athelas said. "They'll keep popping up until the king has to do something about it—either acknowledge or try and prevent the Trial of the Heirlings."

"What's that, then? Some kind of competition?"

"No," said Zero. "It's a massacre. It didn't...it wasn't always like that, though it had the potential. It was only the last two series that took a turn for the worst."

"Someone told me about the last one," I said. "The old king decided he didn't want to give up his throne, so he killed all the contenders."

"He was also the first to slaughter all the contenders in the Trials," said Athelas. "When he was still an heirling, of course. It had been attempted before, but usually one or two escape and live somewhere out of reach. That was the first time every one of them died but the new king."

"Sounds like a nice bloke. I can see why he gets along with Zero's father."

Zero coughed a bit, and I grinned at him, feeling slightly better myself.

"It's all right to laugh sometimes," I told him. "You don't have to choke on it."

"Both of you see what you can make of the scene and the bodies," Zero said to Athelas and Jin Yeong. "I'll take the pet home."

"How come you're testing me?" I asked suspiciously, as the other two went back into the house. Zero had brought me here, not because he needed me, but because he wanted to see if I saw something that I shouldn't be able to see. I wanted to know why.

"The incumbent king," Zero said, continuing on with his previous subject as if I hadn't spoken, "deciding that he didn't want the cycle to change the next time it began to occur, went down in Behind history by slaughtering every heirling as it appeared, along with every human-Behindkind child within reach."

I looked curiously at him, wondering what made this the safer topic for discussion, and asked, "Is that what you reckon is happening again? With this bloke that's going around murdering people, I mean? He's working for the king to get rid of potential heirlings before the Trial wotsit can start?"

"It seems more likely now," said Zero, a crease forming between his brows. Instead of taking to Between, he used the gate, and I followed. "But there are still too many things that don't add up: nothing leads back to the king that I can find. In fact, until I—until recently I wouldn't have thought there were signs of the cycle starting again. He wouldn't have had the knowledge that it was time to look again. More, there are an even number of humans and Behindkind dying.”

“Athelas said that humans can be heirlings, too, though.”

“Technically, they can,” he said. “Logistically, it’s highly unlikely. I was born into a powerful family, and my mother was pregnant with me during the purge that the current king made. Half-humans are routinely slaughtered without question Behind at the best of times. Full humans without magic to protect themselves, and without even a basic knowledge of the worlds Between and Behind? How could they survive?”

“Well, maybe it’s humans the king *thinks* are heirlings?”

“I would like to see his basis for thinking so,” Zero said. “I’ve considered it, Pet; I even still consider it now. But it was unlikely, and I turned most of my attention to other possibilities.”

“Reckon that other possibility has turned its attention to other heirlings?” I asked.

Zero’s eyes flicked back to me. “I beg your pardon?”

“Athelas says you’re an heirling, too. What if the murderer really is going for heirlings and decides to have a pot shot at you?”

“He’s very welcome to do so,” Zero said, smiling derisively. “It would be pleasant to be able to come to grips with him so easily.”

“Oi,” I said, as something else occurred to me. “How come you didn’t get knocked out in the last round of contenders, then? Thought you said your mum was pregnant with you when the last round was going on. If the king killed off any kid that looked like they had a bit of human in ’em, how come you survived?”

“Technically, only *those born heirlings may take part in the trials*,” said Zero. “And since I wasn’t yet born, they had no way of knowing I would come out so. But my father took steps to assure the crown of his loyalty despite that.”

“Yeah,” I said, thinking about the only time I’d interacted with Zero’s father and shuddering a bit. “But having met your father, I would have thought that that involved killing you, and you’re not dead. You’re *not* dead, right?”

He gave a very short huff of a laugh. "The amount of power needed to keep a dead human interacting with the world is said to be equal to the life forces of two or more persons. I would assume that it would take significantly more in my case. I am not dead."

"Okay, so your dad did something that convinced the king it was okay to keep you alive when he killed all the other part-human kids. What did he do?"

"Once a king has solidified his rule against all other contenders, no one can challenge it."

I frowned at him, trying to figure out how that worked out. "How long's that take, then?" I asked. "It's not like you can stop someone's baby from coming for long enough to solidify—you can't stop someone's baby from coming out, can you?"

"A period of twenty years has to elapse without challenge for a king to be secure in his rule."

"Then I still don't understand, because that would mean that he'd have had to stop you from being born for twenty years, or kill you. You said you're not dead, so—"

"Exactly," he said, briefly. "My father temporarily stopped my mother's pregnancy by putting her into suspended animation."

I stared at him, sick to my stomach. "He just…put her to sleep for twenty years?"

"That would have been a mercy," said Zero. "No. He put her body in a kind of stasis, but her mind was awake; it had to be, to keep…everything functioning. To keep me alive. She was awake for twenty years, pregnant and not able to move. I think—I think that's how I remember her voice. I remember her talking to me for longer than I remember being able to see things. By the time I was old enough to remember her properly, she was dead."

"Athelas said," I said, hardly able to breathe, "Athelas said that he killed his parents. Is that something that happens a lot in your part of the world? Are all fae parents like that?"

"Ask what you really want to know," Zero said, but he hadn't moved away from me.

"Didn't you want to kill him? Your father. I w—maybe I would. I don't know."

"I learned very quickly," he said deliberately, "that what I wanted to do and what it was possible for me to do were two very different things."

"Athelas said something like that, too," I said, confusingly glad and disturbed to find that we were already walking toward the front door of my house. This last murder had really been close.

"Athelas and I learned some things together," Zero said, leaving his boots at the door.

There was a lot less blood on him than there had been on Jin Yeong, even after he let drop the glamour he'd been using. There was still enough on his shoes to make a right mess of the hallway, though, and I was thankful for his thoughtfulness.

"How come you lot were apart from each other when I first met you?"

"I separated from him because I wanted him to have a chance to do something apart from me," Zero said. "He's been with me since I was literally in the womb, and for someone that says he doesn't get attached, Athelas is...particularly loyal. Especially when it comes to me."

"Noticed that," I said. "Bet you had your own reasons for separating, too."

Athelas always had multiple reasons for what he said and did, and despite the fact that I held Zero to be marginally more straightforward than Athelas, I was pretty certain he tried to kill two birds with one stone as often as possible.

"This arrangement," he said, nodding toward the linen cupboard door. "It's not a new one."

"Yeah, I gathered that," I said. "Athelas told me—well, he mentioned someone who used to help humans. That was you, right?"

"Athelas talks...a great deal too much," said Zero, stripping first jacket and then bloody shirt from his back.

"Maybe from your perspective," I said, a bit sourly. Athelas might not be as silent as Zero, but what he lacked in taciturnity he made up for in sheer opaqueness. You never knew what was important with what Athelas did say until it came crashing down on your head at a later date. "You told me about it yourself, too; I just guessed that you were one of the two blokes doing it—didn't think it was likely that Athelas was the other one. So what, you had a revelation? You decided you didn't want to be with your family anymore and just started out on your own?"

"I was young, then. And for a little while, despite everything, I was optimistic. I thought that I might be able to forge a different path."

"And back then you didn't seem to be worried about being human."

"It occurred to me when I was younger, in the strength of my human emotions, that attempting to save humans was a worthwhile exercise."

"Yeah? What changed your mind?" I didn't mean to sound sharp, but that's how it came out. "Got less worthwhile?"

"Because no matter what I did, no matter how hard we fought, they died."

"What *all* of 'em?"

"Enough of them."

This time, I meant to sound sharp. "What, you've got an account book that balances how much effort it takes versus how many of them you can actually save?"

Zero closed his eyes briefly. "I couldn't live like that any longer. And then—"

"Your dad got wind of what you were doing, eh?"

"I didn't try to hide it. I wanted him to know that I didn't belong to him and that I was going to make different choices with my life. That...turned out to be a mistake. The man I worked with was a lot like you: when I told him that I couldn't do the work anymore, he just couldn't understand. And perhaps I went mad for a while, because—"

"—'Cos you stayed," I said. "I know he's dead. I s'pose your father got to him?"

"Yes," he said shortly. "And that was the end of helping humans."

"And you just stuffed down your emotions and decided that you weren't ever going to help humans again because it hurt too much."

"The payoff and the expenditure were too far misal—"

"Can you try to talk like a human for once?

He stopped talking, and for a while I saw something very close to despair on his face. He turned that look on me and said, "I couldn't keep going like that. It would have killed me."

"People don't die of heartbreak," I said. "They don't die from having to feel too much, either. Sometimes they wish they could, but—"

"I wasn't strong enough for it."

"Nobody's strong enough for it!" I said. Maybe I yelled it. "You don't have a monopoly on feelings, you know! Everyone has to feel stuff they don't want to feel! They learn to deal with it! They don't just give up—some of 'em have to keep living with it, and guess what? They don't die from it!"

Zero smiled, very faintly, but it was a distant, bitter smile. "If there's anyone who knows that, it's me," he said.

"Sorry," I said, more quietly. "But you can't just give up on helping people because it hurts when you can't save them. Not when you know it's the right thing to do. You have to learn to deal with your feelings: you don't get to just refuse to deal with 'em because you're half fae and you've been told all your life that your fae side doesn't have to do that. It's about flaming time that you lot admitted that you've got as many emotions as us humans; you just don't know how to live with them, so you've made some nice little excuses about why you don't have to."

"That could be true," said Zero, with less ice and bitterness, and a hint of humour instead, "but do you think I could shower in peace, Pet? I'd prefer not to be harangued while washing."

"Right," I said, realising finally that not only was he only half-dressed and standing in the bathroom, but that I'd followed him right to the door in the heat of the moment. "Sorry."

I saw a proper grin just before he closed the door in my face, so I yelled through it, "It's not flamin' healthy, squashing down emotions! Next time it'll be you exploding!"

CHAPTER TEN

I PUT A BIT OF WORK INTO CLEANING UP THE SHIRT AND THE trousers Zero tossed outside the door after a while, then left them soaking in the laundry sink to do a bit of work on his jacket. It wasn't like I needed to do it; I was pretty sure that there was some kind of magic in the jacket that repelled most things, and it was already working on cleaning itself, but I wanted to be doing something. Or maybe I just didn't want to think about that room again. You'd think I'd start to get used to it after a while, but there always seems to be something different about the bodies; enough to make it hard to get used to. I've seen a few of these ones now, and even though they're all technically the same, there's something just slightly off about each one.

I mean, apart from being dead with their insides being on the outside. And this one had been a bit more horrible than the others in one way and another.

All in all, I was glad when my phone rang, pulling me away from blood and leather, and Morgana's voice said cheerfully in my ear, "I stopped two more attacks on my firewall this morning!"

"Is that what you're doing up at this time of day?" I asked her, glancing toward the windows. It was barely light; maybe six in the morning at the latest. "Someone's still trying to get into your computer?"

What was Blackpoint playing at?

"Yeah, but I don't sleep much in the early morning, anyway," she said. "I wanted to see if you'd found out anything else."

"Got some addresses to check out," I told her. "Got a good idea which one to start on, too. Once the others get back, I'll divide 'em up and see what we've got."

"Did you get what you wanted from your friend after you left yesterday?" she asked.

That was about when Zero came out of the bathroom with just a towel around him and casually strolled through the living room toward the study that was his bedroom.

"Heck!" I said, as soon as I recovered from the shock. "Can't you blokes wear clothes around the house?"

"Who's not wearing clothes?" Morgana demanded. "Is JinYeong—"

"I didn't want to leave a blood trail through the house to get clothes," Zero said, his voice slightly perplexed. "I thought you'd be happy about that."

"Yeah, but—okay, fair enough." It wasn't like JinYeong didn't routinely do the same thing. Usually with a smirk.

"If it bothers you, I'll put some spare clothes in the bathroom," he said. "But for now, I trust the sight of my bare chest won't be likely to give you nightmares and hope that you'll recover very soon."

His eyes were definitely bluer when he turned and continued on to his room.

"Sarcasm doesn't suit you," I called after him. More loudly, I added, "And you gotta tell me where you got that scar across your back, 'cos you can't tell me Athelas didn't try to look after it for you!"

"What was all that about?" asked Morgana. I could hear the smile in her voice—well, grin, anyway. "I thought it was dark, scowly, and handsome, but it looks like the ice prince is in on it, too."

I took the phone away from my ear and stared at it, then put it back to say, "In on what?"

"Pet, I think Zero likes you."

I took the phone away to stare at it for a bit longer, then burst into laughter.

In my ear, a very annoyed Morgana said, "Pet!"

"That's the dumbest thing I've ever heard," I said, leaning against the kitchen island to hold myself up in my laughter. "Maybe you should go back to sleep. I think you're a bit too tired."

"Pet, I'm serious!"

I hiccoughed a bit, and suddenly things felt a lot less funny. I cleared my throat and hastily pulled away from the bench to remove myself and my phone call out into the back yard where we wouldn't be overheard.

"What the heck are you on about?" I asked, keeping my voice down, just in case.

Her voice sounded so reasonable. "Don't you ever wonder about how he looks at you? And how he's always making sure you're safe? Not to mention that he's making an effort to listen to you, *and* he's teasing you while he's half naked and don't tell me that *that*'s a thing he does to a lot of people."

"What are you—that's the weirdest thing I've ever heard!"

"You'd better check and see that he thinks the same way, 'cos the way he treats you isn't the way a boss treats his employee. I mean, I've been wondering about it for a while, but this just—"

"He's learning humour," I said, hunching my shoulders uncomfortably. "And he's always teased me, it's just that he doesn't do it as obviously as other people. He's learning about hum—about the way normal people laugh at each other. It's not because he's—he's fallen in love with me. Why would you say something like that?"

"Because it looks obvious to me, and you're ridiculously oblivious. He even lets you insult him and irritate him because he knows that's how you show affection."

I collapsed again, this time against the wall of the house, my brain seething but entirely deficient of words. "That's—*no*," I said, at last. "It's ridiculous."

"I mean, I know he's a bit older than you, but it's not like he's not *very good looking* and I reckon you'll find he'll age very well, so —what *now*?"

At first I couldn't stop laughing long enough to answer her, but when I managed to gather enough breath, I said, with tears of laughter in my eyes, "Oh yeah, he definitely ages well! Like a flamin' cheddar! Can we not talk about this? It's weird and I'm pretty sure he'd clip me over the ears for even thinking about something like this."

"Fine," said Morgana, and I was pretty sure that her black-lined lips were pressed together. "But I'm going to have heaps of fun telling you *I told you so* when you come here and tell me that *someone* has suddenly kissed you and—stop *laughing*, Pet!"

"Your makeup's sunk right in and damaged your brain," I said. "That's the only thing to explain it."

"How *old* are you? I'm the teenager here! If anyone should be acting like a kid, it's me!"

"I'm eighteen, which means I'm still a teenager," I pointed out. "And there's no way Zero is—oh heck, here comes trouble. I gotta go."

"Bet it's tall, scowly, and handsome," Morgana managed to say just before I hung up. She sounded smug.

The annoying thing was that it *was* Jin Yeong; he appeared from the back door as if he'd come out to look for me, and he probably had. He'd probably be wanting breakfast soon. Worse than that was the fact that my face felt red and tight, and I couldn't tell if it was because I'd just been laughing, or from the dreadful embarrassment that Morgana's suspicions had brought out.

Was it actually true? No, it couldn't be. Zero was...Zero was a back to stand behind; a voice that reprimanded. He was also very decided in his prejudice against humans, even if he was half human himself. There's no way he'd lower himself by thinking—liking—no. It was impossible.

I hunched my shoulders a bit, and Jin Yeong tilted his head to narrowly observe me.

"What is wrong with you?" There was that particularly accusatory tone to his voice again; he'd been using that tone quite a bit, lately. "You are blushing."

"I'm not blushing," I said, shoving my phone into my pocket. "It's time for breakfast."

I WAS STILL FEELING A BIT WEIRD AND UNCOMFORTABLE AFTER breakfast, so it was easy to bring out the cards I'd found at Blackpoint's place and chuck them on the table.

"Unless you lot found more than I think you found at the crime scene, we should have a bit of time to check out these addresses," I said.

"How very industrious of you, Pet," said Athelas, picking up the couple of cards at the top of the pile. "It should be a quick reconnoitre, don't you think, my lord?"

"Easily done," Zero agreed.

"This one is mine," I said, pinching the orange card. There was no real reason to take it except the game had been orange and this was orange and somehow that made a connection in my brain that seemed meant-to-be. "We'll be a bit quicker if we split up."

"Take Jin Yeong with you," Zero said.

It was surprising enough that he'd let me do it without protestation, so instead of complaining about having to take a spare vampire with me, I just grabbed Jin Yeong's tie and pulled him along with me. I wanted to get out of the house.

Jin Yeong coughed, but followed. In the hall, he recovered his tie with a scowl and a sharp tug, and said, "My ties are not to be touched."

"What about cut in half?" I asked, backing through the door and into Between in one fluid movement that would have scared me at its familiarity and ease if I'd thought about it for too long. "Sautéed? How d'you feel about poached?"

"Do not poach my tie!"

"Pickled it is, then!" I said, hurrying along. I was elated and scared at the same time: elated that Zero had given me my own task—well, hadn't stopped me from pinching it, anyway—scared that he would come after us because he'd changed his mind.

Behind me, I heard Jin Yeong muttering—something about turning me into a little kimchi—but by the time he caught up with me, he was as suave and sauntery as usual.

This time, instead of the rich area along the waterfront or the older suburbs toward the north, we followed the hilly incline of Cascade Road up in a meandering, westerly direction that took us toward Fern Tree but not quite there. It was all sloped, thin roads with cars parked along the sides of the road and trees arching their greenery over the top, and old stone houses with concrete walls or two-storey wooden heritage townhouses.

It was a familiar walk—recently familiar, which was more important. This was the way, if I wasn't mistaken, that I had followed the old mad bloke that night. My eyes flicked toward the telephone post closest, and sure enough, there was a little bottle-cap sitting there in the dirt, red and grubby.

I slipped my hand into my pocket to feel the bottle top there, my interest kindling, and looked ahead for the next bottle-cap. What was the bet it would be along the road we would have to walk to find the address we were searching for?

Jin Yeong glanced down at me and said accusingly, "You have something in your pocket. Show me."

"Got a map," I said cheerfully, taking the cap out of my pocket and flourishing it at him.

"Where do you dig up these things?" he muttered. "Who gave this to you?"

"An old friend," I said. "And if you tell Zero, I'm gunna mess with your cologne bottles so that some of 'em have holy water in 'em."

JinYeong muttered under his breath and stopped walking. I kept going, but he pinched the back of my shirt and tugged me back by the nape until I was standing next to him again.

"Ask me *nicely*," he said.

"Oi," I said. "This is me best shirt!"

"It is ugly."

"Yeah, but it's comfortable. Look at you—you're beautiful but annoying. Comfortable and ugly is—"

"Ask me nicely."

"It's more fun to threaten you," I pointed out.

He actually thought about that for a moment before he shook his head. "No. Ask me nicely."

"What, will you keep a secret if I ask you nicely?"

He considered that for a moment, then lifted his nose and said precisely, "*Kurolgae.*"

"Oh." I mean, it wasn't as much fun as threatening him, but if he was likely not to tell Zero stuff when I asked him nicely—but then, I knew exactly how trustworthy JinYeong was when he was pretending to be nice. I said suspiciously, "I don't trust you."

JinYeong's eyes grew wine-dark and stormy. "I refuse to be threatened."

"For a Behindkind bloke you don't seem to know how threatening works," I said. "*I* threaten. You *get* threatened. There's no right of refusal here."

Still, it wouldn't hurt to do things a different way for a change. Of the stormy face beside me, I asked, "Please don't tell Zero. Keep it a secret between us, all right?"

"*Kurolgae,*" he said again, so smugly that I regretted asking him straight away. "Then follow me!"

"You don't have the address," I said in annoyance, but he was following bottle caps now.

I shoved the bottle cap back in my pocket, hoping I wouldn't regret letting out as much as I had. I hadn't told him it was the old mad bloke, but it wouldn't be too hard for him to figure out. I didn't particularly want either Zero or Athelas knowing that the old bloke was still hanging around so nearby.

JinYeong was even more sauntery in his smugness than he had been before, so it was easy to catch up with him again. We didn't have far to walk, though. A few minutes later, we stopped between two mailboxes, JinYeong frowning up and down at the street and me doing much the same at the letterboxes.

"That's weird," I said, standing in the dappled shadows between those letterboxes: they were numbered forty-six and fifty. "There should be a forty-eight here."

There wasn't, though: there was a fence around number fifty that came right up to the nature strip, and there were a couple of wooden pegs in the lawn of number forty-six that I would have taken for boundary pegs if they'd been up by the fence. Two letterboxes, and neither of them the right one.

"There," JinYeong said, pointing at the narrow expanse of grass between the pegs and the fence. "We will go there. That path is trying to hide."

"Reckon it's a bit fatter than it's pretending to be, too," I said, staring at it. That gap between boundary pegs and fence was just wide enough to walk along, and further down it looked like we'd have to squeeze between two fences. "It's not Between, though. What is it?"

"I think," he said, eyes scanning the way ahead, "that it is magic. But it is not fae magic."

"You know much about magic?"

"I am immune," he said. He thought about that, and added, "Nearly immune."

"That's a nice trick," I said, impressed. "How's that work?"

He didn't answer me straight away, and I grinned.

"What, even magic finds you annoying enough to just avoid you?"

Jin Yeong sent a small scowl in my direction, but it lacked his usual heat. "Magic is usually targeted upon living things," he said, and started down the path ahead of me. "It is a flaw in the magic user."

"Oh," I said. I had the odd suspicion that I'd hurt his feelings, which was an unusual sensation. I kept forgetting that Jin Yeong was technically dead; he's almost always pretty warm when he's sitting next to me. I trotted after him and said, "Yeah, but you're only technically dead."

He looked across at me, and there was a faint glow to his eyes that I didn't understand. "I am *warm*," he said, in a self-satisfied way that I didn't understand either. "Am I not? I am warm."

"Yeah, you're warm," I said, side-eyeing him. "You're also weird."

Ever found an old, overgrown yard because you walked down the wrong path and ended up in a forgotten cul-de-sac with just one house and lots of wild lawn in a circle all around you? Because that's where we ended up, only instead of a cul-de-sac, it was a narrow strip of bitumen with a concrete curb on it but no road to curb—just that bit of bitumen. Like a road had been cut off somewhere and the end bit had just been dropped here for the fun of it: the severed aglet from a shoelace. A giant, cracking concrete wall grew up a bit behind the monstrous growth of lawn, and behind that was a whole, messy jungle of trees and shrubs that tangled in the space between wall and house. And *what* a house.

It looked like it had once been a school-house, and maybe it had; a red-brick rectangle of three storeys and very many windows. When we got closer to the double-gated main archway that led into the place, I could see that the entrance to the house was also double-doored, with a faded banner of some sort painted over it.

Oh yeah. This place had definitely been a school at one time.

"Front gate, or climb over?" I asked Jin Yeong. I couldn't feel anything Betweenish to the gate, but I was worried that if there was magic, I wouldn't be able to see it. I could usually see when Zero was doing weird stuff with his spells, but I wasn't exactly sure why, and sometimes it took a little while to realise what I was looking at. I wanted to know that I'd be able to duck in time if something magical was thrown at me.

"I have already showered," he said coldly.

"Front gate it is, then," I said. "But if we get caught sneaking in, it's your fault."

The gate wasn't unlocked, but as we got closer it was obvious that it was one of the big ones with huge spaces between the bars that looked nice but weren't much chop at keeping anything smaller than a barrel-chested bloke out.

"Ridiculous," said Jin Yeong, writhing through without even touching the bars. "It is insulting."

"Maybe they didn't expect anyone to be able to get in," I suggested. I'd seen this place before; always in the middle of a clump of houses, and *always* from a distance. To get here, however, had been a lot harder than it seemed. "Reckon most people would never find it. I wonder how they get their mail."

"Perhaps no one is here," he said, gazing at the house.

"Yeah, or maybe it's glamoured to look rundown and empty," I said. "Let's not walk down the driveway, anyway. Don't wanna make targets of ourselves."

"Of course not," he said coldly, and led the way through the trees.

We came up to the house under cover of trees and shrubs, but went for the front doors anyway. There might have been a glamour on the house, but the front doors were definitely broken-down and only half there. I couldn't feel any magic to them, either, so that was a relief.

Still, a definite chill came over me as soon as we stepped into the darkened vestibule, and it felt like a bit more than just your usual damp-house chill. I saw the faint outline of stairs to the left, and a landing that stretched around and across in front of us, and the impression of colonnades further in to support that upper level.

"Stop," said Jin Yeong, edging his shoulder just slightly in front of me to enforce the command.

I opened my mouth to ask why, and then my eyes got used to the dim light and I saw what he'd already seen.

Don't know what I expected when walking into the place, but I definitely didn't expect to be the centre of attention for the muzzles of five drawn and coolly aimed guns. Didn't expect the couple of cross-bows, either. It sounds funny, but the sight of those arrow tips pointing at me from taut bowstrings was somehow more terrifying than the guns.

"Oi," I said, trying not to have a heart attack. "Reckon you could point those things somewhere else?"

"I'm not sure what else you expect when you break into someone else's house," said the woman slightly closest. The leader?

"Walked in, actually," I said. "The doors weren't locked."

"That," she said, stepping a bit closer and tilting her head, "isn't exactly what I meant. Step forward, please."

"So long as that lot don't try to shoot me," I said. I pushed at Jin Yeong's shoulder: it resisted, then moved aside to let me step forward—and, as I realised a moment later, into the light from an open window somewhere further in that lit a diamond in the dusty air like a torch.

The woman's lips parted and I heard the muted sound of indrawn breath around the room.

"It's you," she said, gazing at me as though I was the missing puzzle piece she'd been looking for all afternoon. "It's actually you! You finally got here."

What, had we gotten lucky enough that they were actually

expecting someone right when we arrived? Someone who looked...exactly like me. No way.

"Yeah," I said vaguely. "It's me. Reckon you can put those down now?"

She lowered her gun and the others followed suit. "I can't believe we've finally got The Pet here," she said. "Put 'em away, guys. I told you we were expecting her."

Heck. It was actually me they were expecting. *How* were they expecting me? How did they know I was a pet? Why were they calling me *The Pet*, like the Queen or the Archbishop?

"How'd you know I was on my way?"

"We didn't know it was specifically today," she said, holstering her gun. In the clarity of the light, her hair gleamed red instead of black and I saw the tightened muscles in her arms and stomach beneath her t-shirt. Her face, belying that hardness, was round and pleasant everywhere except in her watchful green eyes. "But we put out the word to try and get you here. I'm Abigail."

"Pet," I said, even though she already knew, offering my hand. "What do you mean, you put out the word?"

"Got a bottle cap?" she asked, grinning, as everyone else in the room put away their weapons and gathered around to shake my hand.

I hadn't expected that, either.

"The old mad bloke one of you?" I asked Abigail. It was kind of nice to think that he might have somewhere to belong, these days: maybe he could get a bit less mad with help and a family.

"He's—well, he's a friend, I suppose. Not really one of us; he's a bit mad for that. But he comes in handy when we need someone to deliver a message—he's got a way of getting in and out of places without being seen."

"Yeah, noticed that," I said. "Why'd you want to see me? I don't know you."

"You know enough to be here. We should have a talk."

"What are we talking about?"

Abigail's eyes swept over Jin Yeong, assessing him from head to foot, and he preened just very slightly. "Who's this?" she asked. "I was told you'd be alone. I'm sorry, but unless he's family or a significant other he has to be separately vetted before he comes into the house."

Heck. It wasn't like they were going to believe that he was a relative, and there was no way I was going further into a house bristling with cross-bows and guns without backup.

"Boyfriend," I said. Luckily, he was close enough that it was easy to slip my hand into his without making it obvious. I waved our linked hands at her, prompting an irritated mutter from Jin Yeong, who tugged down on his cuff with his spare hand when I dropped our linked hands to our sides again. "That count?"

"Yeah," she said. "But don't try to bring anyone else here—especially not those *owners* of yours. We can pack up and move in a second, but we'll be *very annoyed* if we have to do it. We don't like people with loose mouths."

"He comes everywhere with me," I said coldly, instinctively. I had some sort of advantage here, and I didn't know what it was or why I had it, but I was going to make sure I made the most of it. "If you've got a problem with him—"

"No problem," she said. "We know he's not fae; he would have set off our defences if he was. Like I said, family and significant others are allowed—so long as they're human. He's fine."

I blinked a bit and tried to recover before she noticed my surprise. So they didn't know about vampires? Or they just couldn't tell who was a vampire and who wasn't?

"What is this nonsense?" said Jin Yeong to me, in un-aided Korean.

I was grateful to know it, anyway: if this bunch of humans could tell fae from human, they could probably also tell when Behindkind were manipulating Between. "Dunno," I answered, in Korean. "Just follow me."

His eyes flicked up toward the ceiling briefly, but he didn't try to walk away or pull me away with him, so I figured he'd follow along for now. His hand linked with mine was something of a comfort, too.

To the others, I said, "Sorry, he doesn't speak English."

"Come into the house," Abigail said, turning on her heel. Most of the others flanked her, but a couple of the biggest waited until JinYeong and I started following, then flanked us.

"Thought we were already in," I said. That explained the weird, Between-but-not-quite-Between feeling to the outer shell here: there must be a house inside a house.

"It's part of our security," she said over her shoulder. "The more layers we have, the more easily we can escape while fae are stripping them away."

I wondered if Zero had ever thought of doing that to the house. He'd probably know it was possible, but I wondered if he'd ever had to think about actually *doing* it; was there ever a time he'd felt so at risk that he'd have to make plans for desperate escape? I couldn't picture it, but I'd met his dad: if there was anyone who could hurt someone as powerful as Zero, it was his dad. There must be some sort of system in place.

We followed Abigail away from the cracked front doors, the concrete radiating cold beneath our feet—was that more magic to discourage unwary people from camping out here if they somehow managed to make it in?—and down through mould-spotted walls. That was real enough, but the feeling I got off of it wasn't a normal feeling of cold or repulsion; it was too strong and too unreasonable. I even saw JinYeong hunch his shoulders in discomfort.

"What's all this, anyway?" I asked. "The magic, I mean. It's not fae magic."

She drew in a breath too fast. "So it's true! You can see it!"

"It's not really seeing," I said. It was like Between; seeing the tiny crinkles and folded edges of reality being warped rather than seeing the actual thing itself. "But it's different from what I'm used to."

"That's because it's human magic," she said. "In here. We can sit down in here."

"I'm told that's not possible," I said, even though I knew better. It made her grin again, and I added, "Yeah, I know. They're always saying stuff like that and they're pretty often wrong."

"Not everyone can do it," said Abigail. "That much is true; and everyone's at a different level. But there's enough of us who can work enough magic to make a difference. Sit down. We're not going to shoot you."

"Not yet," said a girl in a school uniform.

I shot her a nasty look; she *would* be one of the ones who had a crossbow. I sat down anyway, and JinYeong, still standing, prowled a little way away—getting into a strategic position if it came to a fight, I thought.

"Right; introductions," said Abigail. Gesturing to the left, she said rapidly, "Curly, Jake, Ezri, Donna."

A bald bloke, a skinny hipster, the schoolgirl, and what looked like a checkout chick alternately nodded or waved. Not that impressive, I would have said, except I'd seen 'em with guns, and young Ezri the schoolgirl was still very much attached to her cross-bow.

On her right were Sam, Sheila, Dennis, Mack (as in *truck*, apparently, by the size of him), and Barb. JinYeong and I said hello back, which was mostly me making an awkward sort of wave and JinYeong smirking in a slightly-less-annoying way than usual.

"Got that message a little while ago," I said to Abigail, deciding that it was all or nothing, and that I might as well go for it while I still had some element of surprise. "But I actually came to ask you about Blackpoint today."

That made her face close up, guarded and suspicious. Heck.

Maybe I should have thought about it a bit longer before I charged in.

"On whose behest?" she asked, in a voice like granite.

"My own," I said. "But I s'pose you could say I'm here in my official capacity, too."

"Why is your...your *owner*," she spat the word, "interesting himself with Blackpoint? I'm not about to share information with fae."

"We're just trying to make sure Blackpoint's okay," I said. "We took on a job from a human friend of his to find him and make sure he's all right. Found his place and he was already gone. It looks like he was attacked."

Abigail looked grim, but unsurprised. "He hasn't answered messages for the last two weeks or so," she said. "We knew something was off."

"We're trying to find him, the same as you," I said, taking another stab in the dark. "It doesn't have to be fae versus humans. We can help each other."

"Fae only help themselves," said Ezri's cold young voice. "You ought to know that."

"Yeah, and all humans are dumb," I said, shrugging. "Heard that before? It's not true, but it doesn't stop 'em from saying it. They make a lot of stupid mistakes because they believe it."

"What are you trying to say, Pet?" asked Abigail. Her chin was still firm, but I was pretty sure there was a bit of amusement in her eyes, too.

"I'm saying that if you lump 'em all in together, you're gunna come unstuck. There are fae and there are fae."

"If you say so," she said. "The problem is, they're still fae."

"What about Blackpoint?"

She stared at me. "What about him? He's human."

"Yeah," I said, even though I was pretty certain he wasn't. "But what about the game?"

"What, you think he couldn't have made a game like that if he wasn't fae? He's lived most of his life in their part of the world. He knows it pretty well by now."

Heck. Well, there was a nice bit of info that I hadn't had a minute ago. So Blackpoint himself had been the creator of *City Fae*, had he? He wasn't just running around in it and making himself suspicious to the Behind world while he tried to warn humans.

I glanced at JinYeong and saw that he was leaning with his shoulders against the wall, arms crossed and a darkly amused smile curling his lips. When he met my eyes, one eyebrow went up slightly, so he must have thought I was doing all right. He had settled against that wall as if settling in for the night, and his eyes were dark and amused, which meant I didn't have to worry about him interrupting unless it came to a fight.

"That'd explain it," I said, but I'd come to wonder if it was something else. I had wondered briefly if Blackpoint could be a human so exposed to the taunts of fae that he had begun to believe that as a human he was inferior; but if he was actually the maker of the game, my earlier suspicions were likely to be correct.

If he was human and really believed the fae point of view that humans were inferior, why would he make a game to expose the fae—slowly, methodically, bit by bit? Someone who looked up to the fae wouldn't do that.

I drew in a deep breath and wondered about a different kind of mindset. A mindset a bit more like mine, which saw Behind-kind in general and Fae in particular as a dangerous, corrupt, and ultimately conniving race. A point of view which, if it had occurred in a Fae male, might cause far more problems than just divided loyalty; which might cause the kind of divided mind I'd seen in the messages that Morgana had shown me.

Was it possible that there was a Behindkind out there—a Fae man, for instance—who so much hated what he was that he saw it as a disease to have been born in the world and species he'd been born in? Was that why he was fighting so hard to help humans and warn them about the world Behind? I thought so, but Abigail obviously still believed him to be human.

The question was, would Abigail still be willing to align herself with him if she knew what he was? I doubted it. That was a shame; I had been hoping since we first met Abigail that she would be a sure clue to finding Blackpoint.

I waved at the place around us. "What are you guys doing here, anyway? You've got a nicely hidden HQ, pretty good weapons, and you're doing a better job with magic than I've seen some fae do. It's a lot of work."

"We're a go-between," said Abigail. "Ambassadors."

"Yeah, except Behi—fae don't know about you." That wasn't a guess; it was a certainty. There's no way they would still be here, still alive, if Behindkind knew about them. "You're not really ambassadors if you're only connected to one side."

"If they know about us, they'll kill us."

"Yeah," I said. I already knew that; it was why I had asked the question I'd asked. Abigail and her crew weren't ambassadors, whatever else they were. Nor did I think they were really go-betweens, for the same reason that you can't go between two sets of people when one set of people doesn't know you exist. I tried an easier question. "How do you blokes know about the fae?"

"That was *City Fae*, too," she said. "That was the big eye-opener for all of us here. It's the thing that connects everyone."

"It's a game, though."

"Yes, but it's a game that had too many parallels with the real world—*and* someone has threaded riddles and easter eggs through the whole thing. Someone wanted humans to know about the fae, and we took the challenge."

"So you all started out playing that game?"

"Every one of us. We all came to realise the truth of it in our own ways; Curly found it because he started matching up real-life parallels to odd things he'd already seen, and followed his nose. He lost his house, and none of his friends recognise him anymore.

Sam found the riddles early on and went on to look for all of 'em; opened up some very useful video files that he thought were faked at first. Then someone sent a troll to pick him up from school where the underpass gets really shadowy—he got out alive, but he's missing an arm. He was nearly dead when I found him."

Sam cheerfully saluted me with his remaining arm: he was a burly teenager with a lot of freckles and a happy-go-lucky kind of look that reminded me of a golden retriever.

"So you're more of an underground railroad than a bunch of ambassadors," I said. "You get humans out safely when they're in trouble."

Abigail laughed. "We're trying to get the word out, too," she said. "That's why I said we're ambassadors. It's not enough just to save the humans who are in danger; we want the whole world to know what's happening. We want to be able to fight back as more than one person at a time."

I had to catch my breath before I said, "That's...that's kinda dangerous, you know?"

Abigail's chin got even firmer, which was pretty flamin' impressive. "We know. We're all prepared to die."

"Yeah," I said, "but wouldn't it be better to live? Does everyone need to know about the fae?"

It wasn't like I didn't sympathise, but I was pretty sure that humans *all* knowing about Behindkind wasn't the best way forward. When humans are involved with Behindkind, it's usually in one of two different functions: chattel, or as willing, well-paid assistants who don't mind what they do to their fellow humans so long as they get paid.

"Like what you're already doing," I added. "The world needs humans who are alive, who can help out other humans. So long as you're doing that and not trying to broadcast the entire fae world to the humans, I'm pretty sure you can fly under the radar."

She looked at me for a while, her straight, dark brows pinched together, before she said, "The world deserves to know."

"I think the world deserves to not get slaughtered by fae," I said. "And I dunno if you can have both of those things together. Even the ones...even the fae who are trying to help have divided loyalty when it comes to humans telling other humans about the fae world."

"If we get enough people who know, we've got a better chance," she said grimly. "We could really use you here, Pet. I know you're...entangled...but we might be able to help you with that."

"Let me think about it," I said, getting up. There was a tug at my heart to join with other humans who knew the world we were in, and who actually cared about saving it, but there was a tug against it, too—perhaps three of them.

My psychos were just beginning to seem slightly less psychotic —or maybe we were just beginning to understand each other a bit better. I wasn't quite sure which one it was, or if perhaps it was a combination of the two.

And as much as I cared about Abigail and her rag-tag bunch of humans not getting killed, I wasn't sure if their interests in helping humanity and mine were any more correctly aligned than mine and the psychos' were.

"All right," she said. "At least give me your phone, for now."

I passed it to her, but I watched pretty closely to make sure she did nothing else except add her phone number into my contacts.

"This'll do for now," she said, and gave my phone back. "But if we have to move suddenly, we might not be able to find a way to keep in contact with you."

"I know," I said. "Don't worry, I'll find you if I change my mind."

CHAPTER ELEVEN

JIN YEONG WAS AS SILENT ON THE WAY HOME AS I WAS, WHICH was nice. I had a lot to think about, and judging from the odd, side-long glance he sent in my direction, he was doing a bit of his own thinking; probably most of it about how much he should be telling Zero.

When we got to the front door, I said to him, "Don't worry, I'm gunna tell him everything."

I'd already asked Jin Yeong not to talk about enough stuff. Agreements with him might not be the same kind of binding that they were with Athelas, but I didn't like the idea of making too many with him, regardless. I had the feeling that they might have a completely different downfall to them altogether.

Zero and Athelas were back only a few minutes before Jin Yeong and I were; their multiple addresses had been far less exciting than our single one, at least to a surface look, and they were discussing their lack of results when we walked into the room.

"Nothing?" I said exultantly. "Well, wait until you hear what we've got to tell you!"

Jin Yeong, smirking, continued on upstairs and Zero listened without interrupting while I gave him a run-down of what we'd found out. When I finished telling them everything we'd seen and heard that morning, he sat back in his chair, arms folded, and thought. Seated in his own chair—who had cleaned it? I hadn't had a chance since Jin Yeong vacated it—Athelas did the same, his left hand alternately lying flat against the arm of his chair and lifting and turning slightly as if to grasp something before he remembered he didn't have it.

Either I was getting better at reading his moods, or he was trying to train me to get him tea without having to ask for it. I was betting on the latter.

I left them to their thinking and went off into the kitchen to make up a tea-and-coffee tray.

"Got a theory," I said, when I came back in with the tray. I mean, if I had their attention with the tea tray, I might as well take advantage of that.

Zero's eyes grew bluer. "I should really start to place money on my predictions," he said.

"It would do you no good, my lord," said Athelas. "I wouldn't take your bets."

"All right, so I'm easy to read," I said. "Whatever. You know how everyone except the Enforcers seem to think he's human?"

"I've not heard anything prove otherwise," said Zero. "And you just told us that he's responsible for making that game—what Behindkind is there who can do something like that? It's human technology."

"I believe I'm inclined to agree with the pet in this case, my lord."

Zero's blue eyes rested on him. "Oh, are you?"

"There is too much malice in this to be a human. A human might have such malice and act thus, but not with such a knowledge of what he's up against."

"And it's not like fae can't learn to use computers," I pointed out. "They just don't because they think it's no use. Well, Blackpoint knows it *is* useful, and he's made sure that when he starts exposing the fae, he's doing it in the safest possible way."

"It would seem that it is no longer the safest way," murmured Athelas.

"Yeah, but he got away with it for a flamin' long time," I told him. "*City Fae* has been out for about two years now, and Blackpoint has only just disappeared."

"The question is, *why* would he do such a thing?"

"Reckon I might know that, too," I said, and told them about the messages. "And it's not like North isn't doing much the same when it comes to the Palmers, even if she isn't directly exposing fae."

"No, North is more likely to prefer my own methods," said Athelas, sipping his tea. "She has no interest in changing the status quo, per se; she is more interested in helping out on a case by case basis. I do wonder how your new human friends would feel about Blackpoint if they knew he's fae."

"They'd drop him like a hot brick," I said. "I reckon, though —I reckon that if we could satisfy 'em that not every fae is a bad fae, we could have a pretty useful partnership. Sorta convince 'em not to go putting gunpowder under everything that looks like fae so they don't get taken down by the Enforcers or whatever, and make use of the fact that they know a bit of what's what and how to keep their heads above water. I mean, you said we could use Five, and I reckon Abigail and her lot will be just as useful. And if we don't reach out to them now they might end up dead after all."

"Perhaps it would serve you well to remember your weaknesses," Athelas said. "In general, it's a good idea to know them. People are so fond of taking advantage!"

I gazed at him for a good while before I said, "Pretty sure your idea of weaknesses and mine are different. What ones are you talking about?"

"Does it never occur to you that this habit you have of

befriending stray dogs and taking in wounded humans is something that might come back to serve you badly in the end?"

"You mean someone could pretend to be in trouble just to get closer to me?"

"That, amongst other more likely ploys," he murmured. "I believe you haven't yet forgotten JinYeong's gambit to get into your good graces?"

I scowled. "Thought you said he wasn't pretending?"

"I did indeed," Athelas said. "And hence my warning: actually vulnerable people may yet cause you damage. A truly injured person seeking help may still be a danger to you. Injury or vulnerability alone don't prove the good intentions of a person, and as we've had opportunity to see, you are far more inclined to succour the injured and vulnerable than the healthy."

JinYeong strolled back into the room, one hand in his pocket, for what seemed to be the sole purpose of sending a dark, murderous look in Athelas' direction as he crossed the room. That gaze lingered as he sauntered into the kitchen, but Athelas was unmoved. If I'd had any doubt about the fact that any of the three of them could hear everything said in the house, this would have removed any doubt.

I poured another cup of tea for Athelas. "You mean that if you were trying to get close to me, you'd purposely let yourself be injured so that you could get to me?"

"A sympathetic gaze is so much easier to work with than a suspicious one," he explained. "That is worth some physical injury, after all."

"You're really scary sometimes, you know?" I said, gazing at him, and heard the rumble of Zero's chuckle.

"If you're only just discovering that, Pet," Athelas said, "I really fear for you!"

I stuck out my tongue at him and trotted back toward the kitchen with the teapot. It wasn't that he was wrong about my *weakness*, if that was what we were going to call it; it was more that to a normal person, something like that shouldn't *be* a weakness. A desire to help people who were hurt shouldn't be something that another person could look at and decide to use as a way to get close.

And yet, the world was what it was; not what I wanted it to be. And there were people like that in the world—or at least, there were definitely people like that Between and Behind. It would do me good to remember Athelas' advice. Zero had once said something very similar to me about the kind of people I thought of as family, and even if I hadn't wanted to hear it at the time—even if I didn't quite agree with all of his conclusions now—it struck me that I was going to have to be more careful.

I was in this to help humans, and I wouldn't be much good if I couldn't tell the difference between people who needed help and people who were just trying it on. I didn't want to become like my psychos, their empathy and feelings surgically removed, but I couldn't afford to be misled by mine, either.

As I stepped up into the kitchen, I saw the fluttering edges of Between around a softness in one of the walls.

"What the heck!" I said.

There was no sign of Jin Yeong: only the faint remainder of his cologne lingered in the kitchen. But on the kitchen counter was an ancient port bottle that shouldn't be where it was, and that definitely shouldn't have had the sun shining through it to show its emptiness.

From the sink, I could already smell the richness of port with something lighter beneath it. Something that also shouldn't be where it was.

I took a step toward the sink and copped an eyeful of its contents.

"Dear me!" said Athelas from behind me, his voice lightly amused. "It seems as though you've been teaching the vampire bad habits, Pet!"

"Don't blame this lot on me!" I said indignantly. There was

no subtlety to it at all: in the kitchen sink was the entirety of the lavender earl grey stash I had bought for Athelas—soaked in the contents of the last remaining bottle of Athelas' ancient wine.

The whole lot was ruined; tea and wine, completely scuppered.

"If I was trying to annoy you, I'd be a lot more clever about it," I told Athelas.

The glint of a smile appeared for a moment. "Pride, or fear of repercussions?"

"Both," I said, scooping up handfuls of the boozy tealeaves to put into the bin. "But mostly pride. How old is he, anyway?"

"And yet, there's a charming bluntness to it, don't you think?"

"I wouldn't have called it charming," I said. "But then, I don't kill people for a living, either."

"Neither do we, Pet; neither do we!" Athelas said affably. I didn't trust that assertion, but he added helpfully, "Jin Yeong does it for the enjoyment, I'm quite sure; Zero from a sense of duty. As for myself...well, let us call it survival, and perhaps a little enjoyment."

"That doesn't make it better," I said, taking his cup. "You're not supposed to enjoy killing people."

"Ah," he sighed. "But then, there's such satisfaction in a job well done, don't you think?"

"Your work ethic is messed up," I told him severely.

His shoulders shook gently. "Do you really think so, Pet? Well, perhaps you're right. I take it I can't expect a decent pot of tea for the remainder of the day?"

"Get ya some more when I go shopping," I said, heading back toward the living room. "If I can find it. It's a local tea field and it's not huge, so they don't produce too much."

"Your taste in tea is surprisingly good," said Athelas, following me. "I shall trust you."

It shouldn't have left me feeling so pleased, so I tried to hide the fact that I was pleased by going up to check on the game download I'd gotten from Blackpoint's office.

There were still five hours left on it, which meant that the computer's math left something to be desired in either its first or its second prognostication, so I left it running with Athelas' spell churning around me and put in the CD of footage Detective Tuatu had talked me through burning. I wanted to know when the game had disappeared from the wall—that orange game that had made me choose an orange card, which had brought me right to the doorstep of a group of human resistance fighters.

I skipped day to day until it was there in one shot and gone in the next: a bright patch of orange in one, blank in the next. I grinned to myself and prepared to skip through the footage hour by hour. Even if I hadn't gotten anything else from Detective Tuatu, this was a good thing to have learned about reviewing footage. So long as I had a point of reference, it was easy to find—Abigail.

"Flamin' heck," I said aloud. It was Abigail, all right; walking into Blackpoint's computer room alone, wary, and inclined to be jumpy. I slowed the footage right down to real time and watched her scan the room with a quick but thorough eye that made me think she hadn't been in the house before.

She focused on the game pretty swiftly, though; and *that* made me think that she had come specifically for the game and hadn't just taken it because she'd realised something about it.

"So you two had an agreement, did you?" I muttered to myself. If the fantastical thing I was thinking was right, Blackpoint had been not only clever, but brilliant. "I bet you did. You knew they were trying to do something with the info you've been putting out, and you probably needed a backup plan if things went wrong. You brilliant fae, you."

I disentangled myself from the spell around the computer with a bit more difficulty than I expected, and headed back down the stairs to find Zero and Athelas in the living room again.

"I've got it!" I told them gleefully. "She said—Abigail said he was the one who developed the game, and there was a special version of it on his wall in the video surveillance; all black and chrome and orange."

"Both sets of Behindkind went past it without remark," Zero pointed out. "I remember it distinctly."

"Yeah," I said, "but that just means there was nothing of fae magic to it. And—"

"And I have no recollection of seeing it on the wall in person," Athelas finished for me.

I grinned at him. "Exactly. So in between two different bunches of Behindkind visiting the house and us getting there, someone came in and pinched it. And guess who I saw on the security feed, coming in and taking it off the wall the day after Blackpoint disappeared?"

"The human woman," Zero said, with a very faint, frustrated sigh.

"Got it in one."

"Now that is certainly interesting," murmured Athelas. "She breaks into a fae residence without being caught—which is in itself highly suspicious—and takes nothing with her but a human computer game?"

"Unless she was his way out, and he left instructions with her to take it with her," Zero said slowly.

"Oi!" I said. "That was my idea!"

"It wouldn't be the first time that Fae have used a human as a way out," agreed Athelas. "He could have written her into the security spells: that would explain why none of them went off when she went inside."

"Hang on," I said, scrambling to keep up. "You both agree with me? You think he's stuck in the game, too?"

"I don't know if it's possible," said Zero. "I don't know enough about human computers and the way information is disseminated through them. But I think it very likely that if it's possible, that's what's happened."

"Me too," I said, trying to catch my breath. "Just didn't expect you to agree with me! Flaming heck, now I know we've all gone mad. But the game itself wouldn't have had to be magic, just the bit that gets him *in* there, and he already did that before they got in, so—"

"Everything we know of him suggests that he runs first and asks questions later," Athelas offered. "I think it likely that he ran away. As to *where* he ran away, I have as little idea about that as my lord, but I support the idea that he somehow found a way into his own game. It is something that wouldn't necessarily be suspected by Behindkind who might be after him."

"Looks like us going back to see Abigail," I said, rather gloomily. Abigail hadn't told me everything she knew: she hadn't even mentioned the half of it, and that didn't bode very well for any potential partnership, even if I were persuaded to leave the Troika. Bitter with myself, I said, "They must have had him all along. I didn't expect it because she's so much against working with fae! Heck. She even—Abigail even laughed at me when I said they were a kind of underground railway. I'm an idiot."

And I'd thought—I'd been quite certain that Abigail wouldn't have agreed to have any dealings with Fae, even if they were helping humans.

"I was of the impression that these humans were only interested in helping other humans," Athelas said, echoing my thoughts. "Blackpoint was fae; of that we're now certain."

"Indeed, but what was his biggest crime as far as the king's concerned?" Zero pointed out.

Athelas smiled. "A fae who was hell-bent on opening up the world Behind to humans would be a boon for a group of humans attempting to expose the dark underbelly of things to the human world."

"You said," Zero said measuredly to me, "that you weren't special. You said that there were many humans like yourself."

Athelas murmured, "Fortunately, you are unique."

"There's some truth in it," said Zero, ignoring him. "But don't make the mistake of thinking that these humans are interested in righting all wrongs: they're no doubt interested only in righting human wrongs. They would have rescued Blackpoint because he was useful to them."

"I know," I said, though I said it a bit sadly. "But I don't expect you blokes to be perfect, either, yanno?"

"A distinct relief to me," Athelas said. "I fear it is a burden I could never bear."

"However," continued Zero, "they are more orderly and driven than I had given them credit for, if they have offered and effected aid to a fae in order to expose the world Behind."

"Glad you approve," I said, grumpy and trying not to be. It wasn't like Abigail had actually lied to me. In fact, she'd told the truth the whole time she was talking to me, and had lied only by omission, if you could call that lying.

"Take Jin Yeong with you," Zero added. He must have seen the utter astonishment on my face, because he added, "They don't like Behindkind. You'll be much more useful by yourself—or with Jin Yeong."

"I s'pose at least they don't know about vampires," I said. That came out a bit grumpy as well.

"Try to keep it that way," he said, pinning me with a look. It was one of his icy looks; no arguing with it, though every now and then you could slide beneath it. "When humans discover the world Behind, Fae are usually the ones they find first."

"Or merpeople," I muttered. "Having bar mitzphas."

"I would very much doubt that they know of the existence of anything other than fae," Athelas said. "Our little merpeople hiccough was easily cleared up before it became a problem, and other Behindkind aren't heftily featured in *City Fae*."

"It was nearly a problem for North and Detective Tuatu," I said, but I was grinning. By the time we'd arrived on the scene of that little episode, Tuatu and North had mostly taken care of it. Prepackaged mermen, fresh and stroppy, ready to face Zero when they were unwrapped. That soon took the edge off them. "Anyway, I'd better text Abigail and go find this stroppy vampire to—heck. What do they want *this* time?"

Someone was knocking at the linen closet door.

Zero sighed, and something twitched inside the house, dampening the feeling of life inside. I could still feel that Zero and Athelas were in the house, and that JinYeong was not, but I had the feeling it wouldn't be the same from inside the cupboard—or wherever it was that our visitors really were. A sort of *not at home* notice.

"Indeed," said Athelas, smiling. "Perhaps we should all go on this outing after all, my lord. Our contacts seem to have some idea of what is happening, which would indicate that a swift end to this business would be more expedient than allowing the pet to try her hand."

"What else was it going to be?" I demanded, offended. "You saying I would've taken ages?"

"A learning opportunity," Athelas said. "Must you jump down my throat, Pet? You'll notice I didn't belittle your abilities—I merely expressed sorrow that you had had an opportunity taken away from you."

"Yeah, thanks. Right, I'd better text her; she'll be savage if I take you lot 'round to her place."

Zero gave a brief nod: evidently his new, thoughtful consideration of my part in the team extended to trusting me to deal with humans as I saw fit. I hastily texted Abigail before he could change his mind, very careful not to mention the two fae who would also be wanting to speak with her.

Athelas enquired, "And what of JinYeong?"

"We'll leave without him," Zero said briefly, as a second knock sounded. "I want this business over and done with so we can report it and move on to our own work."

"If you wanna report it, why don't you let Palomena come along with us?" I asked, grinning; but I followed them out without complaining.

I liked Palomena, but I was pretty sure that if she came with us to question a group of humans who knew far too much about fae, she would need to report that to what she would think of as the appropriate authorities.

And now, taking the lead to bring two of my psychos to meet Abigail, I realised exactly why Zero had meant for me to go with Jin Yeong in the first place. If he went; if he saw the humans with Blackpoint, he would have to report that. If I went, he would be able to report that Blackpoint was safe to Morgana, while at the same time giving the vaguest of reports to the golden fae. So long as Blackpoint didn't pop up again with another game to make more trouble, there was no reason to chase someone who had, on video footage, apparently been taken captive by a random assortment of Behindkind just before the golden fae himself got there.

If Zero didn't come face to face with Blackpoint, there was good reason to report that he'd been taken captive already. If he found out otherwise, his agreement with the golden fae would leave him needing to report as much.

To my relief, Abigail answered my brief text with an even briefer one: *St David's. 30 mins.*

It didn't stop her trying to run as soon as she saw who was with me, though; how she knew what they were, I don't know, but she knew.

Athelas laughed and pierced through Between like a hot knife through butter, emerging unhurriedly right behind Abigail and seizing her by the shoulders.

"Inside," said Zero, and when he shut the door of the church, it stayed shut.

"Let me go!" Abigail said. "I have nothing to say to scum like you!"

"Rude," I said, and that made her glare at me.

Athelas allowed her to go free, and she had a gun on him in two seconds flat, her weight shifting to her back foot.

He said, "I really advise against shooting me. It's an inconvenience that makes me rather annoyed."

"Is it still an inconvenience if the bullets are webbed with moonlight?" she tossed back at him.

"My dear child, I have been pierced through with moonlight before; and yet here I stand."

"I don't believe you," she said. "I've seen what this stuff does to fae."

"You lied to me," I said, and just let it sit there in the cold silence of the church.

She stood there without a word for a while, but it must have weighed on her a bit because she eventually said, hastily, "I didn't lie to you! I just didn't tell you everything. I didn't know if I could trust you or not, and it looks like I can't."

"Look, I could have brought them back to your place," I said, annoyed. "I didn't, because I'm trying to respect your group. And if you're talking about trust, you might not have lied to me, but you were being pretty flamin' careful about what you said. You could have at least told me that Blackpoint's safe."

"We don't know if he's safe," she said. "And I'm not going to talk about him with fae."

"Then talk about it to me," I said coldly. "Because I've got a friend who's still worried that he's going to turn up dead, and that's not okay with me."

She had the cheek to ask, "Is your friend really human?"

"I think you know," said Athelas, very softly, "that even if our Pet is soft-hearted, we are quite capable of questioning you in a more...ruthless manner."

It was the tiniest flinch—not even a full shutter of the eyelid, and he was already on her. He swept her around by the wrist until her back pressed into his chest and her gun arm was pinned across her own chest where it pointed harmlessly over both of their shoulders and at the ceiling.

Abigail strained to get free but soon gave up, panting.

"I know," she said, glaring every bit of her hate over her shoulder at him. "Don't worry, I'll tell you the truth. I don't want one of those little worms in my ear."

"I don't tend to use little worms," Athelas said pleasantly. "There are so many more effective ways of getting truth out of humans!"

Did he look at me as he said it? I wasn't sure, but I had the brief impression of drowning in grey eyes before I was blinking at Abigail again.

"Like I said," she said to me, with something of a gasp, "I'll tell you the truth. We want to find Blackpoint, too. He has information we want."

Zero looked as if he could have had something to say about that if he ever were inclined to say stuff, but as usual, he didn't say it. That, as far as I was concerned, was a good thing. He could only have been going to say that any information Blackpoint was going to sell to humans on the manners and ways of life of Behindkind—or even the existence of Behindkind other than Fae —was not something he would allow to fall into human hands; and that would not wash well with Abigail.

"We had a plan in place," she said. "He knew the Enforcers were getting too close for comfort, and we knew if that happened, it had to look like he'd been killed or taken."

Athelas laughed softly. "He informed on himself to a bounty group!"

"Yes," she said. "There had to be someone to blame. Once everything blew over, I was supposed to get in and pick up that game and get him out. He told me he'd already keyed me into the security system and that nothing would go off; just a quick retrieval, in and out. I didn't understand until I was actually in there that he was meant to be in the game itself."

"Yeah, we figured that out," I said. "We didn't know it was possible until now."

"Neither did we," she said. "We're starting to get used to magic, and we've always known about technology, but this kind of lacing electronics with magic is something we've never seen before."

"You're not the only ones," said Zero, somewhat grimly. "Where is Blackpoint?"

She wouldn't look at him, and it wasn't until I repeated the question that she answered.

"That's the thing," she said, looking at me. "He was meant to be in the game, but he wasn't in it by the time I got to him. At start-up, the game went through a special start-up process and everything with me, so I knew what was meant to happen. It just never happened. I don't know if something went really wrong or if he had to escape the game another way, but he wasn't there."

"Heck," I said. "Maybe he got lost."

"Maybe," she said. "But he's not in the entire game. I should know: all of us played it continuously for a week trying to find him in any of the explorable areas, and in any of the bonus hiding spots we had codes for. We even went online—we thought we had him once, but it turned out to be nothing."

"So he got out somehow on his own, you reckon?"

"We suspect so," she said. "And if so, it was a good thing. We think he'll contact us as soon as the fae stop looking for him. If not, we'll go back to the house and try to check his computer."

"Where else could he have escaped?" Zero asked, frowning. "Could he be in the electrics in the house somewhere? The electricity flows through all the devices and equipment in the house, does it not?"

The electrics of the house, or...or...

Oh heck. Abigail really hadn't known Blackpoint was fae, and he must have realised too late that he couldn't trick his way into her headquarters without giving that away.

Which meant that Blackpoint must have been waiting for another exit. Another person to give him a way out of the game...

"Your guess is as good as mine," Abigail said. "I'm only just starting to get used to magic—I don't know how this stuff works."

"Don't think it's magic," I said. "Well, not exactly. Um. Zero? Reckon we should get back and have a bit of a look at that um, new bit of equipment you lot had installed. I thought we had five hours, but it doesn't seem to do maths very well, and I've got the feeling that we might be getting a visitor or something pretty soon so—"

Zero, who had been listening with a frown, uttered a stifled phrase that I was pretty sure was Behindkind swearing, and said, "Very well. You, human—"

Abigail shoved Athelas away as he released her, her gun rising until it was at the ready again. "What?" she spat.

"Keep your mess away from my pet," he said. "If you need help, come directly to me. I'll do what I can."

"I won't need your help," she said.

When we were still just a little way from the house, there was a dull kind of *pop!* and the window in the top floor lounge room shattered outward in a spray of glass and singed, fluttering pieces of curtain.

"The *heck?*" I said, stopping in my tracks before I ploughed into Zero, who was also standing stock still.

"I greatly fear," said Athelas, his voice rather faint, "that my spell may have had some...unintended effects on the computer."

We all three looked at each other for half a breath, then took off running. I don't remember if we used the door or went right through the wall, and I don't remember passing through the living room downstairs, but I heard the drum of our feet as we tore upstairs, and I saw the charred bits that shouldn't have been there at the top of the landing, tiger-stripes in the carpet with sharp edges of not-quite-real magic.

At the doorway, I smelt smoke-edged cologne and my eyes flew to the crumpled suit that looked as though it had been flung carelessly across the room—and maybe it had been.

"Dead?" asked Athelas, as I dropped down on my knees beside Jin Yeong.

Black eyes opened a slit to glitter up at me accusingly. "Why are you...always...blowing me up?"

I opened my mouth to point out that I hadn't been the culprit either time, but something caught my eyes across the room, and that was the end of that.

"Heck," I said. The other two looked at me, and I tilted my chin at the blackened pool of rapidly cooling plastic that puddled where the computer had once been. "Jin Yeong might not be dead, but I reckon the computer is."

CHAPTER TWELVE

I cleared my throat. "You remember telling me to be careful that I didn't download a virus?"

"I remember," Zero said, through his teeth.

"No need to kill me with a look," I complained, carefully lifting Jin Yeong's head from the carpet a few centimetres. There was a bit of blood there, but his head was still in one piece. "It wasn't me that blew up the computer, it was Athelas! We didn't download a virus, but I reckon we downloaded a flamin' slippery fae who wasn't sure of his welcome with the humans. I just remembered when we were with Abigail that if he really was fae *and* hadn't told her *and* found out about her fae-warning magic that he couldn't have come out there. So he had to come out *here*, and Athelas' spell has—"

"Yes," said Athelas. "It has, rather, hasn't it? I wanted to be sure of destroying anything untoward that came through, but I didn't count on our quarry being *quite* so accomplished."

Zero looked around at the mess grimly. "He's made quite the mess, if it really was him."

"There has certainly been someone here," Athelas said.

"Those—they're not char marks from the initial explosion. They're footprints."

He was right: what I had taken for scorch marks were actually footprints, heading toward the stairs.

"Heck!" I said, amazed. "How much current was going through his body to do that, d'you reckon?"

"A lot," said Jin Yeong thickly in Korean, without trying to translate it.

He tried to sit up, and I gave him a bit of help that made him snarl when I got too close to the lump on the back of his head.

"*Hyeong*," he said. "There was an electric man here. He came out of the computer and touched my chest with one finger. One. Finger."

Athelas and Zero exchanged a look.

"Impressive," Zero said. "Between that and your magic, Athelas, it's a wonder we have a house left."

"Show us," I said, twitching Jin Yeong's lapel away from the singe-mark that was in his shirt, black and curl-edged.

He snarled at me, but unbuttoned the shirt and showed us the blackened mark on his chest: it was already healing, but it still looked pretty bad.

"Gotta learn that trick," I said.

"No," said Jin Yeong, rebuttoning. "You will *not*."

"Oh well," I said. "At least I can tell Morgana that her friend's safe. Reckon I can also tell her for sure who's been making forays on her firewalls lately, though I won't be able to tell her why or how. *I* don't even believe it."

"Very nimble," Athelas said. "He would have tried to go for friendly humans once he knew Abigail's *safe* headquarters were guarded against fae. A very good thing he didn't get through to your young friend Morgana, Pet."

"Yeah," I said, but I was still a bit worried. "Hopefully it stays that way."

. . .

I WENT TO SEE HER, JUST IN CASE; I COULD HAVE CALLED HER to let her know he was fine, but I wanted to make sure Blackpoint wasn't trying to get back into her life like the sneaky fae he was. He might have been scared off for a while, but I wouldn't count on it staying that way. What I did count on was his absolute determination to succeed and survive in the work he'd chosen for himself.

Daniel was already with her when I got there, the two of them playing a video game and eating chips.

"So this is why the boys are complaining downstairs," I said. "They kept on saying they could smell chips and that they weren't allowed to go upstairs."

"You look as though you've had a bit of a day," Daniel said, pausing the game. "Want a chip?"

I helped myself to a handful, and said with my mouth full, "Got some good news and some bad news."

"You found him?"

"In a manner of speaking. He's not dead," I added hastily. "But I don't reckon you'll be seeing much of him. He's on the run at the moment and I think he's trying to be careful about who he contacts."

"Thank you, Pet," she said. "Will he be all right?"

"He'll be fine," I said dryly. "He knows what he's doing enough to give Zero and Athelas the run-around, so you shouldn't need to worry about anyone else finding him. He's the one who made the game, by the way: *City Fae* is his baby."

Morgana, her eyes kindling, said, "He *made* the game? No wonder he knew where everything was! No wonder he knew all the ways to make it work for him: he made it and then wandered around in it just talking to people and playing!"

"Yep," I said. "Turns out he was also passing information in the game. There was an um, company that he worked for who didn't much like that happening, and they came after him. They'll be looking for him and he'll be trying to figure out how to keep spreading info, if you ask me."

"He was a whistle-blower?" said Morgana.

I couldn't help grinning, because in human terms that was exactly what Blackpoint was. "Yeah," I said. "I really wouldn't worry about him, Morgana. I've got more of a chance of dying on the job than he does, I reckon."

Daniel was looking at me, so I explained, "He's like Zero."

"He's like *what*?"

"You heard me."

"What's that supposed to mean?" Morgana asked. "And don't think I've finished talking to you about Zero, by the way. You—"

"It means that he's deep waters and hard to get a grip on," I said hastily. "Look, if you're gunna start that again, I'm going home."

"All right," she said, grinning. "But you'd better keep coming to see me now that you've come back once; otherwise I'll send Daniel to get you again."

"I'll walk you out," said Daniel. There was a bit of a grim tone to his voice that made me pretty sure he was going to ask me exactly how I planned to keep Blackpoint away from Morgana now that the fae was running around free. I saw it in his eyes, but he didn't get the chance to say it, because a moment or two after we shut the door, the hall darkened with a shadow that I'd seen at this time the other day. It passed right in front of Daniel as well, but I'm not sure he saw it like I did.

"Heck," I said. "It's back again."

"What's back again?"

"Didn't you see the shadow?" I asked him. "Saw it the other day, too."

"I think this life is starting to get the better of you, Pet," Daniel said irritably. "You're seeing things—that's not a good thing in our world, either, you know."

"It's not things, it's *one* thing in a layered kind of...ah heck."

Daniel looked sharply at me. "What is it, Pet?"

"It's the same kind of thing: the same kind of shadow, I mean. It led to the bodies at the other place—there was a shadow because lots of 'em died in the same place and he hid 'em there for years before the murderer exploded him. It's a shade."

"You're going to have to explain a bit better than—actually, no, I don't want to know about exploding bodies," he said hastily. "Anyway, there are no bodies here."

I wasn't sure if the firm tone was to assure me or himself, but it was vaguely comforting.

"I would have smelled them," he added.

"Yeah?" I asked, and my voice was a bit scratchy because I had to push through that offer of comfort to the unpleasantness behind. "How old would they have to be before you didn't smell 'em?"

"They'd—" he stopped, and said a bit more quietly, "At least a few years, depending. And they'd have to be upstairs, where we don't change to wolf."

"I'm not saying your boys have stashed a few bodies," I said. "But what about before they got here?"

"Fine," said Daniel shortly. "Where is this shadow—shade going?"

"Upstairs; beside that cupboard at the top of the house."

"Where the kids play?"

"Yeah," I said again, and my voice was flat.

"If anything dangerous gets to the kids, she'll murder me," Daniel said, and headed up the stairs, two at a time.

The cupboard wasn't booby-trapped, as I'd half thought it would be—in fact, there was nothing in it at all, and that was weird, because I'd seen 'em taking balls and skipping ropes out of it.

"Dodgy," I said, trying to grin. I shifted a bit to let the light into the cupboard, because there was something scratched into the back of the cupboard. "What's that? A list?"

"Names, I think," Daniel said, his eyes sharper than mine for shadows. "Seven of 'em. They've got dates beside them, too—1901, 1902—heck, they put there a while ago."

"Seven?" I asked, and my voice broke.

Daniel reached in to touch the carved names and said grimly, "The back's loose."

He struggled with it for a moment or two, and I prised away at my side of it, my fingers going white at the tips; then the whole thing came away in a cloud of dust and plaster-board particles. We fell onto our backsides; coughing, eyes watering, breathing in the dryness of particles, and a hollow yawned.

I fanned a clear space in front of my nose, still coughing, and when the air finally cleared enough to be able to see without my eyes watering, I saw a muddle of cloth and grey smoothness that looked like a face but had too much blankness to it.

My stomach turned over.

"What...what is it?" I asked huskily, kneeling.

"You should know a body when you see it, by this time," said Daniel shortly.

I took in a breath of must-and-bone scented air, and leaned forward. It looked like a tangle of hair and bone and cloth, and I suppose that's what it was, now. Originally, it must have been a person—no, originally it had been *people*. Because there was bundle after bundle, one tumbled over another and heavy with dust. Whoever the bundles were, they'd been inside the walls for quite a while.

"How many are in there?"

Daniel snapped, "I don't know, Pet; I've seen as much as you have!"

He'd gone back to being the crabby, stand-offish werewolf I'd met at the start, and I wanted to know why. There was something here bothering him more than the fact that there were bodies in the walls of Morgana's house.

"They're only skeletons," I told him. "Shouldn't they have a bit more meat on their bones if they're bodies? How long have they been here?"

"A while," he said grimly. "They don't smell dead anymore; they just smell like bones. They're not—they're not very old, either."

"Oh," I said quietly. That's why some of the bundles were so small. That's why Daniel had gone all hackly. "Are they all kids?"

"All of them," he said. "Help me get them out."

We laid them out on the floorboards of the attic, side by side, as they came out. Careful not to lose the bones of one inside another if we could help it, careful not to tear the ancient, delicate fabric that still clung to them. In the end, there were seven of them; four boys and three girls, if the clothing was anything to go by, varying in height and material.

"Flaming heck," I said, wishing that it didn't feel like I was breathing in dusted bones. "What are we supposed to do with this lot?"

"Let the police know about them," Daniel said. "That's the first thing. This is something that we can't do by ourselves."

"Yeah?" I said. "Well, I reckon there's something a lot more important to be finding out."

Because I knew the floral pattern of the tiny dress on one of the tiny skeletons, and I knew the little britches on another of them, too, despite the fact that they were riddled with mould and moth-eaten. I'd seen them at twilight, with the last golden sunlight drifting warmly through the weave of the fabric, both skirt and trousers, and I'd seen the kids in them—very much alive.

Only they hadn't been alive, because their bones, so old and fragile, were right here.

"What's more important than knowing how these kids got shut up in the walls, Pet?"

"For a start, we probably want to know how it is that Morgana's been seeing ghosts all this time," I said grimly. "Because I've seen the two kids that those clothes belonged to, and I wouldn't have said they were dead. Morgana's been seeing 'em for years."

Daniel opened his mouth, and I was pretty sure that he had a hot reply to return, but he shut his mouth instead. After some time, he asked quietly, "You sure it's them?"

"Yeah," I said. "They only come out at first and last sunlight, too: I never see 'em any other time. I'll ask Athelas about that, but I bet that's a ghost thing, same as the layered shadow."

"I haven't seen them at all—just the things they chuck at me. I wouldn't recognise them if I saw them."

"They must have known you'd smell a rat," I said. "Or a body, I suppose. Or...do you think they know they're dead?"

"They've been trying pretty hard to take me along with them," Daniel said. "So I'd guess that they know."

"I'm not saying we shouldn't go to the cops," I said, even though I was pretty sure that was exactly what I was saying. "Just...we need to make sure of a couple of things."

"You think she knew all along? Morgana, I mean. Do you think she knew and just didn't tell us?"

"Dunno," I said. I didn't feel hurt: I wouldn't have told Morgana that I could see ghosts if I could. There was a heck of a lot I hadn't told her—still wouldn't tell her if she wasn't already a part of this world. But it was beginning to look a bit like Morgana *was* part of this world, in some weird way.

At the very least, she could see ghosts, even if she didn't know they were ghosts. And I was beginning to wonder about that, too.

Daniel nodded, a frown creased between his brows. "I don't think she knew," he said at last. "About any of this: the deaths, the skeletons, the kids being ghosts."

"Yeah," I said. And that worried me, too. Because if she didn't know, there were other questions that needed to be asked. "Heck! Don't do that!"

The bones tinkled again, as if a breeze had passed over them and sent them tumbling, and Daniel said, "It wasn't me. If you're playing tricks, Pet—"

"You're not allowed in there," said a thin voice. The one I thought of as a younger Jin Yeong appeared beside me and pointed accusingly at the bones. "Those are *ours*."

"Yeah, I know," I said. Without the golden haze of sunshine at the end of day, I couldn't see him as properly as I ought to be able to; his body as well as his voice was thin, stretched, and see-through. More, I could see Daniel through him, and Daniel was sitting in shock, his mouth open. "Daniel, this is one of the kids. I suppose you didn't know about ghosts before this, either?"

He shut his mouth and said a bit hoarsely, "Nope. No one tells us werewolves anything. We're supposed to drag ourselves up with no help and no information."

There was the shifting of air again, and Daniel pulled back from the bones as the children stepped from the cupboard, passing through the bones to gather around us. To my relief, they didn't seem murderous—I had the feeling that as thin and stretched as they were at this time of day, they couldn't do much to hurt Daniel.

"You moved us," said one of them reproachfully. "We're not allowed to go out. She said we gotta stay where we're put until she comes back and lets us out. That's what she tells all of us when she brings us here."

"Kid," I said, "I saw you dancing out the other night."

"Yeah, but that's not really us going out," he said. "That's just the fluttery inside bit of us. She didn't say anything 'bout that, and we were so bored in there when she stopped coming to play."

"You lot know—" my voice dried out suddenly, and I couldn't make the words come out. I swallowed a bit and tried again. "You lot know you're dead, right?"

Young faces looked at me in a range of different expressions: resentful, resigned, and fierce.

"It's rude to say stuff like that," said the first boy. "We do all right. So long as we don't leave the house, we're fine. We've got Morgana. She helps us with stuff, so we help her."

"I know," I said. "But Morgana, does she know?"

"'Course not!" he said scornfully. "As if we'd tell her! She's already got it hard enough. You've gotta put all this back—if it gets taken away, we won't be able to move around the place as easily as we used to. She needs us to get stuff done."

"She has me," Daniel said.

The air grew thicker at once, and the outdoor light that was always switched on up on the roof flickered.

"She doesn't need you!" said at least three of the kids, kicking up dust at him. It seemed like that was all they were capable of moving at the moment. "We're already here!"

"Was that you?" I asked, looking up at the light. "The light, I mean?"

"'Course!" said one of the older kids at the back.

"We keep the house running," said the little girl. "See?"

She clicked her fingers, and the party lights along the top of the awning came to life, one by one, in an orderly row.

"We just keep things connected," she said, shrugging. "Electricity is easy."

What was it that Zero had said when I asked him if he had been dead? *It takes at least one or two people to keep another person interacting with the world once they're dead.*

"Ah heck," I muttered. Because now I wondered, very much, exactly what else around the house the kids were powering.

"Oi," I said to Daniel.

"What now?" he asked wearily. "*Stop* kicking dust at me, you little warts! We should be calling the cops, Pet."

"Don't reckon we can do that just yet."

"Why?"

"Well," I said grimly. "I don't reckon these are the only skeletons in this flamin' big cupboard of a house. C'mmon, let's put these ones back. We've got another place to check first."

. . .

"PET, I DON'T THINK WE'RE ALLOWED TO BE HERE!" WHISPERED Daniel, his eyes darting around the darkened room and more yellow than their usual hazel.

I poked him in the ribs and made him yelp. "Don't go changing in here!" I hissed. "It's not your werewolf senses I need in here—"

"Oh," he said, in a very different voice. "I don't think you're right about that, Pet. There's something very old and dead in here —not as old as the kids, but still pretty old."

"Yep," I said, short and hard. "Reckon that's Morgana's parents."

"*What?*"

"Reckon they're dead, too. I just remembered that I only ever saw Morgana's mum round about golden hour, too. I figured they were reclusive and didn't want to talk much, but now that we know about the kids...."

"Why don't the lights work?"

"Dunno," I said, but I had a pretty good idea. If the lights worked everywhere else in the house and they weren't working here, then they didn't work for a reason. And that reason prob-ably wasn't looking pretty right about now, if Daniel was right about a very old and dead smell. "Don't try to turn 'em on again yet, okay? I'm going to try something instead."

"I bet *that*'ll be good," he said snidely.

"Come out!" I yelled into the room, and he jumped. "We need to talk."

There was silence; the kind of heavy silence where you know you've been heard and the other person is just thinking about whether or not they're going to reply.

Daniel muttered, "Well, that was useful."

"Come out," I called again. "We know you're there; we know you're dead. You don't have to hide from us."

"That," said a nasal male voice severely, "is *rude*."

"Yeah, so I've been told," I said. "You gunna come out?"

"We can't," said the male voice. It sounded like it was pleased about that, in a spiteful sort of way. "It's the wrong time of day."

"That only goes for normal people," I said. "We're not normal people."

"Speak for yourself," said Daniel.

"You're a flamin' werewolf," I said. "What the heck are you talk—"

It shouldn't have been a surprise, the way they came out of the shadows around the edges of the room, trailing darkness that was almost blood-red. A moment before they had been almost laughable; disembodied, querulous voices with personalities to match. Now they were menacing, inky, coiling things without a completely solid form, different from the thready presence of the children.

I saw a rorschach blot of the same woman I'd met in the hallway one night, her hair high and loose on her head in a Gibson-girl style, the rest of her trailing in ribbons of sticky darkness that might have been black and might have been blood-red.

"You're looking a bit, um...faint today," I said. I mean, I know we'd said we knew they were dead, but it was still a bit of a shock to see her this way instead of the way I'd seen her in the golden hour.

"Why have you called us out?" she asked. "Howard, why did they call us out?"

"Because we're trying to figure out a few things," I told her, squaring my shoulders. After everything I'd seen in the last year, it was stupid to be afraid of what amounted to a ghost or two, even if they looked more horror than gothic. "And because I'm pretty sure your daughter doesn't know you're dead."

"How did you know we were dead?" asked Howard, his voice more querulous than before. So this was Morgana's father. She'd got her looks from her mum, for sure.

"Met quite a few other ghosts," I said. "Recently. Once you know, it's pretty obvious."

Not to mention the fact that now that my eyes were adjusting to the gloom, I could see the patchy remains of two people in the room: one at a desk and the other in a seat by the shuttered window, they seemed to have mummified from the little I could see of them, and I didn't much want to get closer and verify the guess. No doubt that was why Daniel hadn't smelled them through the whole house.

"You'll have to have a word to your pack," I muttered to Daniel. "So they know that old bones and jerky smell can mean bodies, too."

"Shut up, Pet," he muttered.

I didn't blame him. If I *could* shut up in horrible circumstances, I'd do it a lot more often, I can tell you. Life'd be a heck of a lot more comfortable.

"We have never been obvious," said Howard, with a disapproving frown.

"And it's very rare that people can see us at all," Morgana's mother added, soft and languishing.

I remembered the bit of the nightmare that Morgana had told me about, and I wondered if this soft, delicate woman and the quizzically-browed man could possibly be as bad as I thought they were.

"You've been hanging around here for a while, haven't you?" I asked them. That worried me about as much as everything else in this place did—but it all made sense in the midst of the worry.

"So long!" sighed Morgana's mother. "Never resting, never stopping, never able to reconnect with the world."

"What keeps you here, then?" I asked.

"Love for our daughter," Howard said, smiling gently.

I stared at him. "What a crock! You don't even go down to see her!"

He coughed in surprise—a residual human instinct, I suppose, since he didn't technically have the pipes for that kind of thing.

"We—we can't be easily seen!"

"Neither can the kids, and they still go to see Morgana. They get along really well, actually. It's not as though she can't see ghosts, after all."

"Well, I'm busy with my portfolio, and Gloria needs peace and quiet for her book."

"She was never a noisy child," said Morgana's mother, her voice just above a whisper. "Poor thing! She's suffered for so many years alone; it makes me feel sick every time I think about her."

The melancholy on her face was beautiful and perfectly drawn in light and shade. Like her hair and her clothes, it was effortlessly elegant and infinitely sad. It should have made me feel that way.

I found that it irritated me instead. "Yeah, but not enough to make you go down and *see* her!"

She looked at me with that same gentle melancholy. "You don't understand. Our entire existence is for her."

"Yeah," I said, more slowly, "that's something you're gunna have to explain a bit more. How long have you two been powering Morgana? It's gotta have been more time than it looks, 'cos I reckon you two have been dead for a long time—since the 20s at least, probably. Your fashion is newer than the kids' is, but not by much."

"Time passes like a river," Gloria whispered. "We never know one decade from the next and the days flow into each other without beginning and end."

"No, but what does that mean?" interrupted Daniel. "If they're…if they're *powering* Morgana that means she's…she's—"

"Yeah," I said quietly. "She's dead, too."

"No," said Daniel.

I put my hand on his arm, but he shook it off, and I was left clinging to a pinch of his sleeve instead. "I'm sorry."

"She can't be dead! I would have smelt it! I would have—she's *warm*, Pet! How can she be warm if she's dead? She has a heart-beat! There's no—there's no body!"

"We keep her heart running," said Gloria, with that sad, lingering smile I now realised I hated. "Heart running, blood pumping through her own body. She's no ghost."

There was a bite to the last sentence, even in her soft voice, and I thought I understood it.

"The night you both died, someone came into the house, didn't they? They offered you a choice, I reckon."

Howard's eyes sharpened on me. "How did you know? He said we could save our daughter and die, or let her die so that we could live." He shrugged, and looked away from me. "I suppose you can guess what we decided. We didn't know that he would kill her, too, anyway."

"You sure about that?" I asked. "'Cos I'm pretty sure that's not how it went. I heard you were offered the choice and made a different decision."

That's what I remembered about Morgana's nightmare, and I had reason to know that nightmares weren't always just nightmares.

I must have looked at them with something very close to bloody murder in my eyes, because when I said through my teeth, "*Tell me the truth*," Gloria gave a gasping laugh.

"He would have killed her anyway," she said, still breathlessly. "We knew that. And even if one child died, we could always have another one. It was no choice at all."

"She at least can eat and drink," said Howard bitterly. "We're stuck here without so much as a cup of coffee to comfort us—she can eat and drink, and move around the house. She has a body."

"You've got a body, too," I pointed out coldly. Imagine being bitter toward the very slightly better position of your kid!

"He didn't tell us that we'd live on by losing our souls bit by bit to feed our dead daughter," Gloria said. There was no bitterness in her voice, just a sense of injury. "So long as she lives on in this house, so do we. *I've killed her*, he said afterwards, *And you'll live for a long time yet, but she's more alive than you'll ever again be. I trust you'll enjoy it.*"

"Well," I said, "I hope you do, too."

"Wait!" Howard said. "You're not going? I thought you were going to help us!"

"No one can help you," Daniel said, his voice gravelly and harsh. "Your souls were lost long before you sold them to buy your lives. I hope you rot and wither away in darkness for the rest of time. And when I find a way to separate her from you, you will die."

"Don't—you can't do that!" cried Gloria, her voice growing fainter as we walked toward the door. "We'll die! You can't separate her from us!"

I opened the door, and Daniel turned back with a particularly toothy grin. "Just watch me!" he said. "C'mmon Pet. It stinks like the dead in here."

I followed him out, cold and sick. I thought I had had a small, glimmering idea of the murderer's sense of humour now; the twisted, convoluted mind of a person who had used and then killed a human murderer—the same person who had also offered sordid hope to a pair of parents who didn't deserve to be parents, then snatched it out from under them with a fae trick.

I had no doubt in my mind that they were one and the same person. And if the murderer that Zero and Athelas were after was also the person who had murdered Morgana's parents, then he was also the one who had murdered my own parents.

And I wondered—I wondered very much—if they had been offered the same choice that Morgana's parents had been offered.

CHAPTER THIRTEEN

"Why didn't any of you tell me that ghosts are real?" I demanded, as soon as I got home. I felt very badly done by, and annoyed to boot, because despite everything, it had still been very hard to prevent Daniel from calling the police and having all of the bodies carted off.

Fortunately, I had enough annoyance at my three psychos to keep me going. If I'd known of the existence of ghosts before now, I liked to think that I would have discovered Morgana's secret a lot sooner.

Zero paused his sharpening, then resumed. "I didn't know."

"But you know *everything*," I said, with a bit more snideness than was probably warranted.

He shot me a very blue look, and said, "Are you admitting that, now? That I know everything? Does that mean you'll be more obedient from now on?"

I grinned. "Depends on what the orders are. Oi. Athelas."

"Yes, Pet?"

"You know about ghosts?"

"Let us say that I had an inkling," he said. "However, the subject is still under discussion Behind as much as it is in the human world: some Behindkind refuse to believe in their existence, others are more...open-minded. We know of shades, but those are quite different. In any case, what humans would think of as ghosts aren't quite the reality of the situation."

"I am dead," said Jin Yeong, without bothering to translate for me. He shrugged. "Yet I walk. It is natural for echoes of people to exist. Your friend does not look like a ghost."

"I don't think she's dead," I said. "I think she's mostly dead."

"She's a zombie," Zero said. No surprise, no sudden realisation: I wondered how long he'd known. From the start, maybe? "There's also a lot of discussion about them, but no one doubts their existence. We just don't know how they live on when they should be dead, nor how it is they consume their sustaining energy."

"Brains, I've heard," I said, a bit shaken. I'd been hoping that Athelas had been joking with me about zombies until I learned that Morgana's parents were powering her. "Reckon I would have noticed, though; and it's not like she could have gotten it into the house without Daniel knowing, right? At the moment, she's feeding off her parents' souls, as far as I can tell."

"I've yet to hear that zombies have to eat brains in order to survive. Human consumption, yes; and for optimal performance, yes. Survival, no."

"Maybe they're like vampires and just like doing it," I said.

"I do not eat brains!" said Jin Yeong indignantly, while Zero said, "Vampires need to drink blood in order to live. Zombies can live without brains, even if it's not their ideal state. For vampires, the first feed is the most important and they require a certain amount to remain living."

"The enjoyment," said Jin Yeong, with a very sharp smile, "is a bonus."

"Dunno why you're turning up your nose at brains, then," I remarked. "Oi. Did you know, too? About Morgana being a zombie, I mean?"

"I don't know what a zombie smells like," Jin Yeong said. "Why would I know that?"

I pointed at Zero. "He did."

"One feels that you would have been equally as petty if he had known it," Athelas said. "As for me, I can safely say that I learned nothing more from going to the house than I would have if I hadn't gone. I was, of course, aware of the existence of zombies."

"Yeah, but you didn't see Morgana," I said. "You're excused. Also, I'm gunna need information from you so I'm not going to reef into you or anything."

"I'm delighted to hear it," he murmured.

I turned back to Zero and said accusingly, "*This* is the kinda stuff I wanted you to tell me about. *This* is what I'm complaining about!"

"Oh," said Zero. "But I thought it would hurt you. It's my job to keep you safe."

"This is tearing-off-a-bandaid hurt," I said. "Not stab in the stomach hurt. It's something I needed to know."

He frowned. "Needed to know? Why?"

"I've got to ask her about it—or tell her, if she doesn't know."

"She's a human. If she knows about it, we have to do something about it."

"Pretty sure she's Behindkind," I pointed out. "Otherwise, what about Jin Yeong? You'd have to consider him as a human, too. She exists between worlds; not dead, not alive. She's obviously Behindkind."

"The law is fluid when it comes to both zombies and vampires," murmured Athelas. "But I believe if my lord were to... express a preference for a certain type of treatment, it might very well set a precedent."

"Yeah, but you can't say it's against the law."

I looked expectantly at Zero, and he took it in silence for quite some time before he said, with the faintest edge of irritation, "No. I can't say it's against the law."

"Well," I said.

"However, I *highly advise* not doing so."

"I know," I said. "I don't want to tell her either. But I don't think we've got a choice: it's too big."

"There's always a choice," said Zero.

"Yeah," I said grimly, "but they're usually all bad ones."

ZERO MAY HAVE DISAPPROVED, BUT HE DIDN'T SEEM WILLING TO let me go alone to Morgana's place when I went the next day. Jin Yeong, just as inexplicably, sauntered alongside me the whole way there, and when Zero stopped outside Morgana's door and silently leaned against the wall opposite the door, he came into the room with me.

Daniel waited downstairs—prowling more than pacing. When we got there, he'd said, "You want me to—? I mean, I should come in."

"No," I'd said. "If she takes things badly, she'll need someone she can talk to afterward."

It wasn't as if I thought that would change things between them. They'd had an easy friendship from the start, and Morgana had been playing with ghosts for goodness knew how long—she shouldn't be too put-off by being friends with a werewolf.

Still, now that I was here in the room, it was hard to believe that I could pull this off. I didn't even know where to start. Funnily enough, it was easier to start things off with Jin Yeong standing behind me, even though he didn't say a word. He just stood there, the pressure of his hands on the back of the chair inclining it slightly toward him.

"What's up, Pet?" Morgana was dressed a bit more sombrely than usual today: her eyeshadow was all deep purple with dark green edges, her lips matte black, and the night-dress she wore was long-sleeved and high-necked in unrelieved black. "You're looking serious. I thought you found Blackpoint? Did something happen to him after all?"

"No, he's safe," I said, smiling in spite of myself. As if we could have pinned down such a slippery thing as Blackpoint! He might hate his own kind, but his methods of dealing with people were pure fae: trust no one, and never stop the sleight of hand. "You might hear from him again, who knows? He's the one who's been trying to get through your firewalls, so if you want to talk to him you'll have to open up a bit."

Now wasn't the time to mention exactly how and why Blackpoint had been trying to get through to her. What I had to say was going to be tricky enough to tell her without getting into side-issues. By the time it was less complicated, she would probably be ready to talk to Blackpoint on an equal basis anyway.

"So that's who it was!" she exclaimed. "If I'd known—"

"It's probably a good thing you didn't know," I said. "He made a bit of a mess of our home computer with his games—you don't know what it might have done to yours."

"He would have had a bit of a fight for it," Morgana said. "I'm not too sloppy with a computer either, you know, Pet."

"I know," I said, wandering over to the window and gazing across at the building there. It was old, but not too old: maybe thirty years or so. Before it had been built there was just a big, blank wall there, the remains of an old factory that was too tall to see around but too empty to be interesting.

"Reckon you must have been glad when they pulled the old factory down," I said. "It would've been pretty boring to look at that every day."

"Once it shut down, there was no fun in it," she said sadly, sealing my heart in ice.

So it really was true. I'd known it was, but it was breath-taking hearing her speak so casually about something that had happened over thirty years ago when she looked as young as she did.

Going back to my chair took too long and left me feeling tired. "I s'pose it blocked the view, too," I said.

"It was all right when there were people working there," she said readily. "Then I could watch them coming and going from work. But when it was empty, it was just a blank in the scenery. That place is much nicer."

She seemed to think about what she was saying for the first time, and added, "Anyway, I'm glad it turned out like this. I wouldn't have met you and Daniel if it wasn't for someone building a normal house there and someone else deciding they wanted to turn it into a hospital."

"Yeah," I said. "Oi. That reminds me. I've been meaning to ask you how long you've been in this place by yourself?"

Her eyes lifted to mine; cautious, questioning. She knew she'd slipped, but she didn't know what I knew, and it was impossible for a normal person to know what I knew. But still she wasn't sure.

"I'm not by myself," she said. "I have Mum and Dad upstairs, and the kids are always around. And Daniel and the others are downstairs now."

"Yeah, but before the boys got here, how long?"

"I don't count days," she said, her shoulders tense. "It's no use; it just makes everything seem longer."

"Seems odd, doesn't it?" I said sadly, wishing I could be kind but unable to be so. "It probably didn't even occur to you that it was weird for you to live for so long until tv was invented. How long ago was that?"

She fidgeted. "Don't—don't, Pet!"

"I even asked you about your period and you had an answer for that because you were trying to explain it to yourself, weren't you?"

"I don't—I can't get out of the house," Morgana said, her black lips drooping tragically. "Does it matter if I live a bit longer than other people? Aren't I allowed to?"

There it was: the smallest crack to wedge my fingers into. I'd seen those cracks in Morgana's façade before, but I had excused them; ignored them.

"You've been here a heck of a lot longer than most of the other people around here—since the 20s, as far as I can tell. It must have started to get really hard to justify that when you got the internet as well."

She looked down at her hands. "I suppose you think I'm dead or something. I don't blame you. I've wondered about that before, but the kids could always see me, so…"

"No," I said, "you're not dead. Well, you are dead, but you're not a ghost: you're a zombie."

"That sounds very like me," she said, trying to smile. "Nice and dark. How do you know? I thought I was dead—no, I didn't! I'm not dead, Pet! It's ridiculous! How can you know that?"

"I know it because I know the kind of people who know the right kind of things," I said. I jerked my thumb at Jin Yeong and added, "He's a vampire."

She spluttered a laugh. "That's obvious," she said, but the laughter quickly drained from her face. "Wait, you're serious."

"I am always serious," Jin Yeong said.

"Prove it," she said to him.

Jin Yeong stared coldly at her, folding his arms; he stepped deliberately from behind my chair, put his heels together very precisely, and then, to my huge surprise, caused himself to rise about a foot in the air.

"Heck!" I said, nearly falling out of my chair. "You didn't tell me you could do that!"

"It is obvious," he said, flicking a quick glance at me. "I do so when I am fighting. You should have seen it."

"Not up and down, you don't!" I said firmly. I would definitely have noticed it. So a certain amount of levitation went into a vampire's speed and dexterity, did it? No wonder Jin Yeong was so effortlessly abandoned when he literally threw himself into a fight.

"Is it enough?" he asked Morgana.

"Yeah," she said, as though her mouth was dry. She cleared her throat and said, "Come back down please. I mean, it is pretty obvious with his looks, I suppose. What about your Zero?"

"Zero's fae. Him and Athelas; you haven't met Athelas, though."

She looked at me defiantly, and that was familiar and a bit off-putting. It took me a while to realise that it was because I was usually on the other side of it, and when I did, my heart dropped a bit more.

She said to me, "That doesn't mean you get to tell me what I am."

"I think you already know it," I said. "You've been wondering for years why you're different from other people; you must have been."

"I wondered," she said uncertainly. "But there was always something to explain it all, and—and— Did you—did you tell Daniel? You didn't tell Daniel, did you?"

"Daniel already knows," I said. "He's—he'll be fine with it. He's waiting downstairs."

"He's *fine* with me being a *zombie*?"

"There's a whole other world out there," I said. "Daniel knows that."

That made her fingers twist back into the bedspread. "I don't —I don't think I want to know about another world. And if you think I'm up for eating brains you've got another think coming."

"Um." My psychos had given me some very specific information about that. "Actually—"

"Don't joke about it," she said quietly.

"I promise I'm not. I was told that if you can find a way to make yourself eat them, you'll be able to get around without— without another power source."

Morgana had to know about what she was, but there were some things I would never tell her. I would never tell her how her parents had once chosen to save themselves instead of her; I would never tell her that they lived a shell of a life, their souls sucked away a little more every day to keep her interacting with the world. Souls sucked away and hating her more and more with each day.

"You think Mum and Dad are dead, don't you?"

"Yes," I said. There was no way to make it better. "You're the only thing keeping them here, and it's about time they moved on. The kids are dead, too—but they're not really connected to you and I don't think you could get rid of them if you wanted. They're sorta...echoes of kids, bouncing around the place."

"They're..." She whispered it, "They're dead too?"

"Sorry."

"Sorry doesn't change that, Pet!"

"I know. But I'm sorry anyway."

I stopped to let her think about it for a while, and she just looked blankly across the room and out of the window.

After a bit, quietly, I said, "You said—you said when you were younger you felt trapped here. There's a bit more freedom for you if you can work with your body; Athelas says that once you start eating...you know...once you start eating properly for a zombie, your body will be useable again."

"That's not comforting!" Morgana said. It was more of a strangled squeal, her eyes dark with saltwater. Her chest rising and falling too fast, she said, "Pet, what makes you think you can come in here and tell me I'm a monster, and that I can't have what I want unless I let myself be one! What did I ever do to you?"

The last sentence rose to a scream, and drawn by the noise, Zero opened the door. Morgana glared at him, but he crossed the room and stood beside me anyway.

At him, defiantly, she said, "I don't know what I am, but I'm not a zombie. I've never even thought about eating brains. It's stupid!"

"There are other forms of human consumption," said Zero, his blue gaze levelled at her.

I shoved him a bit more vigorously than necessary. "Stop it! Morgana, your parents—"

"Stop!" she said, and her voice wobbled. "I'm not saying things aren't…unusual. But I'm not a zombie. I can't eat—I can't do that."

"It's not just that," I said. "The fact of being a zombie, I mean. If you can accept who you are and work with it, you can get out of the house—you can walk again! You're only weak because you've been trying to keep living like a human."

"If I walk again, will my parents go away?" she asked, one of her hands pressed to her chest right at the breastbone, as though she couldn't breathe. "No, don't tell me. I don't need to walk; I just need to stay here. I need to figure out the nightmare and the kids and the other stuff…and I can't do that if I'm always scared about what'll happen if I go outside. Vampires and fae? I've got enough problems without that."

"I know it's scary at first—"

"Why did you have to tell me? I didn't need to know, Pet! I was happy here!"

"Because you don't have to be stuck *here*," I said. "If you—if you work with your state, you can do something about it—and it's no good telling me you don't want to. I know you do. And you've gotta see that it's not safe to not know."

"It's more dangerous to know!" she flashed at me. "You brought a *vampire* to see me! Your Zero is *fae*. And now I'm a zombie who has to eat brains to be able to walk? I won't!"

"*Ya,*" said JinYeong, showing his teeth and startlingly understandable. He said, "Why are you blaming her? She didn't do this to you; all she did was tell you the truth."

"I'm already dead!" Morgana shot at him. "You think your stupid teeth are going to frighten me?"

"His teeth can still do some damage to your body," said Zero warningly, while Jin Yeong stared his outrage at Morgana.

"Don't threaten my friends!" I told Zero in exasperation. "Look, can you lot wait outside for a while?"

Zero gazed at me for a moment, then silently nodded. Jin Yeong tried to protest, but when Zero seized his arm he allowed himself to be dragged toward the door with no more than a token snarl.

Morgana, her eyes not meeting mine, said, "You too, Pet."

"Morgana—"

"I don't want to talk to you right now," she said, even more quietly. "I have everything I need here. I don't need to go out. If I stay here I can still see Mum and Dad; I can still see the kids."

"Morgana—"

"*Please*, Pet."

What else could I do? I joined Jin Yeong and Zero outside the door, and clumped grimly downstairs again.

To Daniel, who was waiting at the foot of the stairs, I said shortly, "Reckon she's gunna need you. She's angry at me and a bit scared, but I reckon she'll be fine with you. Just don't push it right now. Treat her just like normal; don't try and make her understand."

I didn't stay to watch him hurry up the stairs; I headed out of the house, Zero and Jin Yeong behind me, and turned my face toward home. At least Zero didn't try to say *I told you so*, and I appreciated that.

It wasn't fair of me to mizzle off to my room and ignore everyone. They were probably expecting tea and coffee, and it wasn't like it was their *fault*.

Right now, I could understand how Morgana felt: it felt as

though the Troika had taken something precious away from me, and I knew I must look the same to her right now. I didn't want to see them; didn't want to see the great big gash in my world that had once seemed safe, despite all the little cracks I'd always known were there. It had been my normal, and like Morgana, I'd avoided looking at those little cracks for a very long time. Now the cracks had been dwarfed by the giant slash in reality that was the Troika, and for a little while I felt as though I didn't want to see them. I wanted to go back to a time when I might have been able to be friends with Morgana without knowing about stuff like fae, Behindkind, and ghosts or zombies.

But then, I wouldn't have met Morgana if it wasn't for the Troika: I would have still been nipping in and out of my house under cover of darkness, trying desperately to save up enough money to buy it for myself and as desperately trying to avoid the Nightmare every night. Trying to ignore the fact that nothing about my life was normal even though I tried to pretend it was.

Because once you saw that there was more to life than you thought, it was like a bandaid had been ripped off. Everything exposed to the light and air and starting to itch and scab. Morgana had chosen to back away from the sudden influx of light and retreat into her safe world. I had chosen to focus on that light so much that it had conveniently blinded me to the old way of life and the old things. Neither of them were particularly healthy ways of coping, and they each had specific costs: to escape a horrifying new world, Morgana had to face her own self and her own nightmare; I had to plunge headlong into a wild, terrifying world outside of myself that might kill me at any moment if I was to keep running away from the memories of my old life. We each ignored one danger for the other, and tried to comfort ourselves by pretending that our danger was the better danger to face.

My own room should have been comforting. I could still hear the psychos moving around downstairs; I even heard when Athelas left the house, though that was more of a feeling than hearing. It wasn't comforting, though. Instead, it was dark and dreary and cold, and I felt as though I could feel the walls growing around me, so I went back downstairs.

Zero was just stepping down from the kitchen when I wandered past the linen cupboard, a cup of coffee in one hand with a plate of biscuits balanced on top and something weird and magicky in his other hand. He looked vaguely guilty for a moment, as if I'd caught him raiding the kitchen, then the expression smoothed away into his normal emotionlessness.

Deliberately, he looked away, stepped right down into the living room, and crossing the carpeted floor silently, just as deliberately sat down on Jin Yeong's side of the couch. He put down his coffee and biscuits, and without looking at me leaned back into couch, magic flickering between his fingers.

I stared at him for a while before I moved. Zero doesn't give hugs, you see; but he does accept them occasionally. This was probably about as close to an invitation as I would get. So despite the fact that I didn't want to see another Behind-kind today, there was no one bigger or broader or more huggable than Zero; no one who was quite so comforting even if he was part of the problem for which I required comforting.

I curled myself up on the couch beside him, leaning into that huge, broad side, and let my head rest against his arm. If I slouch against Jin Yeong, I can lean against his shoulder; otherwise I have to tuck it into his shoulder. With Zero, there was no hope of ever reaching high enough for that; it was all cotton-covered bicep beside my ear.

I don't remember when it happened, but at some stage Zero drew out the magic in his right hand with his left, dropping me in against his ribs as his arm extended. I made a surprised little grunt but shuffled up a bit closer again and went back to staring at nothing in particular. I couldn't properly see the magic and I didn't particularly want to have to think, either. It was nice just to sit there and listen to the heavy beat of Zero's heart through his ribs.

Zero didn't try to shuffle me back to a more comfortable distance when he finished with his magic; just draped his arm over me instead, like a heavy security blanket, and stretched his legs out in front of the couch at an angle to avoid the coffee table.

There was a mutter of Korean from the direction of the kitchen, and a swift, about-face of pinstripe in my peripheral vision. I was too sad and content and comfortable to say anything rude or inflammatory, so I ignored it and kept listening to the steady thump of Zero's heart.

A few minutes later, JinYeong marched out of the kitchen, across the living room, and set down a mug of coffee in front of me. He also glared at Zero, which didn't seem to move Zero much by what I could see when I glanced up at him.

I picked up the mug to sniff at the coffee cautiously and said aloud without actually meaning to, "Doesn't *smell* poisoned."

JinYeong narrowed his eyes at me and said menacingly, "*Drink. It.*"

"Yeah, that's not at all suspicious," I muttered, but I sipped it anyway. To my surprise, it actually tasted good. Not as good as what I could make, but not bad for a person who routinely drinks blood. It surprised me to find that it wasn't hard to smile at him. "Thanks."

"I," said JinYeong, with very great emphasis, "am *warm*."

I stared at him. "You were normal for about two seconds. What the heck are you talking about now?"

"*Warm*," he said, and padded away upstairs.

Zero and I stayed as we were until I remembered to ask, "How did the golden git take everything?"

I felt his ribs move slightly with the soft snort of laughter. "I might have known that you'd find out he'd been here."

"Don't think the house likes him," I explained. I'd been staring aimlessly in the general direction of the linen closet since watching Jin Yeong stalk upstairs, staring at a coiled, furled section of Between that was as tightly wound as a muscle protecting itself. They must have had a visit while I was at Morgana's place the other day. I yawned and added, "It's all tight around the linen closet."

"He didn't take it well, but he had no reason to distrust me when I said that the video evidence pointed to Blackpoint being taken captive by a mob of unknown Behindkind who had been tipped off to his location and knew he was likely to be wanted by king and country for a reward."

I hugged him. "Thanks."

"I also told him that since it was too late for my kind of trace recordings, the human evidence was the only thing acceptable as any kind of proof at this stage," Zero added repressively.

"Would've hugged you if you'd told him everything, too," I said. "It wasn't an exchange. I know you've got your own laws and rules you have to play by. I'm thankful you're even doing this much."

"Is that why I was harangued earlier?" he enquired, but when I looked up at him, his lips were faintly curved.

"Yeah," I said. "It's an expression of love."

And suddenly that sounded weird, because I heard Morgana's voice in the back of my mind saying, *He knows that's how you show affection.*

Heck. When had things started to get weird?

I asked hastily, "How come it took you so long to start helping humans again, anyway? I know you said it's hard on you, but that never stops you helping me or worrying about me, so I know it must have been eating away at the back of your mind."

"You think that I'm emotionless and dangerous to humans, but Athelas is—"

"Yeah. Reckon he's broken. Don't reckon he'd be a liability when it comes to doing as he's told, though."

"Perhaps. Perhaps not."

"You wanted to make sure he was safe to be around humans?" I asked. That was actually a pretty fair consideration.

"And then," he said deliberately, "there is the issue of *you*."

"Who're you calling an issue?"

"I knew that if I began this business again, it would draw my father's interest—and the king's interest. And for the time being, I very much prefer that my father and the king not know about you."

"Bit late for that now," I remarked.

Zero's eyes closed for a brief moment. "Yes," he said shortly. "That is exactly my point. I would also very much prefer other Behindkind not to know about you."

"Lots of 'em know about me," I said. "But they all still think I'm your pet, so—"

"Even Behindkind have been known to get fond of their pets," Zero said. "I prefer not to give anyone reason to think that you can be used as leverage when it comes to me. All in all, now did not seem to be a judicious time to begin that particular enterprise anew."

I leaned against his huge warmth silently for a few moments before I poked him in the ribs. "Oi."

"What?"

"Glad you decided to do it, anyway."

"I had very little choice in the matter," he said. Maybe he saw my grin fade, because he added, "There was a legacy I have always wanted to pick up again when I thought myself strong enough. And it seemed as though the time had come. Don't read too deeply into it: I'm not a champion of humanity or anything of that kind. I'm cleaning up a section of the world in accordance with the laws of my kind."

"Got it," I said, as my phone buzzed against my left hip from the pocket.

I still squeezed his waist one more time before I let him go, because even if I didn't read too deeply into it, he was still helping. Then I slid my phone out of my pocket to see who was texting me. A small part of me thought briefly that perhaps it could be Morgana, but when I tilted my phone and the black screen flashed into life, it was an unknown number that glowed up at me.

Below the number, neat and tidy, a text said, *Thanks for helping me out. I'll be seeing you.*

"Heck," I said, causing Zero to shift slightly.

Because the last word of the message was simply a signature.

Blackpoint.

www.ingramcontent.com/pod-product-compliance
Lightning Source LLC
Chambersburg PA
CBHW070009120726
47909CB00003B/854